THE 419 CODE

AMAKA DE

Published by

MELROSE BOOKS

An Imprint of Melrose Press Limited
St Thomas Place, Ely
Cambridgeshire
CB7 4GG, UK
www.melrosebooks.com

FIRST EDITION

Cover designed by Richard Chambers

ISBN 978 1 906561 71 0

Printed and bound in Great Britain by:
CPI Antony Rowe. Chippenham, Wiltshire.

FSC
Mixed Sources
Product group from well-managed
forests and other controlled sources
Cert no. SGS-COC-2953
www.fsc.org
© 1996 Forest Stewardship Council

CONTENTS

INTRODUCTION   v

CHAPTER 1: OH NO, NOT 419   1

CHAPTER 2: AFTERMATH OF THE BIAFRAN WAR   8

CHAPTER 3: BAABA'S FAMILY   10

CHAPTER 4: BAABA DREAMS OF LAGOS   16

CHAPTER 5: BAABA'S DISAPPOINTMENT   40

CHAPTER 6: THE POLICEMAN'S DAUGHTER   44

CHAPTER 7: NEWS FROM LAGOS   63

CHAPTER 8: BAABA'S TRIP TO LAGOS   66

CHAPTER 9: BAABA'S EARLY DAYS IN LAGOS   72

CHAPTER 10: BAABA'S APPRENTICESHIP IN FRAUD   74

CHAPTER 11: BAABA QUALIFIES IN WAYO   78

CHAPTER 12: OGO BITES OFF MORE THAN HE CAN CHEW   86

CHAPTER 13: OGO'S JAIL SENTENCE   93

CHAPTER 14: BAABA ENDS UP ON THE STREET   94

CHAPTER 15: BAABA'S LUCK CHANGES   97

CHAPTER 16: BAABA JOINS THE POLICE FORCE   98

CHAPTER 17: BAABA APPREHENDED FOR BRIBERY   100

Chapter 18: Baaba is Saved by

      Section 419 of the Criminal Code   104

Chapter 19: Baaba Invents a New Line of Wayo   105

Chapter 20: Baaba Exploits Women   109

Chapter 21: Baaba's Devious Act   112

Chapter 22: Baaba Visits the Village   116

Chapter 23: Baaba Takes His Love to Lagos   121

Chapter 24: ChiChi Settles with Baaba in Lagos   124

Chapter 25: ChiChi's Enlightenment   127

Chapter 26: A Father's Wrath   130

Chapter 27: Baaba Preaches 419   139

Chapter 28: Baaba Transforms 419   144

Chapter 29: ChiChi is Apprehended by the Police   151

Chapter 30: The Wedding   159

Chapter 31: Baaba's Transformation   161

Chapter 32: Baaba Plans Polygamy   172

Chapter 33: Baaba Takes 419 Beyond Nigerian Borders   174

Chapter 34: ChiChi Leaves for England   180

Chapter 35: ChiChi Divorces Baaba   185

Chapter 36: Baaba Degenerates into Drugs   186

Chapter 37: A Village Boy Turns into

      a National and International Villain   187

INTRODUCTION

THIS IS A STORY ABOUT cheating; about fraud.

It is a personal story.

'419' is a particular fraud that originated on the African continent, in Nigeria. In a reasonably short period of time, it grew to an international fraud that had ensnared thousands of people in what became known as 'Advanced Fee Fraud'.

Just as you cannot fully understand the man without first knowing the boy, to appreciate how this fraud could mushroom as explosively as it did, it is important to understand a little bit about Nigeria.

Nigeria is located in the west coast of Africa. At the last UN census in 2005, the population was estimated at just over 130 million. In 1960, Nigeria claimed it's independence from Britain with three main regions; the Hausas and Fulani in the north, the Yorubas in the south west and the Igbos in the south east.

Nigeria is blessed with a natural resource – oil. This provides the main income but has also been the main source of conflict.

In 1967, the Igbos tried to break away from the federation hoping to be in control of the oil which was in their territory. Biafra was born. The rest of the country could not sit back and allow the Igbos to monopolize the country's biggest resource. The opposition finally resulted in the 'Biafran War'. The Igbo's independence lasted three years with the death of two to three million people. This bitter war ended with the country near total collapse.

For the Biafrans, necessity led to a burst of creative energy. After the war, that creative energy took on other forms, which brings us to the story of 419.

The aim of this book is to trail the historical events that led to the birth of this cancerous fraud.

Deception, or *wayo* as it is known in Nigeria, has been in existence since the birth of man. Certainly it was deception on the part of the snake in the Garden of Eden which led to Adam and Eve's fall.

No one should be naïve or foolish. Fraud is part of our character as people. However, the extent to which simple fraud gave birth to 419 is truly remarkable. At first, our hero simply modified and modernized *wayo* into something more efficient and effective. Even he did not know that he was giving birth to a monster.

Chapter 1:
Oh No, Not 419

ChiChi was exhausted. Her legs ached. She had too much on her mind. She fairly collapsed on the edge of her bed and gave herself a moment or two to just relax. When she looked up, she saw that the clock on her bedroom wall read 10.30 p.m. She immediately calculated in her mind the *most* sleep she would be able to get. Her conclusion: not enough! Especially if Bobby didn't turn down the volume of his stereo. "What was it," she wondered, "about teenage boys and loud music?"

With a sigh, she lifted herself from the bed and walked down the hallway of her semi-detached house.

"Bobby!" she called out before she was half-way down the hallway. "Bobby!"

No answer.

She raised her voice even more as she approached the door to his room. "Bobby, please turn down the music!" she called as she pushed his bedroom door open a crack.

Almost immediately, the volume of the music went down. A young man – a boy still, she wanted to believe – looked up at her with an open, good-hearted expression. "You look tired, Mum," he observed.

She nodded. "I am," she said, not bothering to explain that it had been his music that was partly to blame for her still being awake. "Bobby," she went on, "please wake me by six, all right? I have a meeting in South London at nine and I don't want to be late."

Bobby frowned at his mother. He knew that she relied on him to organize certain aspects of her life and as much as he enjoyed having the responsibility sometimes it rubbed him wrong. "Mum, why can't you just use the alarm on your mobile?" he asked, his voice still raised to be heard over the music.

She shrugged and leaned against the door frame. "I've told you, I don't know how to set the alarm on my phone," she sighed.

Exasperated, Bobby raised his arms in some combination of resignation and agitation. "Mum," he said, "I showed you last time." He was showing his teenage impatience. He was anxious to turn his music back up – a little. He was relaxing himself when his mother came into his room, and he didn't enjoy being disturbed any more than she did.

"Well," she said, sounding defensive, "I can't remember what you showed me. And even if I did," she continued, "I wouldn't know how to turn it off."

Although Bobby was often frustrated that his mother didn't embrace

1

technology, ChiChi was perfectly happy to remain somewhat ignorant about all the new doodahs and gadgets that seemed to be bombarding her at every point in her life. She often wished her life could be *simpler*, not more complicated. She liked her mobile just fine but she only wanted it to do what a phone was *supposed* to do – make and receive calls. Everything else was simply an annoyance. Actually, it was worse. Although she didn't admit it to Bobby, she was frightened of all the different features on her phone. She thought that she would ruin the phone if she tried to use one of the features and did something wrong.

"You *can't* break it," Bobby had reassured her more than once. "Even if you do something wrong, I'll be able to fix it."

While that thought *was* reassuring, she would much rather simply not take the chance.

Though clearly exasperated, Bobby also knew that he wasn't going to convince his mother to change. Certainly, not this evening. So, with a roll of his eyes, he told her not to worry. "I'll do it in a minute, Mum," he promised. "I'm just doing some recording for my friend first, okay?" With that, he got up and half guided, half pushed her out of his bedroom. As soon as she was in the hallway, he closed the door behind her.

She stared at the closed door for a moment, feeling some anger bubble up. But the truth was, she was too tired for anger. So, with a sigh, she turned and trudged back to her bedroom. She half laid down, half collapsed onto her bed, waiting for Bobby to finish and come in to set the alarm for her.

No sooner had her head hit the pillow than the volume of the music rose back up to its previous level. She shut her eyes tightly and tried to ignore it.

Whatever else, she simply could not afford to be late to her meeting the following morning. She wanted to leave herself plenty of time to make her way to South London. She would have to take the Tube and she had a healthy mistrust for London's system of public transport. She had yet to have got anywhere important in a hurry when there wasn't some delay somewhere in the system, throwing off her schedule completely.

"There are delays on the *whatever* Line due to …"

Oh, that horrible, calm voice! She thought of it with dread. She would recognize that voice anywhere, the one that came from the speakers in every Tube station in London. Always with the announcement of a delay – in a very clear voice – and always with a garbled voice explaining the reason for the delay.

She was quite certain that the Tube authority planned it that way just to frustrate users like herself.

No, ChiChi was of the 'old school'. She would much rather arrive at her destination with plenty of time to spare and wait there.

"I'm going to have to wait *someplace*," she reasoned. "I might as well wait there as well as here. At least that way I won't have to worry about making it to my meeting on time."

She was a very prompt person. It annoyed her when anyone was more than a moment late. Part of this was integral to her basic nature. She was an impatient person. But part of it was also the way she was raised. She'd been taught that being prompt was a sign of respect.

Therefore, she never liked to keep anyone waiting. This, of course, was a lesson that Bobby seemed not to have learned with any diligence.

She was pondering the problem of 'today's young people' not being prompt. She was so engrossed in her thinking that she didn't even hear the music stop. As a result, she was a bit startled by the short knock on her door, followed by Bobby pushing it open a bit.

"Mum?"

"Yes, love."

He stepped into the room. He perched on the edge of her bed and reached for her mobile on the night stand. "I'm setting it for six, right?"

She nodded. "Thank you," she said.

He shrugged, continuing to move his fingers over the keys of her mobile.

"You'll have to remember to turn it off again when I get home," she said. "I don't want to wake up so early after tomorrow morning," she said.

He looked at her as if she was from another planet. She simply did not 'get it' at all. "Mum, you only have to go to *settings* in the menu and set it to do whatever you want it to do.

"It walks you through each step."

"Yes, yes," she said sleepily. "I'm sure it does." She adjusted herself against her pillow. "But I don't care about settings. I just want to get my calls." More than once she had watched Bobby playing with his phone, getting music to play, or his ringtone to change or some other such trick. In her heart, she envied him and his generation, with their ability to use technology. Back in her own school days, students had not even been allowed to use a calculator.

"Now, the whole lot of them don't even have to think," she sighed. The simplest problem was solved for them. She sometimes worried if they'd ever be able to work their way about anything without a computer.

Whatever, she needed to get some sleep. She did not even take note of Bobby leaving her room after he'd set her alarm, or the fact that he'd given her a light kiss on the top of her head before leaving.

The following morning, she awoke with the alarm and immediately got ready to leave. She wasn't taking any chances. True to form, when she arrived at the Tube, there was an announcement informing passengers about serious delays on the Northern, Circle, and District Lines.

"I knew it," she muttered to herself as she got in the queue to purchase her ticket. "There must be something about me and the Tube. I must jinx it." She sighed. She almost hoped that was the case. She couldn't imagine there being delays every day.

As she got to the front of the queue, she had gotten herself into a real froth. In fact, she was quite sure that she hated the Tube.

"I can't be late," she told the person in the ticket booth. "It's a very important interview."

The ticket seller was not interested in hearing her tale of woe.

But ChiChi knew that if she were late, she would get into a panic and become even more nervous than she already was. The fact was, every interview made her nervous. That was why she worked so hard to make sure that everything was in place. It gave her some sense of control. But if she were late – and for a reason far beyond her control – she would simply lose it.

What, after all, would a potential employer make of her being late? Even with a valid excuse? Being late demonstrates irresponsibility and lack of discipline. A potential employer would certainly *appear* to accept appropriate excuses, but how could he ever take you seriously? Being late simply tells him too much about you – and nothing good either! And so what if the train *was* running late. Wouldn't you have to take the train to work *every day*? Would that mean you would be late every day?

Feeling a heaviness in her heart, ChiChi bought her ticket and trudged down the steps to the platform. She tried to make her way into the large crowd that had formed to wait for the next train.

Oh, how she hated crowds like this! But there was nothing to be done. On most days when *she* didn't have an important place to go – when the trains ran on time – there were no crowds. But today … late trains. Crowds. Horrible!

No matter what, she *had* to be on the next train, no matter when it arrived. So, inch by inch, foot by foot, she fought her way through the crowd, making her way to the place on the platform where the first carriage would stop. She had taken the train many times and she knew that the first carriage tended to be less occupied. Crowds have their own psychology and herding instincts matter. The majority of the people clump together in the middle.

She didn't have time to be part of *this* herd!

Suddenly, the crowd came to life. There was noise further down the tracks. A train! A train was coming. Suddenly, people were pushing and shoving in all directions. It was like getting batted about by a wave in the rough sea. But she held her ground and, when the train came to a stop, she managed to fight her way into the first carriage.

People continued to crowd in, and she found herself mashed beneath a tall man's armpit the entire way to Kings Cross. For a moment, she was panicked that she wouldn't be able to get off the train to change at Kings Cross, but she managed to fight her way off the train and out to the platform.

Thank goodness there seemed to be no delays at the Kings Cross station – and no crowds either. She walked through the station, following the signs, to her next train. The nearly empty train arrived promptly and she got on. She had a seat to herself and immediately took out her newspaper and opened it to the Horoscope page.

She religiously read her horoscope every day but *this* day, being so important, meant her horoscope had even more significance. She hurriedly turned to the page where Jonathan Cainer, the astrologist, wrote his column.

Her fingers fairly trembled as she looked to see how her day – and interview – might go. "Aha!" she thought to herself as she read the horoscope: *be on the look out and watch every little detail today. You cannot go wrong if you do; but if you don't, you will miss a very important message.*

The horoscope made her even more resolute. "I will have to listen to the interview questions very carefully," she thought to herself. "And I will most definitely not rush to answer."

She sighed deeply. She felt better now. She had a sense of what she could *do* to make the interview go well. She felt herself relax a bit. Not all the way. She was still nervous but at least she had a sense of how to go forward.

Having read her horoscope – and reread it to make sure that she'd understood it correctly – she turned her attention to other sections of the paper. As she glanced through the various articles, one caught her attention. 'Banks warn staff and customers of a Nigerian scam referred to as "419".'

She read it again. Curious. She creased the paper and began to read the article itself. In it, the reporter wrote how the banks were advising their customers against responding to any email or letter from Nigerian businessmen claiming to have inherited large sums of money from a dead wealthy parent or uncle. The article even included a sample of a 419 letter.

The reporter had concluded his article with the words: *Beware! This is a get POOR fast scheme!*

She found the article a revelation. When she finished reading it, she looked around her to see if any of the other passengers were reading the same article. She felt the colour drain from her face. She was stunned. Of course, she had friends who had received these letters, but she couldn't believe that 419s had become so prevalent that an *international* bank had to warn its customers against falling victim to them.

Unlike others on the train – or anywhere else – reading the article, ChiChi was in the unique position of knowing how the fraud started in the first place. Part of her wanted to laugh out loud. She couldn't believe that it had escalated to this level. But she did not laugh. She felt an overwhelming sadness come over her, knowing that the article only contributed to a terrible image for Nigeria.

"America might be the home of the free but now people will think of Nigeria as the home of the fraud," she thought sadly. Suddenly, her thoughts were no longer on her upcoming interview but rather went back many years to her childhood. For she had grown up in Nigeria with the man who started the fraud in the late 1970s and who coined the term 419 to identify it.

She had not given it much thought then. The Biafran war had only ended a few years earlier. The country was in shambles and the Igbos were desperate to survive and rebuild their lives.

She lived at the time in Lagos, the capital of the country.

Her thoughts continued to drift into the past until an announcement came over the speakers in the train, letting the passengers know the next station: her stop.

She forced herself to focus on the present, on getting through the station and to her interview. "I must think about today," she told herself as she walked through the station and on to the street. There, she stopped to look at a map and get her bearings. She made her way to her interview and back, trying to focus on the immediate. However, in the back of her mind, she could not completely erase the image of those numbers. 419. They were there, always, like a shadow.

Back on the the train going home, she returned to the newspaper article and read it over and over, committing it almost to memory. Beware! This is a get POOR fast scheme!

My goodness.

She could not bring herself to get rid of the newspaper and that article. She kept it in the drawer by her bed, sometimes taking it out and reading it before going to sleep. For weeks she kept it there. Months. She found herself researching the fraud in other articles. She had Bobby show her how to do a search on the Internet and she began to research there as well. There seemed to be more and more warnings on the Internet and in the newspapers about the fraud. In Britain and in America. There were articles about how Britain was working with Nigeria to deal with the fraud and how it had affected people's lives and the image of Nigeria abroad.

As much as these articles captured her thoughts, none captured her attention as much as the many and varied articles about how the fraud began. "They've got it all wrong," she told herself whenever she would read one of these articles. Sometimes she was astonished at just how wrong the reporters and writers were.

She even thought that the articles *about* the fraud represented another kind of dishonesty or fraud. "How can they write this stuff?" she wondered, knowing just how wrong they were.

Over time, she realized that she would have to set the record straight. But then she felt discouraged. She was not a writer. How could she be expected to write the story? And, once written, how could she ever get others to read it? The more she read on the Internet, the more she got to become familiar with self-publishing and e-books. Maybe that was something she could do?

Still, the more she learned, the more she learned that even self-publishing was not an easy task.

Frustrated, she wanted to give up her idea to write the story but, somehow, the idea wouldn't give *her* up. She decided that she would write the story of the origin of 419, even if it didn't get published. She would write it to pass on to her children. Or, if they didn't read it, she would write it if only to satisfy herself that she had written down the truth.

For two years she struggled with her desire to write her book. More than once, she told herself that it was a silly idea and to forget it. But every time she tried to forget, there would be another story about the 419 men from Nigeria to remind her and to prompt her anew.

So, on a Saturday morning, she finally took the plunge and began to write. There were many false starts but slowly the story started to take shape. She started to write down her experience with 419 and put all her emotion into the words. She hoped that people would read her story and maybe understand the history of 419 a bit more – and in doing so, would understand Nigeria a bit better. And understand her as well.

That was her hope. That is her hope.

For here is her story …

CHAPTER 2:
AFTERMATH OF THE BIAFRAN WAR

IT IS HARD TO IMAGINE what life was like when the ugly Biafran war finally drew to a ragged close. Those Biafrans who managed to survive mostly ended up being driven by the fighting from the towns to the villages. The valuables they left behind – and there were many as the people barely had time to escape with their lives – were looted by soldiers on both sides. The towns remained ghost towns and the people remained in their individual villages until the fighting drove them from their villages as well, turning them into wandering refugees.

It was only with the news that the civil war was finally over and the constant artillery bombardment had ceased that the people began gradually returning to their villages; a trickle at first, and then more and more.

Along with the civilians, the Biafran soldiers were also beginning to come out from their hiding places. Many were suffering grievous injuries. Most were suffering from traumatic shock. They returned to a world as devastated and devastating as that which the civilians had confronted.

With rubble all around them they had no choice but to begin to rebuild.

Like many others, Baaba served in the Biafran army and the air force. At twenty years of age, he had already seen enough cruelty for a lifetime. He had fought bravely but returned home to a devastated village. His village was very remote, far from the nearest town.

('Baaba' is not his real name. We shall call him this because it means 'boss' or 'father of all'.)

Like the others, Baaba's parents had also come out of hiding to return to their village. They could not believe what they saw. Everything, everything had been destroyed. There was nothing.

Without school buildings, parents and teachers organized classes under trees, out in the open, for their children. Village elders encouraged this for two reasons. One, the children needed some education. But also, it was important to keep the children busy so that they stayed out of mischief.

Of course, there were many parents who could not concern themselves with the education of their children. For them, education was a luxury. They had to worry about how to feed themselves and their family. They had no idea where their next meal would come from.

And there were many, more than who liked to admit it, who doubted in their heart of hearts that the war had really ended.

Despite his parents' desire for him to return to school, Baaba was one of the ones who refused. It was not that he would not have benefited from an education.

But he had been an officer during the fighting. He had commanded others in the Air Force. He simply could not bear the humiliation of sitting in a classroom to be instructed like all the others.

After enjoying the privileges of his rank, he could not bear to be 'no better' than the others – even if it was true. No, what he needed was some quick and easy way to make money. He had no time to 'waste' in school.

In truth, Baaba refused to go back to school because he could not take instruction from anyone, let alone the teachers. At school, disruptive behaviour earned corporal punishment. Students were openly caned if they misbehaved. Baaba could not submit himself to such humiliation. Punishments also included facing the wall or standing on one leg for a given time.

"This is foolishness," he sneered to his friends, looking at the children and young people returning to the classroom. "We are men. We have fought like men. Can we be expected now to simply learn as boys, to be treated as children?"

Even worse, although his village had its own primary school, the only secondary school was some four miles away, in another village. There, he would have been forced to sit with others as an equal, others – some of whom he'd commanded.

No, it was impossible. And, truth be told, he didn't have the patience for it any more. War will do that to a young man. It will rob him of the patience and innocence necessary to learn the old way. It will make him hard and callous. It will make him see the world differently than he did before the fighting.

Very differently.

When he was a boy, Baaba used to think that the large Iroko trees that shaded his village from the sun watched over everything he did like giant, wise men. No more. Now he appreciated them for their protection from the blazing sun and for the home they provided to the birds singing night and day. But he would never again view them as benevolent giants that watched over him and protected him.

The natural world was no longer safe or dangerous. It had lost its magic for Baaba. Much of life had lost its magic for him.

"I am a man now," he said to himself. "I am no longer a boy."

And it was true. He was a man. And a man's world is different from a boy's. But before the war, a boy was ushered into manhood by tradition and culture, by the care of the village elders and under the watchful eyes of the Iroko trees.

In a time of war, a boy becomes a man by the terror of seeing a friend's innocent body pierced by shrapnel. In a time of war, a boy becomes a man by looking into the terror of another boy's eyes … and killing him anyway.

CHAPTER 3:
BAABA'S FAMILY

BAABA STOOD SIX FEET THREE inches tall. His skin was dark and shiny. He had a long, pointed nose. This feature, more than any other, distinguished him from most of his friends who tended to have flat noses, pressed wide against their faces. His deep, chocolate eyes were intelligent but also troubling. The darkness of them seemed to hide secrets. After the war, those secrets seemed to be even more troubling.

Still, he was a handsome young man. Physically, he was strong and quick. His greatest strength was his legs. He had powerful legs that could carry him far distances. As a boy and a young man, his passion was for football and hours of the sport every day had strengthened his legs until they were capable of enormous gifts.

He had never been an 'easy' child. From his earliest days, he had been more than a handful.

"I do not know what to do with the boy," his mother would cry in frustration to his father. "I hit him with the palm of the tree but he just laughed at me."

Baaba's father would look at his wife with a mixture of annoyance and impatience. The boy was just a child. Why couldn't she control him? But she couldn't. He was constantly getting into fights with other children, some of them a good deal older than him. In many of those fights, he did not stop fighting even after the other child cried out in pain.

Many times, the other child was so badly beaten that his parents would come to Baaba's parents to complain.

"This is not right, for your boy to be so vicious to others," they complained. "We all live in this village. We will have to take the matter to the police if it ever happens again."

Baaba's cruelty and strength were a dilemma to his parents. He had a temper that seemed to flare out of nowhere and which had a violent expression that he could not seem to contain.

In an effort to find a way to help their boy, they brought in an exorcist to perform the rituals that would relieve Baaba of the demons that seemed to have control over his soul.

"These temper tantrums and destructive ways must end," his father said to his mother. He shared the belief of Baaba's mother that Baaba was the incarnation of a dead relative who had been a murderer in life.

Baaba's mother had arranged the exorcism. Despite her own difficult nature – in many ways, she was as troublesome as Baaba – she did not want to see her son dead in the bush, killed by those who he had tormented.

Although the other villagers were glad to have a solution to Baaba's cruel ways, they felt little sympathy for his mother. She was a difficult woman herself. People who knew her avoided arguments with her. She was a quick-tempered woman with her own violent bent. Neighbours who observed the boy nodded to themselves in recognition of the mother in his behaviour.

Those who brought problems with Baaba to his parents knew that they would have to endure her accusations that the problem was with their child, not hers. Still, even her fierce nature and angry pride recognized that there was something about her child that was incorrigible, something that was beyond her control.

The exorcist used his spells and his potions, uttered his incantations and his prayers. In the end, very little changed.

Mind you, to look at Baaba was not to gaze upon a frightening or threatening-looking person. Quite the opposite. There was a quietness about Baaba, almost a sheepishness. There was much about him that was likable. Indeed, those on his 'good side' were devoted friends.

He was handsome and attractive. The older girls all liked to toy with him. He never spent time with girls his own age.

"Girls," he said with some disparagement in his tone. "A man needs a woman," he added. Never mind that he was hardly a man when he made such boasts.

Still, in addition to his powerful frame, women seemed to find themselves attracted to the hint of danger. Perhaps there is a whiff of adventure about such men – something in their recklessness or their potential for violence. Perhaps women believe that such young men and boys simply need their 'love' to heal them.

Whatever the reason, Baaba had relations with many older girls and women, bragging about his exploits to his friends when they could barely brag about such simple adolescent pleasures as kissing a girl or pressing a hand against her budding breasts.

"That one has a bush thicker than the jungle," he laughed to his friends, pointing out a woman in the marketplace. "I needed my machete to find my way to the goal," he added with a snicker.

"But isn't she married?" one of his friends whispered, glancing at the woman and then back at Baaba.

He shrugged. "And what if she is?" he asked darkly. "If her husband is not man enough for her, then she has to find someone who is."

His best friends, Emi and Nnaa, listened to his escapades with wonder and vicarious excitement. Though both were strong men in their own right, they had none of the presence or danger of Baaba.

For all his swagger and success with women, Baaba was incapable of succeeding in school. He had no patience for the instruction. He certainly was not about to allow 'silly fools' to discipline him for his outlandish and disruptive behaviour.

In some ways, the war 'rescued' him.

Even though almost all his friends returned to school after the war, he could not and would not step foot into a class. Instead, he spent his daytime hours loitering about, roaming the marketplace, enjoying trysts with older women and then, when school was letting out, he would return to find his friends so he could chat and play football with them.

Although she feared for him, and complained about his behaviour to his father, his mother was his fiercest defender to others. If he got into trouble, she would be even more vocal than he in blaming the victim of his violent behaviour.

"My boy would not have beaten him up if he didn't deserve it," was a common refrain.

While it might be a wonderful thing to have a parent who is always willing to defend you, regardless of your behaviour, more often it results in a person unable to take responsibility for his own behaviour.

And, in Baaba's case, it also resulted in his illiteracy. For, while he was loitering in the marketplace, his friends and the others were learning to read. They were learning skills and becoming familiar with ideas.

His ignorance and illiteracy would have a major impact on his life.

Unlike Baaba and his mother, Baaba's father was one of the most gentle souls in the entire village. He was a very peaceful, God-fearing man. He was a local clergyman for the village church. He worked as a civil servant, serving as a court clerk before his retirement.

He was, in truth, something of a timid man who became withdrawn and saddened by the turn his life had taken. His wife bullied him constantly, badgering him with demands and criticisms that were mean and unwarranted. He had learned early in his marriage that it would do him no good to try and fight with his wife.

Besides, it was not in his nature to argue. He was, essentially, a man who sought placid waters. He hated confrontation. As a result, he simply accepted his wife's mean-spirited and wrong decisions in regards to his marriage and to Baaba – all in his effort to maintain peace in the household.

Sadly, his efforts brought him little of that and failed in any benefit he might have wanted for his son.

Unlike most of the other men in the village – certainly those with sufficient financial standing – Baaba's father only had one wife. While the culture tolerated polygamy, he dared not practise it himself.

No other woman would dare accept his offer of marriage, not when that offer was preceded by the reputation of Baaba's mother.

It's important to note that it was very unusual for any man in that village to be bullied so completely and publicly by his wife. Nigerian and Biafran culture placed the man at the head of the household.

The man was lord.

But not in Baaba's home. At least, not when the man in question was Baaba's father. Not surprisingly, Baaba had no respect for his father. He learned early in life that the one he had to please was his mother. She was the one who made the decisions in his house.

Only when he got older and *he* became more demanding did he learn that he could bend even his mother's taciturn will.

Baaba loved his mother's cooking – one of the things she did well that was acknowledged even by her enemies. No matter what he was up to, Baaba found a way to arrive home at precisely the moment when the meal his mother had been cooking was ready to be served.

Or, as his mother sometimes said, "I always know when you will be home."

"How do you know?" he asked her.

She smiled with a gleam in her eye. "A mother has a sixth sense about these things," she teased him, with a coy voice almost like that of a lover.

Baaba was not above using the knowledge of his mother's 'sixth sense' as a bludgeon when she did not happen to have a meal ready for him when he arrived home. "And where is your famous sixth sense now?" he would berate her at those times when his meal was not ready.

"I'm sorry," she said in a quivering voice. She lowered her eyes in the face of her son's anger, showing him the deference and respect she never showed to her own husband.

Of course, no one should be surprised that as much as he enjoyed his mother's behaviour towards him it was not going to serve him well. Indeed, her pampering of him, her respect for him as opposed to her disdain for her husband, all laid the emotional foundation for Baaba's unrealistic expectations of the world around him.

He expected *every* woman to show him the same respect and obedience that his strong-willed mother showed him. He expected *every* man to defer to him, as his father did to both him and his mother.

He expected the world to always have a feast prepared for him.

Although he was illiterate, he was not a stupid boy. It did not take him long to realize that the world was different from his own home and village. However, he was never able to learn the valuable lesson about how to come to terms with the world, and to be successful in the world.

He never learned how to accept that the world did not *owe* him.

Baaba never lost his power over women. He was so much more handsome than almost all the other men in the village that he was always going to be a favourite. Only a couple of the other boys even came close to his physical attributes. One was his dear friend Emi.

As they grew older, Baaba no longer dominated in attracting women and the two often engaged in competition for this woman or that one.

"I will have her before you," Baaba bragged to Emi as they both eyed a young girl just growing into her maturity.

Emi laughed. "Oh, you will be left with her only after I've had her, and then she will know how good a man can really be."

No one other than Emi could ever speak to Baaba in such a manner. But he could and so Baaba laughed. "Perhaps you are right," he joked. "I should let you have her first. That way, she will not be disappointed when you do finally get to enjoy her fruits."

Sometimes, they simply decided that rather than compete, they would share the girls. Many of the girls found the arrangement appealing. Some did not. Some detested the idea and refused out of hand.

"What do you think I am?"

Baaba would laugh. "We know what you *are*," he said. "We're just trying to decide how we want to take advantage of what you are," he added, with wicked glee and no regard for the girl's feelings.

Baaba was interested only in those things that he enjoyed – on his terms. More than anything else, he was also motivated by his boredom. For example, Baaba liked to play football and was on the village team. When he would get bored, he would start with kicking a football around his father's compound. He would then progress to the main village area and then, just to amuse himself, kick the ball directly at someone.

"What's the matter with you?" the victim would invariably ask, recognizing the meanness in the act.

This would result in an argument and eventually a fight.

Baaba's mother, learning of the fight, would rush to the scene and apportion blame on arrival without any care or understanding of the cause. The last thing she was prepared to accept was that her son could possibly have been the offender.

So, with her wicked tongue and nasty nature, she would quickly become part of the fracas. It seemed she and Baaba were of one spirit when it came to such situations. They seemed to thrive on trouble. It seemed to satisfy some deep need they both possessed, or perhaps simply amused them when they became bored.

They seemed to feed off the turmoil that each caused. Baaba's mother would not allow anyone to be critical of her son and her son fought any type of disrespect directed towards his mother. To his mind, his mother was simply the best and could do no wrong. In fact, when someone suggested that *she* was contributing to the problem, Baaba became more incensed and more violent.

Meanwhile, Baaba's father simply refused to become involved in such situations. He remained at home, waiting to hear their report of the disturbance – which was always one-sided and to their benefit – when they returned home.

When he returned from the war, Baaba had a scar on the left side of his head. When his mother saw it and reacted with shock, running her finger along the scar's ridge, he simply shrugged to dismiss the concern.

"I did not get this in combat," he said coolly. "Those idiots could never shoot me," he added, referring to Nigerian soildiers. "No, this was a foolish accident. My friend was cleaning his weapon and it discharged.

"These things happen all the time in war," he went on.

Of course, the explanation was a blatant lie. He had been wounded by enemy fire. But he could not bring himself to admit to it.

Baaba continued to be pampered after the war as he had been before the war. Despite having seven brothers and sisters, he was accorded his own room in his father's thatched mud-house. While the others had to share rooms, as was the custom in large families in the village, Baaba's mother made certain that he was honoured with his very own room and space.

Of course, being the only one with his own room elevated Baaba's sense of privilege. It also enraged his siblings. They were jealous of the special treatment that he received.

"None of this will come to any good," the neighbours said, witnessing the way he was pampered.

"He's a wild boy already," another nodded.

"He needs to be disciplined, not babied."

No one – other than Baaba and his mother – could imagine that her treatment of him could amount to anything other than tragedy.

But his mother justified the special treatment she gave him by her story of his birth. She said that the special bond between them was due to her experiences during her pregnancy and the birth. She claimed that the duration of her pregnancy with Baaba was thirteen months instead of nine.

"He is special," she claimed. "It was a sign from the gods that one day my Baaba would grow up to be an important man in society."

Of course, her prophesy did turn out to be realized, but not in any way that she could have imagined. Rather than gain importance due to his goodness or to his positive acts, he realized this prophecy in the most negative fashion. His future actions brought shame not only to the village but also to the nation. For he was the man responsible for the renaming of the common *wayo* to the infamous 419.

Chapter 4:
Baaba Dreams of Lagos

Lagos was the capital of Nigeria. At the beginning of the war, the South-Easterners fled the capital along with the rest of the population. It was only after the end of the war that people slowly began to make their way back.

While some returned to Lagos, others waited before they were willing to venture away from their villages. The brave and the foolish went to Lagos first. It was only later, when they returned unharmed, that others followed.

Baaba was among the 'third wave' of returnees to make their way to Lagos. A friend, Ochi, had visited his uncle Ogo in Lagos in the school holidays and came back wearing all new clothes, new shoes, new trousers, and a new watch. But most impressively, he took from his pocket a wad of money he had received from his uncle.

Baaba, always looking for a way to make money, was wide-eyed when he saw Ochi.

"How did you get that money?" he wanted to know.

Ochi smiled. It was not often that anyone elicited such an unguarded question from Baaba. Besides, Ochi enjoyed telling the story of his trip to the capital city, embellishing a bit more with each telling.

Baaba listened to the story with a rising excitement in his heart. The more Ochi spoke, the more Baaba was certain that he had to go to the capital himself.

"What does your uncle do for a living?" he asked Ochi when he had finished with the telling. "Does he need a servant?" he added, only half in jest.

"My uncle is a magician," Ochi said.

Baaba's eyes widened. "What? You're joking with me!"

Ochi shook his head. "Not a bit. He is a magician and he makes a great deal of money from his trade." Ochi looked at his friend. "As to working for him … well, you can ask him yourself when he comes to the village."

"When is he coming?" Baaba wanted to know.

Ochi shrugged. "He's coming on holiday in a few weeks. He told me that he would take me back with him to Lagos.." Ochi knew that his uncle wanted an apprentice for his magic.

Baaba listened to Ochi carefully. However, while Ochi spent much of his time bragging about his uncle and how he was to be his apprentice, Baaba's thoughts were already ahead of the story. Ochi's intent in telling the story was for Baaba to be impressed both with his uncle and him. But Baaba focused on another conclusion.

"So," he thought as he listened to his friend, "one can make money in Lagos without going to school."

This realization was almost revelatory. After all, his father had insisted that the only way to earn money was to be educated and the only way to become educated was in school.

Over and over, he asked Ochi, "So your uncle does not work for any body?"

Ochi shook his head. "He is his own boss," he insisted. "And he makes loads of money from the trick trade."

Baaba leaned closer. "So tell me, how does he do it?"

"How does he do what?" Ochi asked.

"How does he do the magic?"

Ochi laughed. "I couldn't tell you that even if I knew. It's a secret." Then he frowned. "But I really don't know. He never took me to one of his performances. All he wanted me to do was to count the day's earnings when he came back."

Baaba felt deflated. He'd gotten so enthused hearing about Ochi's uncle that he wanted to learn more. It was the first time in a long time that he ever truly wanted to learn about something he didn't already know.

He wanted Ochi to tell him more about magic. He was already imagining a scenario where he could learn a trick or two and then go to the nearest town, which was a bit more than twelve miles from the village, and set up his own magic show to make money.

But Ochi was no help at all. He really didn't know anything. Ochi continued to tell him more stories about his time in Lagos so that, by the time he was finished, Baaba was very downhearted. He also felt bitter. "Why can't I have an uncle in Lagos?" he asked himself. "Why is Ochi special? I want someone who will take me to Lagos."

But he had no rich uncle. Although hardworking, his father was poor and could barely afford decent meals. In fact, had he decided to go to school, his parents would not have been able to afford the fees. His father would have had to borrow the money.

But it didn't matter because he did not want to go to school. He did, however, want to make money. Lots of it. And Ochi's story had inflamed his imagination.

He left Ochi and stopped on his way home to see Emi. He wanted to talk about Ochi's stories with someone and there was no better 'someone' than his best friend. Emi would certainly understand his reaction and feelings to Ochi's stories.

After telling him some of what Ochi told him, Baaba looked at Emi. "Don't you have an uncle who lives in Lagos? Maybe he could take us to Lagos to serve him."

Emi considered the prospect. "I do have an uncle there," he admitted. "He's a civil servant." But then he shook his head. "But he's a very selfish man," he said with an expression of distaste. "I don't think I could inquire. He does not get along with my parents at all."

Once again, Baaba had allowed his hopes to blossom and now, once again, he felt deflated and disappointed. "There must be *some* way to get to Lagos," he thought to himself. He realized that his only smart option was to wait until Ochi's uncle came to the village and then ask him himself if he would take him back to the capital to be his servant.

Once he had hit upon that strategy, he knew that he would have to be very vigilant to make sure that he did not miss the visit. So, in a new routine, he began to visit Ochi's house with greater and greater frequency, stopping in more than once a day.

During most of his visits, he waited for Ochi to return home from school – if only to have a sensible excuse for being in the house. While he waited for Ochi, he mostly played with Ochi's younger siblings who were not yet old enough to attend school.

He rarely saw Ochi's mother. She was a very busy woman who really ran the household. She was either out on the farm or in the market. She was the breadwinner of the family and both resented and took pride in the fact.

Ochi's father spent most of his time at home, drinking the local palm wine and chatting to his friends. All in all, it was a household that was familiar to everyone in the village – the hardworking, in-control mother, the lazy, not-in-charge father. The only difference between Ochi's household and Baaba's was that Ochi's mother would never show his father the disrespect that Baaba's mother showed his father.

But Baaba didn't concern himself with any of that. He was constantly trying to devise more ways to be able to spend even more time at Ochi's house. He wished he could spend the night in Ochi's house to make sure that he wouldn't miss the man's arrival.

All of Baaba's hopes for the future were focused on Ochi's uncle. He would be devastated if he missed the visit.

He helped Ochi's mother with household chores, which was unthinkable for Baaba. He would *never* help his own mother with chores. He even volunteered to repair the kitchen roof. A strong wind had damaged the thatch on the roof, leaving it vulnerable to leaking. He would not have helped his own mother repair her roof, but again, here he was enthusiastically volunteering to help Ochi's mother.

He was devious though. He knew that if his offer to be a servant was to be heard sympathetically, he would need a good reference from Ochi's mother. He was smart enough to know that he needed her on his side.

Ochi's mother was shocked by the change in Baaba. Pleasantly, but still shocked. In fact, everyone was. Nobody, including Ochi, could believe the transformation in Baaba in the weeks since Ochi returned from Lagos.

He had been transformed from the bone idle to restlessly industrious. He became a near-permanent fixture at Ochi's house. He only returned home at night to sleep.

"Where have you been all day?" his mother demanded to know. "You don't even eat at home any more."

He ignored her questions.

"You must listen when I speak with you," she snapped. "Where have you been all day?"

He shrugged. He was tired from his labours at Ochi's house – and he was emotionally drained from all his attention to his dreams and plans. "Just leave me alone," he snapped. "I want to go to Lagos."

At that, she smiled to herself. She was certain that her 'lazy' boy would never leave the village. That would require him to become industrious and, to her knowledge, he had not become that. Besides, one did not simply 'up and go' to Lagos. One needed family, someone to guide and help you.

"You have nobody in Lagos," she told him pointedly. "How can you even think about going there?" she demanded.

"Wait and see," he snapped back.

She laughed out loud. "I wish you good luck then, Mr Dreamer!" she said in a mocking tone.

"I'll go, you'll see," he muttered under his breath, beginning to understand how his father felt under her withering sarcasm.

Fortunately for Baaba, he didn't have to wait much longer. Ochi's uncle arrived two weeks later. Baaba was reduced to an admiring bystander as he drove his Volkswagen Beetle into the village, kicking up dust, and a knot of young children behind him. He wore a long-sleeved white shirt and looked dignified in comparison to the men of the village.

Luck was with Baaba that day. When Ochi's uncle arrived he was cutting firewood for Ochi's mother. Looking up and seeing the commotion that the arrival was causing, it took him a moment to get over his own astonishment. But when he did, he gathered himself and rushed to the car as it pulled up in front of the house.

Ignoring the excitement all around and shutting out the screams of the women, Baaba made a small, courteous bow. "Welcome, sir. Let me help you with your bags."

And with that, he went back and forth from the car to the house, making several trips to collect the man's luggage and bringing it into the living room.

Although he kept his eyes respectfully downcast, he watched every move that Ochi's uncle made. He took in his every gesture with admiration, taking note of the way he walked, talked, and smiled. He had already – and subconsciously – begun to mimic his accent. He was impressed with how the women looked at him longingly, including the married women. He did this without envy, for he too looked upon this man as a god from a foreign land.

Baaba watched as the uncle distributed gifts to Ochi's parents and siblings.

"Thank you, Ogo," Ochi's parents said, beaming with pride and gratitude. Neither was blind to the honour that the visit bestowed upon their house.

Ogo was happy to shower them with gifts. Like too many people in the country, the war had taken his relatives from him, leaving him with no immediate family. Having lost his own parents during the war, he 'adopted' the nearest family he could. As Ochi's father was a relation of Ogo's mother, they constituted his only family in the world and he embraced them as though they were much closer than they were.

In truth, Ogo had reason to be close to Ochi's family. They had looked after his parent's compound and kept it clean. In return, as was the custom, they fully expected Ogo to succeed in Lagos and build a 'Zinc house' in the village, one that would be sturdier than the thatch huts that so many lived in.

His parents had hoped that Ogo would marry one of the village girls. That way, when Ogo was off in the city, the wife would remain in the village to look after his late parents' assets and, eventually, his new house.

His parents had been dead set against Ogo making the mistake of marrying a girl from Lagos. She would be unsuitable for the purpose of the marriage. His father had acquired assets, especially land, and a future bride would be necessary to manage these assets.

No one would expect a 'city' girl to show the same respect to the family as a village girl would.

In addition to a wife, he needed children to pass along the family name. If he died with no children, then others, even strangers, could conceivably inherit all the family's assets.

Such an eventuality was simply not acceptable. To maintain his family's honour into future generations, Ogo would have to have children, or at least a child. Such a thing was not an individual decision. It was a family and community matter.

It would be shameful if he did not meet these expectations.

All this went through Baaba's mind as he looked on at the family's reunion. He only wished that he could have been part of the family rather than just a very good friend. Still, he knew that his strategy was sound – he was here and he would meet Ogo.

After several moments, Ogo's attention shifted and his eyes fell on the tall, powerful, and handsome young man who was standing respectfully off to the side. He gestured with his eyes and Ochi jumped forward to introduce Baaba to his uncle.

"This is my best friend, Baaba," he said proudly – for it was true that he was proud. To be Baaba's best friend was a meaningful thing to him. "He has been waiting every day for your arrival," he added.

Ogo arched his eyebrows in curiosity.

"He even refused to go home because he wanted be sure to be here when you arrived," he concluded with a broad smile

Ogo was impressed, both by what Ochi had said and by the way that Baaba had greeted him earlier by the car. He was also favourably impressed by Baaba's physical presence. He turned to the young man. "Tell me, my boy, what is your name?"

Baaba, despite his nature, continued to keep his eyes partly downcast to show due respect to Ogo. Still, he was gratified to note the look in Ogo's eyes when he asked him his name. "My name is Baaba, sir."

"I see, Baaba. And tell me, which village are you from?"

"My village is the one with the big church, sir."

"And your father's name?" Ogo continued, determined now to find out more about this young man.

"Mr Oma, sir." Anyone who had known Baaba through his life would have been shocked at the deference he granted Ogo. They were so used to his disrespect and lack of concern for authority that they would have been astonished. However, they would have missed something very important if all they focused on was Baaba's deference.

He had a plan and a strategy. What should have surprised them – if anything did – was the discipline with which he was following his plan. For it was that discipline that had him working in Ochi's house all these weeks, taking care of every chore he could.

Ogo arched his eyebrows and studied Baaba. "So, you have been waiting for me?"

"Yes, sir, I have."

"Now why would you have been waiting for me?" Ogo inquired.

It was here that Baaba's native boldness found its voice. "Because, sir, I would like to be your houseboy."

At first, Ogo was a bit taken aback by the statement. He looked at Baaba curiously. "But, I don't live in the village, my boy."

"Oh, I know that, sir," Baaba said. "I do not want to be your houseboy here in the village. I want to go to Lagos with you, sir."

Ogo raised his hands in a kind of surrender. "But that is impossible," he said. "You are still in school."

"No, sir," Baaba said quickly, "I don't go to school, sir."

This answer troubled Ogo. "But why are you not in school?"

"Because my parents cannot afford the school fees," Baaba answered, knowing full well that the answer was at best disingenuous and at worst, an out-and-out lie. For his father had made it clear on any number of occasions that he would borrow funds from his church in order to pay his school fees.

Even so, Ogo was not convinced. "But your parents would never allow you to go to Lagos; Lagos is much too far from the village."

"My mother has said that I could go, sir," Baaba said. This time, his answer was a complete falsehood. His mother had never said any such thing and it was unlikely that she would.

Ogo found this to be an interesting subject. 'So, you have already discussed this possibility with your mother?" he asked.

Baaba nodded his head. "Yes, sir. I told her that I was waiting for your arrival and praying for the chance to discuss it with you."

Ogo frowned. "But I had planned on taking Ochi with me," he said. "He will go to a school in Lagos."

Baaba sensed that this was a very important juncture in the discussion. He didn't want to sound too anxious but he wanted to be clear that Ochi coming to Lagos was not a problem in his mind. "I can come with Ochi, sir," he said. "Ochi can go to school. I want to be your houseboy."

Ogo nodded softly. "Okay. We will talk about this later."

"Yes, sir. Thank you, sir."

That night, Baaba spent the night in Ochi's house for the first time. In fact, he did not go home again for several days. With each passing night, Baaba's mother worried more about him until finally she sent his younger brother to Ochi's house to ask him to come home.

"What are you doing here?" Baaba asked his brother angrily.

"Mama sent me to tell you to come home."

"I'm not coming home," he snapped, looking over his shoulder to make sure no one in Ochi's family was listening in on the conversation.

"But Mama misses you."

"Tell her that I'm busy, but that I'm all right," Baaba said before sending his brother on his way.

Meanwhile, Ogo was very pleased with Baaba's company. After five days, he went to Ochi's mother and asked if she would visit Baaba's mother and get her permission for Baaba to remain with him.

Ochi's mother was a bit hesitant, although she didn't tell Ogo why. She had no desire – no one did – to speak with Baaba's mother.

"And, Baaba, will you accompany her?" Ogo said. "I would not want your mother to think that I wanted you to remain with me against your will."

Baaba was thrilled with how things were turning out – although he shared Ochi's mother's reluctance to go and speak with his mother. However, he knew that he would be able to get whatever he wanted from his mother.

To make the task easier, Ogo gave them some very fine gifts and money to take to Baaba's mother. Ochi's mother could have saved herself some concern. As soon as Baaba's mother received the gifts, she was greatly disposed to allow Baaba to remain with Ogo. In her mind, having her son with such a generous person could result in more gifts for her.

Everything was working out just the way that Baaba had hoped. Not only did it seem that he would remain with Ogo, but his relationship to the man was already becoming very close. For while Ochi was in school, Baaba was alone in taking care of Ogo's needs.

From the moment Ochi left in the morning, Baaba was the one to fetch water for the gentleman's bath, to polish his shoes, and to deal with his every need. Baaba polished Ogo's shoes until he could see his own reflection as clear as in the still pond in the back of the village. He filled bucket after bucket of water for the gentleman's bath. He used the heavy charcoal iron to press his shirts.

He held his shaving bowl whilst he shaved.

Baaba was delighted with the role he was playing in Ogo's life. With each passing day, things were turning out exactly as he'd hoped. For his part, Ogo was quite pleased with Baaba as well. More than being satisfied with his behaviour, Ogo took a liking to Baaba. He told him that he looked handsome and that the girls in Lagos would flock round him.

"I doubt that," Baaba said with uncharacteristic humility.

"Ah, but I know how they are," Ogo said, with a twinkle in his eyes. "They will be very happy to meet you."

"If you say so," Baaba said, bowing slightly. He felt happy for the first time in his life. He was glad to serve the older gentleman. More even than whilst doing chores for Ochi's mother, Baaba happily assumed the role of a servant to attend to Ogo's every need and every wish. He genuinely believed that rendering these services to Ogo was a privilege that he was fortunate to have.

The truth was, he admired Ogo and was happy to be so close to him.

Because Ochi left for school in the morning, Baaba had no competition for Ogo's attention during the day. From the time that Ochi left until he returned, Ogo relied exclusively on Baaba. As the days went by, they became closer than master and servant. Ogo came to rely upon Baaba.

Over time, Baaba became his confidante.

Baaba enjoyed his time alone with Ogo. During this time, Ogo would tell him stories of his escapades in Lagos. He would tell him about his girlfriends and the nightlife they enjoyed. Most importantly – and most interestingly to Baaba – Ogo would tell him how easy it was to make money in Lagos.

"I met a man from the Western Region who changed my life," Ogo told Baaba. He went on to describe how this man's influence taught him how easy it was to make money in Lagos.

By the end of his first week in the village, Ogo had a very high regard for Baaba. The two of them had developed a friendship that was warm and trusting. Baaba genuinely liked the older man, and the older man genuinely cared about the younger.

"Listen to me, Baaba," Ogo told him. "If you are able to pass some tests, I think I will take you to Lagos rather than Ochi." The older man looked over his shoulder to make sure no one else could hear him. "You mustn't say a word about this," he went on. "But I would take you as an apprentice instead of Ochi. But pay attention, as much as I like you, my decision would depend on your ability to pass these tests.

"I expect a certain level and standard of service …"

Ogo's words motivated Baaba to work even harder for the older man. It was not difficult for him; he believed that his goal was waiting for him if he did and he was happy to work for Ogo in any case.

Baaba got up earlier than anyone else in the compound to begin his chores. He swept the floors. He started the fires. He attended to Ogo's needs. Even Ochi's mother, for whom he had worked harder than he ever had for his own mother, looked on in amazement at the transformation in Baaba.

She knew Baaba was lazy and had only worked hard for her to meet Ogo. She also knew the trouble he caused in the village, his idleness, and refusal to go back to school. She realized that Ogo was a genuinely positive influence on him.

Ochi's mother was so impressed by the transformation in Baaba that when she happened to meet Baaba's mother in the market, she did not turn and go the other way. She made a point of approaching her to tell her the good news. "I tell you, your son is full of surprises; he does not stop working from morning until late at night."

Baaba's mother was happy with the news and prayed that Ogo's influence had really transformed her son. She thought to herself that he had not been in any trouble since Ogo's arrival. That was a very impressive thing in and of itself.

He was simply working too hard to get in trouble. He had also abandoned his 'bad' friends. He was no longer just hanging around, waiting for something bad to find him.

She was filled with joy and pride about her son. When she arrived home, she announced to her husband, "Baaba is a changed boy; he is doing very well at Ochi's house."

His father glanced up at her and frowned. "Good riddance," was all he had to say.

* * *

Baaba worshipped Ogo. There was nothing that he would not do to earn and hold his affection and respect. When Ogo was in the room, Baaba stood at attention, waiting to receive an instruction or sign as to what he should do. He used everything he'd learned from his army days during the war to show respect for Ogo's authority.

Even when he had the opportunity to sit down, he remained on his feet. He was determined that Ogo would never view him as being 'lazy'. Ogo responded to Baaba's earnest behaviour. "I like this boy," he said many times. And he took him wherever he went.

At Ogo's side, Baaba met many new people; for Ogo visited many friends and relations as he sought to show off his wealth and status.

Baaba stood behind Ogo as he wove the stories of his adventures in Lagos. "It is a wide open city, I tell you. Great opportunity but great danger as well …"

One theme that he constantly returned to in his visits was that, despite his success in Lagos, his desire was to come back to the village, build a house, and get married.

Hearing this, all of Ogo's friends nodded and smiled. Ogo's intention spoke well not only of his own achievements but also of what was most important to all of them – community and family. And everyone could see that he had developed a clear affection for Baaba and was bringing him into his family circle.

There was nothing that Ogo did that was too trivial in Baaba's mind not to be elevated to a great importance by him. "Would you like these?" Ogo said to Baaba one morning, holding three old and worn shirts in his hand.

Had he been holding out three golden goblets of the finest wine in the world, Baaba could not have reacted with any more enthusiasm. His smile lit up the room. "I would love them," he said.

After receiving them, Baaba carefully washed them and laid them out to dry. After that, he always wore one of them, always clean. He swelled with pride, knowing that the shirt had been Ogo's. He felt a little more than 'just himself' when he wore them, like he was wearing a part of Ogo.

With each passing day, he became more dedicated to serving Ogo. He was always at the ready to do whatever it was that Ogo wanted, whether accompanying him on outings or cleaning or cooking.

Ochi saw the budding relationship between his friend and his uncle and he wanted to be part of it. But that would have required him to stay home from school, something his mother would simply not allow.

"But it would only be until Uncle returns to Lagos," Ochi protested.

But his mother would hear none of it. "You should concentrate on your education. That's what you must do. Leave Baaba and Ogo to their own devices," she suggested. "For you, school is what you must concentrate on."

Although he understood his mother's point of view, there was no denying that Ochi felt a bit jealous of his friend and the closeness that he was enjoying with his uncle. On more than one occasion, he'd said something to Baaba.

More and more, Baaba was more certain in his responses to Ochi. He felt more secure in his relationship with Ogo. "Why should I return to my mother?" Baaba demanded. "I did not ask you to go to school, you know. You are a mama's boy. That is why you have ended up in school.

"There was only one choice – school or staying home with us. You chose to go to school. But I have stayed here and now your uncle depends upon me to provide him with necessary services." He shook his head. "I am not going back to my mother."

Baaba's attitude shocked Ochi. He was stunned when he left him. Why, he wondered, had he ever given Baaba so much information about his uncle? Why had he told him about his uncle's life in Lagos? He should never have spoken up. But now he knew it was too late. Baaba was in his compound to stay. His uncle needed and wanted him. His own petty jealousy could not change that.

There was no instant of Baaba being more indispensable to Ogo than in the matter of finding him someone whom he might marry. For marriage was always on Ogo's mind in his village. It was one of the reasons he'd come back – to find a bride. It happened that he had seen a girl who had caught his eye and his interest and he wanted to meet her. He turned to Baaba to arrange it.

"You know that girl, Amaka?" he asked Baaba.

"Of course, sir," Baaba said.

25

"I would like to meet her. She has my interest. Talk to her for me, would you? Find out if she would go on a date with me."

Baaba smiled. He knew that his services in matters of love were indispensable to Ogo and would surely bring him even further into his good graces. "I do not think there will be any problem," he said to Ogo. "Her parents are very poor. You are rich and live in Lagos. She will gladly accept a proposal from you.

"You should speak with her."

Ogo shook his head. "No, I cannot speak to her. You do it. I am not sure she would like me. I cannot bear rejections from women," Ogo confided to Baaba.

Baaba, who had never suffered a rejection from a woman, found it difficult to imagine such a concern, particularly from someone as desirable as Ogo. However, he accepted it, knowing that he would be able to arrange such a date easily. "When would you like her, sir?" he asked enthusiastically, making it plain to Ogo that he had the confidence that Ogo lacked in this instance.

He had no doubt that he could convince Amaka to date Ogo. What Ogo did not know was that Baaba had slept with Amaka in the past; however, that romantic relationship didn't last any longer than any other Baaba had been in. But Baaba's great gift with women was not so much his ability to convince them to have sex with him but his charm in remaining friends even with those girls he no longer was close to.

"Please," he would say to the girls. "I'm sorry if I hurt your feelings."

How could a girl refuse his apology? She couldn't. In the village, the girls liked Baaba. Despite his wicked ways with them.

Ogo was thrilled by Baaba's confidence in regards to Amaka. "Do this for me and I will most definitely take you to Lagos with me and make you my apprentice," he said, a grateful smile spreading across his face.

Baaba fairly jumped with joy. "Please, just tell me where you want to meet with her and she will be there." As soon as the words were out of his mouth, he regretted them. In his enthusiasm to help Ogo, he feared that he had made Amaka sound like one of the easy girls in the village, the ones who would go with any man, any time.

Ogo frowned. "What do you know about her, Baaba? Do you know her well? Does she fool around with men?"

Baaba shook his head. "Oh no, sir," he said emphatically. "She is a good girl. A very good girl. It is just that she is my friend and so I am sure that I can convince her to see you very easily."

Ogo nodded a bit hesitantly. "All right then," he said. "But we must get this exactly right," he went on. "I couldn't bear the shame of being turned down by a girl in the village. In Lagos, I wouldn't care," he added calmly. "But here … well, it would be a terrible loss of face."

Baaba didn't much follow Ogo's concern. He'd been turned down by village girls. Not many, but some. And it hadn't changed his standing. Of course, he was not an important and successful man like Ogo. So, if Ogo wanted this particular girl – and if he was placing so much on dating her – then Baaba was determined to make it happen.

Amaka was a distant relation of the village ruler. While the ruler's family could not help her family financially, as an in-law, he could be very helpful to Ogo, even nominating him for an appointment in the village. Such appointments had many benefits.

Convinced that Baaba could make the meeting happen, Ogo turned his attention to *when* the meeting should take place. After some discussion, they agreed it best to wait until the weekend when people relaxed at home after going to church.

"I think this will be the best," Baaba agreed.

That settled, Baaba waited until Saturday evening to go to Amaka's house to speak with her. He put on one of the shirts Ogo had given to him, settling it snug against his neck, and then headed out to Amaka's house.

When he arrived, he discovered that Amaka wasn't there. "Where is she?" he asked her younger brother.

The young boy pointed in the direction of the river. "She has gone to go fetch some water," he said.

Baaba nodded and then sat down comfortably on the branch of a fallen tree outside the house. He purposefully chose that spot because it was close to the only entrance to the house. Amaka could not return without his seeing her.

He sat, biding his time, for nearly an hour. During that time, more than one person came by and asked him what he was doing. Each time he replied that he was, "Waiting."

His answer elicited laughter and curious looks. Waiting for what? For whom? But Baaba was known to be one of the village's curious members and so he was given wide latitude by some to go about his business.

Finally, he spotted her walking towards the house. He knew it was her immediately. She was walking with a pot of water balanced on her head and a wet cloth wrapped around her body, keeping her cool during her exertions. Even from a distance, he could hear her humming a hymn from church. As she came closer, he could see the blissful expression on her face, as if she didn't have a care in the world.

As she came closer still, Baaba jumped up from the tree branch where he was sitting, flashed one of his famous charming smiles, and called out her name. "Amaka, Amaka, I have been waiting for you," he said sweetly.

Hearing his voice brought her out of her blissful reverie. She eyed him suspiciously. "Waiting for me? Why is that? What have I done, Baaba?"

He laughed easily at her concern. "Nothing, nothing at all," he said.

She continued to view him with apprehension. Why was it that Baaba would come to see her, after their last encounter? They were friends, yes, but that didn't mean that she hadn't been deeply wounded by the way he had treated her. She had fallen for Baaba's charm, believed his charming words, and surrendered to his sensuous ways. He made her feel as if she was the most beautiful girl in the world … and then what happened? Why, he ditched her for the next thing in a skirt.

She had agreed to forgive him but she had never gotten rid of the hurt, particularly because his next conquest was her dear friend. Yes, they were friends. But that didn't mean that she wanted him at her house – or that she wanted much to do with him at all. He was trouble to young girls like her.

At least she had not become pregnant from her dalliance with him. Even now, she trembled with the anxiety that had given her stomach cramps the entire month until she got her period again.

"What are you doing here?" she asked, trying to keep her voice light and cheerful, not betraying the emotions she felt. "Have you not done enough damage to me already?"

Baaba laughed – albeit a bit nervously. "Amaka, we have been through all that already," he said. "I have apologised from the bottom of my heart. What else can I do?" he asked.

Several things came to mind, but Amaka kept them to herself. Instead, she waited, wanting to hear why it was that Baaba was at her house, waiting for her.

Seeing that she was not much interested in small talk, Baaba got right to the point. "I have come to give you good news; you are a very lucky girl," he said brightly. "Of all the girls in this village, Ogo has chosen you as his bride." He did not wait for her to reply, or for the surprised look to finish forming on her face. "Have you any idea how important he is in Lagos, the capital city? He could have any girl he wanted but he chose you." He smiled warmly. "You, Amaka," he said, his eyes twinkling brightly, "you are a very lucky girl."

But Amaka did not *feel* lucky. Rather, she felt more suspicious than ever. "What did you say?" she demanded, narrowing her dark eyes at Baaba. "What have you told him so that Ogo wants to marry me?" She removed the water pot from her head and set it down on the ground. "What does he want with a village girl in any case if he is so high and mighty? I cannot speak proper English and my parents cannot afford the school fees." Even as she was speaking these words, something else was happening. She was growing excited that Baaba might be telling her the truth. Yes, she was 'just' a village girl and couldn't understand why an important man would be interested in her, but being just a village girl made her very intrigued about the interest of this important man.

After all, she had heard of Ogo's visit and had seen him on a few occasions when he visited his friends with Baaba. She had heard the gossip and understood that he lived in Lagos and was rich. Well, that meant that if she became his wife, he would take her to Lagos. He would give her money to help her parents and siblings.

Baaba could see a transformation taking place in her thoughts, but he didn't know exactly what it meant; not yet. She eyed him suspiciously still, but there was a good deal more playfulness in her eyes now. "You are teasing me, aren't you, Baaba?"

He shook his head, but she wasn't convinced.

"I know you, Baaba. You are just using Ogo's good name to trick me into going to bed with you again." She shook her head firmly. "It will not work, Baaba. No way," she added for emphasis.

"No, no, no," Baaba said vehemently. "I am not joking. Ogo sent me to speak with you. He sent me to ask you." He watched her expression change and the smooth skin on her cheeks form a smile. Yes, he knew he could convince her now. "Imagine," he said to her. "Just imagine what it will be like to go to Lagos and see all the beautiful things we only hear about."

Baaba knew that he was being somewhat deceitful now. He had overheard Ochi's mother talking to Ogo about marrying a village girl, a village girl who would remain in the village when he returned to Lagos. "Okay," he thought to himself, he wasn't being completely honest with Amaka. But maybe Ogo would decide to take her to Lagos. That was possible, wasn't it? Of course it was.

Regardless, she wouldn't know for sure until *after* the marriage.

Still, he felt uncomfortable with the deceit. Well, not the deceit but with the possibility that she would somehow see through his message. "When can you come and see him?" he asked hastily, wanting to move the conversation forward.

She rolled her eyes. "Come on, Baaba, I have to think about it." She might have been intrigued by the possibility but she was, at heart, a good and sensible girl. That Baaba had charmed her into his bed spoke more about his gifts than her behaviour.

However, Baaba knew there was danger in delay. Time to think was time to reconsider. "No, no," he said. "There is no time to think. Ogo is going back to Lagos next week." He shrugged as if to suggest that it was not an important matter. "Of course, if you are not interested, he can always pick another girl." He saw her expression change. "I know he wants to find a girl before he goes back to Lagos."

"Why is he in such a hurry?" Amaka asked, again showing her sensible side. "Besides, I cannot decide without talking it over with my mother, anyway."

Baaba felt a shiver of concern. Now her mother would be involved *before* Amaka felt committed. That meant anything could happen. He had to get her committed right away. Strike while the iron is hot! "You know, this is why he came home. He did not want to marry Lagos girls."

Amaka shrugged. "I still have to tell my mother."

Baaba shook his head. "You are putting the cart before the ox," he said. "You shouldn't tell anyone – including your mother – until after your visit. What if you don't like him? You will have gotten her all excited for nothing."

Amaka thought about Baaba's words. They seemed to make sense. Still, he had tricked her before with his sensible-sounding arguments. "No, Baaba," she insisted. "I need her advice."

"I really think it would be better if you met with Ogo first," he said emphatically. "If you like him, then you can talk it over with your mother." He

29

laughed. "Then you will have something to discuss with her. If you don't like him, what will you say? Nothing, and everything is done."

Baaba could feel the perspiration forming on his scalp. This girl was hard work. He didn't remember it being this difficult to convince her to have sex with him. Why was she being so difficult? Maybe it was just easier when he was his own agent rather than someone else's … But it was easy for him. Women fell for his charms and his good looks. It was more difficult to convince them to fall for someone else.

Amaka was giving serious thought to what Baaba had said. It *did* make sense after all. Why should she get her mother all involved if nothing was going to come of the meeting? "Okay," she said after a moment. "But I will not agree to anything until I have spoken to my mother."

"Of course not, Amaka." He laughed in a teasing way that made her feel ashamed. "It's not as if he will marry you after your first meeting."

She looked away from him, feeling foolish. When she looked back at him, her eyes were filled with anger. "I don't trust men any more after what you did to me," she said sharply.

Baaba, who knew he had accomplished all he was looking to accomplish, simply smiled. "I am only a young boy. Ogo is a mature man looking for a wife. You should not confuse my behaviour with him."

She seemed satisfied with his words. "Okay," she said, "I will meet with Ogo next weekend."

Baaba smiled broadly, a genuine, true smile. He had succeeded! He was already savouring his reward. But then his smile quickly faded. If he was to be rewarded for his efforts, Ogo must know about them.

"You must not forget that I am the one who has arranged this meeting," he emphasized to Amaka. "You must tell Ogo to take me to Lagos. This is the reason I am doing this. If you refuse his proposal, I will not go to Lagos."

Amaka smiled in the way that only a woman who held all the cards could smile. She stepped back, looked him up and down, and then nodded her head knowingly. "I knew it," she gloated. "I knew that there had to be something in it for you.

"So, you want to go to Lagos but now you find that you need me in order to realize your dream." She placed her hands on her hips and looked at him with a mocking expression. "You need me," she said again, emphasizing the truth of the statement. "Baaba," she said softly, "you are terrible. You know that."

"You're right," he argued. "I am terrible and selfish. But that doesn't change anything, Amaka. I advise you not to miss this opportunity. You know what they say, 'opportunity only knocks once'. Miss it and you will not get a second chance. So make fun of me if you would like, but remember, Ogo can have any girl he wants. He is a rich, influential man.

"You should look at this as a gift. If he chooses another, imagine how you will feel. You will be jealous of Ogo's future wife wearing all the best clothes and being the envy of her friends. Imagine instead that *you* are Ogo's wife. Then imagine going to Lagos and coming back with new clothes for your mother, brothers, and sisters, and sending money to your mother from Lagos to help her take care of your brothers and sisters. Ogo may even buy a car for you, like a Volkswagen Beetle, and teach you how to drive it, can you imagine?"

The picture he painted filled Amaka with a longing the likes of which she had never experienced before.

Baaba suddenly felt desperate to make everything work. "Please," he said, "please come with me tonight, even if only for ten minutes. I promised Ogo I would bring you." He was imploring her now. Pleading. But in a charming, self-satisfied way that was both endearing and annoying. "Please don't make me to be the fool who has fallen short and not fulfilled his promises."

She shook her head. "Oh no, not tonight," she said hastily. "I cannot go tonight. No."

"Why not tonight?" he demanded. "Ogo is leaving very soon. He only has time tonight." He knew he was lying to her now but he was drunk with the power of his charm and his ability to manipulate her feelings and actions.

"Oh, all right," she said. "But you will have to wait for me to change my clothes. And I will have to tell my mother that I am going to visit my auntie." She looked around as if realizing for the first time how it would look if she spent more time talking to Baaba. "Now you have to go and hide until I am ready." She smiled a warm, teasing smile. "We don't want Mama to see you," she whispered knowingly to her partner in crime.

Baaba clasped his hands together and pressed them against his chest. "Thank you, thank you. You have saved my life.

"I will hide by the Iroko tree near the square and wait for you, please don't take too long." Baaba lifted the water pot and helped Amaka put it back on her head. "Remember. Not too long," he said, and then he headed for the Iroko tree.

"I promise," she said.

True to her word, it was not terribly much longer before Amaka made her way towards the Iroko tree. As soon as he saw her, Baaba smiled broadly. Then, when she came up to the tree, he took her hand and looked up to the sky. "Thank you, dear Lord."

She laughed. "Why are you thanking the Lord?" she asked. "You should be thanking me. I'm the one who has deceived her mother to meet you – and to meet Ogo."

"You are right," Baaba conceded. He looked at her and he felt a deep longing. Amaka had not only changed her clothes but she had put on a bit of make-up to improve on her already naturally beautiful dark face. The dress she wore showed off her womanly curves to perfection. Baaba felt a familiar feeling as he gazed upon her. He took her hand and smiled his most charming smile. "You look so nice, you know," he said, not thinking so much about Ogo or Lagos now. I wish I had money to marry you," he added in a very sincere voice. "If I did, I would not let Ogo or any man touch you." Then he smiled again. "Maybe when I make money I can take you from Ogo."

Amaka gently removed her hand from his. Then, with a shrug, she said, "You like women too much and you have many of them so don't be trying to win me over with your sweet talk."

Baaba opened his mouth to protest but she stopped him. "My brother told me you are interested in that policeman's daughter, the one that just came back from the school in the town."

Baaba looked away, hiding his guilty expression. "That is terribly unfair," he protested. "Your brother should not be discussing boys' talk with you."

She laughed. "I would worry less about the talking and more about what is being said," she observed.

"Well, yes, I do like her and will make sure I make enough money to marry her," he said shyly. "But she is still in school. And her father is a terror so I have to be very careful."

She smiled sweetly, as though seeing this vulnerable side of Baaba was even more charming than his usual confidence. Her smile – and the obvious emotion behind it – alerted him to his immediate mission.

"Anyway," he said, clearing his throat. "That is not my concern right now. Right now, I have to make sure that Ogo marries you so he can take me to Lagos." Then he looked her right in the eye. "When we get to Lagos, you must give me big food like my mother does."

"But I am not your mother," she said, teasing him.

"You will take good care of me though, won't you?"

They joked and talked all the way to Ochi's compound. Along the way, Baaba told her some of the stories Ogo had told him about Lagos.

When they arrived at the compound, Ogo was sitting in a lounge chair with a bottle and a glass of beer on the small table in front of him. He had a blue shirt with an open collar to show off his hairy chest. He was under the impression that showing off his hairy chest appealed to women.

"Good evening, sir," Amaka said sweetly, showing her respect to Ogo as they came closer to him.

Ogo played his part perfectly. He appeared surprised, as if their arrival had not been expected. His eyes widened and then he smiled warmly. "Who is this young beautiful thing?" he asked, turning towards Baaba with a look of astonishment. "Where on earth did you find this queen, Baaba?"

Baaba rubbed the palm of his left hand on his head, a gesture he made when he was feeling a bit naughty. "She is an angel who has fallen from the sky, sir; an angel who I happened upon while making my way back to the compound," he concluded with a sweet laugh.

Ogo smiled at Baaba. "Baaba, please get this queen a chair and a bottle of Fanta," he said in a voice that was both kind and filled with authority. He turned to Amaka. "Or would you like two bottles?"

Amaka's eyes widened. Two bottles? That was a luxury far beyond her family. Her mother could not even afford a single bottle for one child, much less two bottles at a time.

Ogo, of course, had made the offer knowing the effect his generosity would have on the young woman. He watched as the astonishment at his generosity sank in. It seemed as if her personal and family history was playing out in the expression on her face. She had lost two brothers in the war. Her mother struggled to raise six children on her own, with Amaka being the second.

Amaka's mother focused more on her two remaining sons because they were the ones who would secure and maintain the name of the family for future generations. In her family, as in the others, daughters were treated less favourably than sons. This seeming unfairness was simply the result of practical considerations. Girls would eventually marry into other families, acquire new names, and lose their original family identity. The boys would remain, bringing their own wives to their families. They were the ones who would care for their mother in her old age.

Boys had to achieve in order to take care of their families. Girls could simply be married off. As a result, the general attitude in the culture was that girls deserved – and received – less attention and care than boys.

Ogo's offer had its desired effect. Amaka was favourably impressed. Still, she remembered her place. "Thank you, sir, but I will have one only."

She was very conscious of wanting not to appear greedy. She wanted Ogo to like her. Of course she would have preferred two bottles. Not for herself, of course. She would have taken the second bottle home to her mother and siblings. But she was a good girl, a sweet girl. She would never allow her family's poverty to colour the way that Ogo looked upon her.

Baaba could see by the light in Ogo's eyes that he had succeeded in his task. With joy in his heart, his footsteps were light as he hurried to the bedroom to get a bottle of Fanta for Amaka. Some might have thought it odd that the Fanta would be in the bedroom but Ogo kept all his goodies in his bedroom for entertaining his guests – crates of lager, malt drinks, soft drinks, and spirits for the elders of the community or visitors from the village ruler. He also kept Cabin biscuits for the young ones and girls who came to visit him.

Baaba was the perfect servant. He opened the bottle of Fanta and poured it into the glass for Amaka, all the while smiling at her with a big smile. When he could do so discreetly, he winked at her, making sure she did not forget that her good fortune in catching Ogo's eye had a lot to do with him and that his future depended on her.

"For our future queen," he proclaimed as he dramatically poured the liquid into the glass. When he was finished, he set the bottle of Fanta back down on the table. Then he took his usual position behind Ogo's chair, awaiting his next instruction.

He was shocked to hear criticism in Ogo's voice when he said, "You have failed terribly. You can't even serve a lady a drink properly." He made a dismissive sound with his tongue, clicking it against his teeth. "And you want to go to Lagos?" Not waiting for – or expecting – a response, he stood up and took the glass from the table. He stood in front of Amaka and, with a small bow, handed her the glass. "Please drink this, our queen."

Amaka smiled sweetly as she accepted the glass. Then she took a sip of the Fanta and placed the glass back on the table. "Thank you, sir."

Pleased by the graciousness that she displayed, graciousness that equalled her beauty, Ogo returned to his chair. "You must hand the glass directly to the lady and remain standing until she takes the first sip," he said to Baaba with a condescending smile. "This is how it is done in Lagos," he added, in a tone that made it clear to Baaba that he was still being tested and evaluated.

Baaba swallowed his annoyance at being made to feel the fool in front of Amaka, whom he considered himself the better of – after all, he *had* bedded her! – And focused on his need to continue to learn and improve his performance if he was to ever get to go to Lagos.

Ogo and Amaka exchanged some small talk until Ochi's mother, who had been preparing the evening meal, came and asked Ogo if he would like to eat.

Ogo, rather than answering directly, turned to Amaka. "Only if my queen will eat with me," he said, reaching his hand out to touch Amaka's hair. "Will you eat with me, my queen Amaka?"

Amaka averted her eyes, because Ogo's charm genuinely moved her and because she realized that she too was being tested, and, minute by minute, she wanted more and more to pass the test.

"If that is your desire, I would like that very much, sir," she said.

So it was settled. In no time, the meal was brought out and served. Baaba lifted the bowl of water first to Ogo and then to Amaka. Amaka dipped her fingers into the water and smiled to herself. She could not believe that Baaba was serving her water to wash her hands before eating, that he was serving her, this person who had fooled her with his arrogant charm and taken advantage of her innocence. For the first time since he'd worked to convince her to meet Ogo, Amaka believed that the world that Baaba had outlined to her might actually come true.

"It is unbelievable," she thought. "Life is being turned upside down. I will be the queen and Baaba will be my servant."

Baaba was not blind to exactly the thoughts that Amaka was having. Even so, that would not change his behaviour. He took his position behind Ogo, as Ogo and Amaka enjoyed the meal.

Baaba was very conscious not to do anything wrong. He did not want to be reprimanded again. He wanted to pass the test. He did not want to lose sight of his dream of going to Lagos.

One of his duties was to make sure that the diners' glasses were never empty. He did not forget the lesson that Ogo had demonstrated earlier as to how a drink was to be served to a woman. Ogo nodded his head approvingly as he watched Baaba pick up Amaka's glass and fill it before returning it directly to her hand.

Yes, the boy was learning. Ogo was clear in his expectation that Baaba perfect every act and behaviour before they went to Lagos. He had made clear to Baaba that he was being taught and tested all the time and that he needed to pass the tests if he was going to go to Lagos.

Baaba stayed focused and tried his hardest. He poured the drinks with a steady hand and a demure expression. He was quite sure that he had passed the 'drinks test'. After the two had enjoyed some refreshment and food, Baaba once again raised the bowl of water to the two of them, only this time he also presented them with a piece of an old towel with which to dry their hands.

This seemed to satisfy Ogo and to be pleasurable to Amaka. As soon as he had put down the water bowl, he presented Ogo with a chewing stick with which to pick at his teeth.

"Ah," Ogo sighed as he sat back in his chair. As he poked absently at his teeth, he felt fully satisfied – both by the meal and, more importantly, by being in the presence of the beautiful Amaka.

After a moment, Ogo looked at Amaka, who demurely looked away. This pleased Ogo. He turned to Baaba. "Baaba, can you check that the bedroom is tidy," he said. "I would like to speak to Amaka, my queen, privately."

Amaka raised her eyes, suddenly alarmed. "No, sir," she said quickly. "We should talk here, not in the bedroom …"

Ogo considered her for a moment, trying to assess her meaning in her protest. "Are you afraid of me?" he asked. He smiled at her. "I want to marry you. How can you have children for me if you are afraid of me?"

Amaka felt trapped. How could she avoid going into the bedroom with Ogo without insulting him? It was then that Baaba came to her rescue. He winked at Amaka and then turned to Ogo. "Sir," he said, "I believe she is just trying to be nice and proper. I believe that she really wants to talk to you."

Ogo seemed to accept this explanation. "All right then," he pronounced. "Go and tidy the bedroom." He looked at Amaka. "Do not concern yourself with anything, my queen. We will talk and everything will be all right."

* * *

Amaka lowered her eyes and felt the heat rush to her cheeks. Still, she was more comfortable for Baaba saying something. Meanwhile, Baaba rushed off to the bedroom to do as he was instructed. As he tidied the room, he hoped and prayed that Amaka realized how important she was to him. She was his ticket to Lagos. He couldn't imagine that she wouldn't show him her appreciation for all that he was doing for her and her family.

Being Ogo's future wife was a privilege. There were other girls in the village Ogo could easily have chosen to be his bride. But he, Baaba, had made sure that Ogo chose Amaka.

"Everything is ready, sir," Baaba said when he finished tidying up. He bowed and smiled to both Ogo and Amaka.

"Good," Ogo said brusquely. Then he stood up from his chair and groaned softly from the cramps he suffered in his legs. "Okay," he said to Amaka, extending his hand to her. "Let's go," he said as he helped her up and guided her to the bedroom.

Ochi's mother had been watching and discreetly listening to the developments during the meal and, as soon as Ogo and Amaka left for the bedroom, she plied Baaba with questions. "Do you think she will marry him?" she asked urgently. "Did you speak to her?"

"Yes, I have spoken with her," he said, his voice certain. "She likes the idea. Yes, I think she would very much like to marry Ogo," he said.

Ochi's mother nodded. "Good. Yes. She is a good girl. She will be able to care for Ogo's parents' house in the village. She would have no problem concieving, her mother is hard-working and has given birth to many children."

As he listened, Baaba realized that these were her priorities for what made a successful marriage. No romance, just responsibility. Then he froze with fear. He hoped that she wouldn't tell Amaka about the plan to keep her in the village after the marriage. He knew how that would ruin his own plan for taking advantage of the situation with Amaka to earn his own ticket to Lagos.

After all, going to Lagos was the main reason that she was willing to consider the marriage at all.

Ochi came into the compound, and Baaba immediately set upon him to share with him Ogo's intention with Amaka and how that would help his own cause for getting to Lagos. But Ochi seemed uninterested in what Baaba had to say.

"What is the matter?" Baaba asked. "You seem angry with me."

It surprised Ochi that Baaba was able to recognize that someone was angry with him at all. After all, Baaba was so self-consumed he hardly noticed anything going on around him if it didn't directly serve his purpose.

Truth be known, Ochi was displeased with Baaba anyway for taking his place. He had been trying to avoid his old friend for days and the most disturbing thing was that Baaba did not even notice. So Ochi reacted to this latest comment simply – despite his surprise. He shrugged his shoulders and said, "You are now in charge, what can I say?" With that, he retired to his room. The simple truth was, he had had enough of Baaba's stories. Not only did they annoy him, but they made him jealous. Every one of them was about what Baaba would do when he got to Lagos.

Without Ochi to talk to, Baaba found himself pacing apprehensively while Ogo and Amaka talked in Ogo's bedroom. All he could do was pray that Amaka agreed to Ogo's marriage proposal. If she didn't … well, he didn't want to think about what that might mean for his own future.

After a time of pacing, he just couldn't play all his concerns in his head any more. It was tiring him out. He settled down onto a large branch of a tree outside the compound and fell asleep, exhausted by mental fatigue.

Two hours later, he was awakened by Ogo's laughing voice. "Baaba, you are worse than the disciples of Jesus who could not keep awake for their Lord," he said, laughing cheerfully.

Startled, Baaba jumped up from the tree branch, rubbed his eyes, and said, "Good morning, sir," he stammered, trying to collect himself. "I was only closing my eyes and waiting."

Ogo shook his head. "It is not morning, Baaba ..."

It was then that it dawned on Baaba where he was and what was happening. It all came rushing back. The meal. Amaka. The discussion in Ogo's room. His eyes widened with an unspoken question.

Ogo smiled. "You have completed your task well," Ogo said, calming Baaba. "Amaka has agreed to marry me."

Baaba let out a deep sigh of relief.

"Now we have to sort out all the arrangements." Ogo spoke quickly. "We do not have very much time. I will be leaving shortly."

Baaba nodded, disturbed that Ogo had said 'I' and not 'we'.

"I will be going to see Amaka's mother tomorrow, and then the village ruler. I also have to inform the chiefs. For now, you have to take her home to her mother."

Baaba nodded.

"By the way," Ogo added off-handedly. "Amaka insists that she can only go to Lagos if you are going." He shrugged. "So you have to come. I will have to speak with your mother as well to let her know."

Baaba was fully awake now. It took all his energy not to jump for joy. "Thank you very much, sir," he said, grasping Ogo's hand and shaking it enthusiastically. Then he prepared to run off to take care of his next chore.

"Wait," he said. "Before you do anything else, I want you to take Amaka home and deliver her safely to her mother."

"Yes, sir," Baaba said, rubbing his eyes to become fully awake. He put on his shirt and then went to collect Amaka.

As soon as they had left the compound, Baaba turned to Amaka and began to ask her questions.

"So," he wanted to know, "what happened? What did he say?"

"I don't know if I should be talking about any of this," Amaka said coyly, smiling at him. "After all, a wife doesn't speak to another man about what her husband has told her."

"Amaka!" Baaba cried out in frustration. "First of all, it is not the same thing and, second of all, you are not man and wife yet."

She laughed. "I was only teasing," she said. "He said that he will look after my mother and my siblings," she told him.

"That's it?" Baaba cried out. "Certainly he said more than that. You have said that you would marry him. Did he agree to take me to Lagos?"

She shook her head. "Baaba, is it *always* about you?"

He seemed not to hear her at all. Instead, he continued to ask her question after question, not even waiting for an answer.

Amaka drew a deep breath, showing her exasperation at the number of questions Baaba was asking. He did not let her answer one question before he threw the next one. Finally, she could take it no longer. She put up her hands to stop his questioning. "Okay, okay, Baaba. Yes, I will marry Ogo and he will take me to Lagos when he is going." She then went on to tell him that they discussed his future employment in Lagos.

"Ogo likes you very much and he promised me that he would take you to Lagos," she said. She also told him that Ogo was impressed with his intelligence and that he would learn the trade very quickly.

"Did he say how much I could make in six months?" he asked, drunk with his need to know everything about his future.

"Baaba," she cautioned. "You must learn to be patient. You have always wanted to rush everything in life. You need to be careful and thoughtful, or you will find that you've fallen into a trap," she advised him. "Now, you must trust Ogo. He must make arrangements for the marriage. We will be leaving for Lagos in two weeks. In the meantime, Ogo has said that I must begin eating much more. He wants me to put on weight so his neighbours in Lagos will not think me undernourished."

In a short time, they arrived at Amaka's compound. "Well, good bye," he said to her. "Thank you for your patience and kindness. You have been better to me than I have ever been to you."

She appreciated his saying that. But she didn't respond to it directly. Instead, she said that it was because of him that she would be married soon.

"Certainly I am in your debt for your help," she said.

He smiled. "Maybe," he conceded. "I guess we have helped out one another," he said.

"I guess we have."

With that, Baaba waved and left Amaka at her compound.

* * *

The following morning, Ogo was very focused on the many tasks ahead. He instructed Baaba to go to the palm wine tapper to arrange for drinks.

"How many kegs shall I order, sir?" Baaba asked.

"Hmm, let's see," Ogo said, thinking about the need ahead. "Ten," he said. "No, wait, make that twelve. We will need two more for other visitors."

Baaba nodded. "No problem, sir. What day shall I tell them to have them for, sir?"

"Tell them for Saturday morning."

Baaba turned, ready to go, but Ogo was not yet finished.

"When you return, we need to go to the ruler and arrange a day to see the chiefs, Amaka's parents and uncles." Ogo knotted his hands. "There is so much to do this week," he fretted.

"Yes, sir," Baaba said. "We will need hot drinks, sir."

Ogo agreed. "Yes, I know. I still have some bottles of gin and whisky I brought from Lagos. We will go to the town and get some lager, stout, and soft drinks. Tomorrow is market day, so I will ask Ochi's mother to buy cola nut and enough food. It will be up to her to organize the women who will do the cooking," he observed to himself. Then he turned to Baaba. "Is there anything else you can think of?" he asked Baaba, more as a friend than a servant.

"Yes, sir," he said. "Amaka's mother will need money if she is to buy food and drinks to entertain her guests."

Ogo smiled and nodded, grateful for Baaba's foresight. It would have been bad form for him to have put Amaka's mother in such a difficult position. "I will take care of that when we go to see them," he said resolutely. "And I will also give Amaka's father enough money to get the drinks for the elders and his friends."

Ogo was quiet for a moment, going over his endless lists in his head. "Ah," he said finally. "This is all so much. Let's have some breakfast and draw up a full list of everything we need."

"As you wish, sir," Baaba said. With that, he went off to take care of his errands. Along the way, he couldn't help but reflect on his good fortune. "My luck has really changed for good," he thought to himself. "I am going to go to Lagos. Who would ever have believed that things would turn out so well for me?" As he walked along, he whistled a popular Biafran war tune.

* * *

The marriage ceremony was performed. Everyone in the village was happy with the union. After the ceremony, the days just flew by and soon it was time for Ogo to leave for Lagos.

Ochi's mother prepared local food and other delicacies for the newly married couple. These were difficult to find in Lagos because they were indigenous to the village and included spices and herbs to help Amaka get pregnant quickly.

Amaka was instructed on the hows and whens of taking the various herbs and potions. Once she became pregnant, she would return to the village. Her job was in the village not in Lagos.

"Remember, she has to come back here," Ochi's mother insisted to Ogo. "You cannot keep her in Lagos."

Ogo nodded, listening closely to what he was told.

Baaba was also preparing for the trip. His mother had agreed to everything that Ogo had discussed. His dreams were now within reach. He ignored his father's advice to remain in the village and go back to school.

In his mind, there was nothing for him in the village.

His future was in Lagos.

Chapter 5:
Baaba's Disappointment

TWO DAYS BEFORE DEPARTING FOR Lagos, Ogo stood beside Baaba while he slept and, as the first thin light of dawn arrived, he gently shook his shoulder. "Baaba," he said softly. "Baaba, wake up."

Baaba opened his eyes. As soon as he saw that it was Ogo, he sat up straight. "Yes, sir," he said.

Ogo frowned. "I need to talk to you," he said in a tone unlike any he'd used to speak with Baaba before. "Come." With that, Ogo rose and walked from the bedroom.

Baaba quickly rose and followed along after Ogo into his bedroom, rubbing the sleep from his eyes with the palms of his hands. Once they were inside the bedroom, Ogo pointed to a chair and told Baaba to sit down.

"You have been a very good companion," he began, his voice softer and heavier than it had ever been. "You have served me well. Extremely well. You have made it possible for me to marry Amaka." He lowered his eyes and paused. A moment later, he raised his eyes and looked at Baaba again. "I know I promised that if you fulfilled your tasks correctly and faithfully, I would take you to Lagos with me to be my apprentice …"

He paused again, and in that pause Baaba felt his heart sink to his stomach. He leaned a bit forward, listening ever more carefully to Ogo's words.

"Well, I am sorry to say that things have changed a little bit …"

"But …"

Ogo raised his hand to stop Baaba from speaking. "We cannot both travel to Lagos together," he said. "I have to go first. I will send for you to join me shortly after that."

Baaba felt emotion bubbling up in his throat. He wanted to protest but he also knew that it wasn't his place to do so. He was also disarmed by the tone of Ogo's voice. Usually, Ogo was always boisterous and loud. But he spoke this morning in a calm, understated tone. Baaba blinked. Once. Twice. "What did you say, sir?" he asked sheepishly, fearing that he'd simply not heard Ogo correctly.

"I said that I must leave for Lagos without you," Ogo said directly. "I will go with Amaka now. I will send for you when I move from my one-room apartment to a two-room apartment." He shrugged. "Sure you see that I need a little bit of privacy with my new wife if we are to make babies," he added. He shook his head. "There is just not enough room for an extra person."

"So I am not going because of Amaka?" Baaba asked, still having trouble understanding this profound change in his hopes and dreams.

40

"No, no, no," Ogo insisted. "Not *because* of Amaka. I am a married man now. I need the space to be with my wife. It is my decision, not Amaka's."

Now Baaba's emotions and fears began to find a voice. "But … but," he sputtered. "But you will forget about me when you get there," he said, unable to hide his fear.

Ogo's eyes widened in the face of Baaba's emotions. "No, I will not forget about you. I promise you," he said. "Do you not believe me? You trust me, don't you?

"I need you in Lagos to be my apprentice. I will send for you, just as I am promising you I will."

Baaba heard Ogo speaking but he no longer heard his words. All he could think about was that the very person who had been responsible for his wonderful good fortune was now the very one who was standing in the way of his going to Lagos. "If Amaka was not going to Lagos," he thought to himself, "Ogo would not need two rooms and I would be going with him." He focused his eyes once again on Ogo, still conscious of how important this man was in his life. He tried not to think of the cruel irony of his situation. Instead, he tried to focus on what was essential and important about his future.

"Do you have any idea, sir, how long it might be before you will be able to send for me?"

"Oh, not long," Ogo said, leaning closer to Baaba. "A month, maybe a little bit more." He saw the disappointment on Baaba's face and it touched his heart. "The first thing I will do when I get to Lagos is set about finding a two-room apartment. I will do this because I need you as my apprentice." He placed his hands on Baaba's shoulders and looked into his eyes. "You are a very good boy and I know that you will go places with me." Then he smiled an absurd, overly enthusiastic smile. "Don't worry. I promise that it won't be too long."

Baaba could not help but furrow his brow in worry. He wanted to believe Ogo, but his disappointment was so sudden and so deep it was very hard to mask how he felt.

"Baaba, please do not worry," Ogo said. "You are definitely coming to live with me in Lagos. Nothing can stop that."

Baaba nodded his head without saying another word. What was left to say? Nothing he could say would change anything now. "Thank you, sir," he whispered as he turned to leave Ogo's room and return to his own. As he stood in the doorway, he looked bitterly at his own packed bag. The bag seemed to mock him for his naïve dreams and hopes.

He turned and walked away from his room. He stopped and sat down heavily on one of the benches in the compound. Alone with his thoughts, he tried to sort out what had happened to him. He had gone to sleep the evening before, filled with dreams and hopes, and then he'd been awakened from his slumber only to have those dreams deflated. "One minute I am going to Lagos and my future is bright," he thought, "and the next, I am stuck here still." He shook his head.

He didn't know whether to believe Ogo's promise. Perhaps he would but his disappointment made it very hard for him to see a bright side.

Why did life have to be so filled with ups and downs?

"I will have to speak with Amaka about this," he mumbled to himself. "It is all her fault."

He put his hands to the side of his head and he began to sob. Ochi's mother observed Baaba crying and her heart nearly broke for him. She went to Ogo. "Now you must go and talk to Baaba," she told him. "He is crying so sadly."

Meanwhile, Baaba's thoughts became even darker. He feared that Ogo would forget him when he returned to Lagos. "My life is finished," he cried. "There is nothing for me now." The tears poured from his eyes. He wished that Ogo had never taken a fancy to Amaka. Worse, he wished that he had not helped convince Amaka to marry Ogo. But what choice had he? Ogo wanted to meet Amaka. Baaba *had* to make it happen. It was one of the tests he had to pass in order to be able to go to Lagos. And what did he do? He made it happen, that is what he did. He made Ogo's dreams come true.

And now? Now he wasn't going to Lagos anyway.

All sorts of horrible thoughts whirled around in his head. He was terrified that if Ogo went back to Lagos without him, he would forget about him and all the tests he'd passed … and then all his dreams would be as dust. "My life is finished," he cried out again, seeing nothing but darkness ahead where he had once seen the bright colours of Lagos. Why had Ogo had to have fancied Amaka? Why had he convinced her to marry Ogo?

What else could he have done? Nothing.

"He has used me," he decided dejectedly. "He has used me and now he has replaced me with Amaka. It is not fair," he argued to himself. "I have given all I was asked and then some. I met all his constant demands. I passed all his tests. Lord, I went further than I could have done for anyone."

He had never felt so sad before, not even in the midst of war.

Not only were his dreams ruined, but his sense of honour was stained. What would he say to Emi and Ochi? He had boasted like a rooster to them about his trip with Ogo to Lagos. Now Ochi, his own feelings hurt by Baaba's attitude and his relationship with his uncle, would have the last laugh. "Oh, why, why?" Baaba moaned. The more these thoughts swirled in his head, the more tears poured down his cheeks.

It was then that Ogo came out of his room and sat in his lounge chair. He looked over at Baaba and frowned. "Why are you crying?"

Baaba could not answer him. He simply looked up at him with red eyes and tears streaming down his cheeks.

Ogo's brow furrowed in concern and then annoyance. "You do not believe me, do you? You do not believe that I will send for you to come to Lagos."

Baaba flinched. It sounded so harsh coming from Ogo's lips but it was true, that was what Baaba felt. He smeared the tears on his cheeks and then looked down at the ground without saying a word.

Ogo leaned forward and, in a stern voice, asked again, "Why are you crying?" But he didn't wait for an answer. He continued in an even voice, "I always keep my promises. I am considering that, you are a man. This is why I would like to have a separate room for Amaka and me. If not for your sake, I would not bother. You have to come to Lagos because you are wasting your life here in the village."

It was as if storm clouds had parted and blue, sunshine-filled sky was once again apparent. Baaba looked at Ogo and nodded. "All right, sir," he said. "I believe you. I will stop crying but," he added, his voice quivering, "but please, sir, do not forget me here in the village."

Ogo felt some tenderness then for the young man's feelings. He softened his tone. "I swear in my father's name that I will not disappoint you. I like you very much. You just have to be patient for a month," he said. Then he invited him back into his room where they spent some time chatting about his hopes for Baaba in Lagos.

Slowly Baaba calmed down. As he listened to Ogo he felt reassured. Even so, when he said that he believed Ogo he meant that he did not believe that his God would allow Ogo to forget him.

CHAPTER 6:
THE POLICEMAN'S DAUGHTER

WHEN OGO AND AMAKA LEFT for Lagos, everything changed for Baaba. While Ogo was in the village, Baaba's days and evenings were spent attending to his wants and needs. What was more, his constant attention to Ogo was energized by his dreams of going to Lagos. Now, he found himself distressed and withdrawn. He avoided his friends and stayed alone in his room. Ogo's departure made him irrelevant. While Ogo was in the village, Baaba was important because of him. Now …?

One of the sad things was that he had actually become used to working hard. He had begun to enjoy his efforts on behalf of Ogo. He found himself missing his early morning chores for Ogo. He missed the breakfasts he served and then shared with Ogo. His life was now bland. He had no exciting stories to listen to, no leftover food from Ogo to enjoy or to take to his family. But the single worst thing was that he was without hope. His dreams for his future were dark, despite Ogo's fervent promises. Without his hope, he could not see the point in facing each day. He was depressed.

"Have faith," his mother consoled him. "If God did not plan for Ogo to take you to Lagos, he would not have come home in the first instance." Her voice was calm and caring, without a hint of the sadness or doubt that Baaba felt. "It is all God's work, my son. You have to believe He will make it happen."

Although he did not become the believer his mother would have preferred, he did manage, over the course of three or four days, to come out of his room and venture outside his compound. He was surprised to find that the feel of the sun on his face gave him pleasure and the blue sky warmed his heart.

"What a fool I've been," he thought to himself. "The world is always filled with possibilities, even if they are not the ones you expect."

He decided to go and visit his friend Emi, who had tried several times over the course of the previous days to speak with him about his misfortune but each time Baaba had sent him away without seeing him.

"How could I have treated him so badly?" Baaba wondered to himself.

As he walked on his way to Emi, he seemed to be looking upon a new world, one filled with new possibilities. It was just then that he happened to see the policeman's daughter who had returned to the village on holiday. She was coming back from the river with her water pot. She had a cloth wrapped around her body from her chest to her knees.

Baaba felt a shiver of excitement course through him, a shiver he had not felt in some time. "What a beautiful creature," he thought to himself. For the first time in his life, Baaba, the charmer and womanizer, felt himself shy and at a loss for words. He was quite certain he couldn't speak with her. The thought that he was paralyzed in the presence of a girl astonished him. "I can't even bring myself to talk to her," he thought to himself. "I am actually afraid of a girl." Once he got over the novelty of the feeling, he realized that she must be some girl to make him feel that way.

Indeed, she was. Her eyes were sharp, piercing, and beautiful. Her body was gracious and easy. Baaba slowed down behind her, watching her swinging hips as she walked. She walked as beautifully and gracefully as a dream. She was tall, shapely, and dark.

He was smitten with her to the very marrow of his bones. When he arrived at Emi's house, his thoughts were still completely on the policeman's daughter.

"Baaba!" Emi greeted him, his voice filled with joy at seeing his friend. Despite the annoyance that his friends felt at Baaba, having had to endure his endless tales of Lagos and his dream of going there, they all felt it was much worse to see the sad and depressed Baaba. With Baaba so sad, it was as if a light had gone out in the village.

The two friends embraced and then they chatted about Baaba's misfortune. Emi was sympathetic to his friend but he was equally determined to get him to forget about Ogo and Lagos. "Lagos people don't think about village people when they are in Lagos," he insisted. "He used you."

As much as Emi was giving voice to Baaba's own fears, Baaba protested. "No, no. He promised me."

Emi could only laugh. "Promise? What promise?"

Emi's certainty that Ogo had taken advantage of him only served to make Baaba sad again. "Please," he said, "don't speak like that. Don't make it worse for me. I need your sympathy, not that kind of talk."

Emi felt chastised. "You are right," he said, lowering his eyes. "I am sorry. We just have to live on hope," he concluded.

They were quiet and thoughtful for a moment after that but soon their attention turned to a subject upon which they could talk endlessly – and happily. Their attention turned to girls.

"I have heard that the policeman's daughter is back in the village on holiday," Emi excitedly said to Baaba. He went on to confess that he was completely taken by her. "I am arranging for a friend of hers to plan a date."

Perhaps only Emi loved beautiful girls more than Baaba. Oh, it was not that others didn't love beautiful girls but those two loved them as they loved the very air they breathed. When they saw a beautiful girl, they *had* to have her. They felt that their love was total and eternal. Until the next beautiful girl.

Emi particularly loved the girls who had lived in the towns around the village. He had lived in town himself for a time, with an uncle. This was before the Biafran war. He found town girls more interesting and exciting than their village counterparts.

He was also able to speak with them in a knowing and familiar way. In this regard, he had an advantage over Baaba, who had always lived in the village and could not tell stories about the town life.

Of course, as soon as Baaba heard of Emi's interest in the policeman's daughter his own heart sank into the pit of his stomach. Even if he wanted to compete for her affection with his friend, he doubted that he would come out ahead. For all his charm and ability to win girls, he ran a poor second to Emi.

Emi was the one that the girls really fell for. Often, Baaba was the one to end up with his rejects.

Of course, learning of Emi's feelings towards the policeman's daughter allowed Baaba the ability to hide his own feelings about her. Still, he was annoyed by Emi's feelings. Emi already had a beautiful girlfriend. Why would he want another?

Even as he asked, Baaba understood Emi's voracious appetite for pretty girls. They shared that feeling. It was one of the reasons they were such good friends.

Hadn't Amaka expressed her own feelings about that appetite to him only a couple of weeks earlier? But now, his heart was broken. For after all, *he* wanted to marry the policeman's daughter. Hadn't Emi told him that he wanted to marry his current girlfriend? She was from a rich family. He only wanted her for her father's money.

Although he played around, Baaba had no steady girlfriend. Now, he felt not only attraction to a pretty girl but a longing for something more than simply a romantic interlude.

But he couldn't very well say anything. After all, he and Emi were very close friends and had been since childhood. They joined the Biafran war on the same day and served in the same regiment. They both left the Army to join the Air Force. Many of the villagers referred to them as 'the twins' because they were inseparable. They seemed to share everything – clothes, food (they alternated meals between their mothers), and more than once in the past, girlfriends.

But not this time. The policeman's daughter was different. His feelings towards her were different. All he could hope was that Emi's interest in the policeman's daughter would not destroy their friendship. For Baaba was not prepared to lose her.

Still, he was aware of the situation and so he needed to think through his feelings and what he wanted to say before he mentioned anything to Emi. Even though he was smitten by her, he was sensible enough to know that the first thing that he had to do was to talk to her and discover if she fancied him at all.

When he left Emi that evening, he was determined that he would speak with her before Emi did.

In the past, he simply would have gone right up to her and turned on his charm, but he didn't feel he could do that this time. Usually, Baaba had no problem chatting up girls. This girl was different. In addition to her beauty, she was a strong presence. She had a good personality and stood out amongst the other girls. And, he had learned something from Ogo – sometimes it is best to be able to send an intermediary to put things in place. He thought about the people he could approach to help him and he decided upon her cousin Nnaa, who was also his friend.

Yes, he would speak with Nnaa. He smiled to himself, thinking that he had hit upon a very smart plan. After all, it would not seem odd at all that he approach Nnaa. He paid regular visits to his compound as it was. And wasn't it convenient that Nnaa's compound was next to the policeman's? There were days – he thought of them as his 'lucky days' – when he would get a glance of her from Nnaa's compound, but even then he could not summon the courage to talk to her.

There were times he was bothered by his unusual timidity. Other times he found it curious and almost amusing. It was such a unique occurrence. He really didn't know what to make of his timidity when it came to the policeman's daughter. And when he realized that he wasn't merely timid, he was actually nervous to talk to her … well, he didn't know what to make of it at all.

Add to that, she completely ignores him whenever she sees him with her cousin … it added up to a most curious and troubling situation for the usually confident and self-assured Baaba.

His thought was that it would be easier for him to finally speak with her if he could find a way to get her out of her father's house. Perhaps it was her father, the policeman, who made him nervous? Could that have been it? Baaba considered this and then rejected it.

No, it was the girl herself.

All of these thoughts were swirling in his head when he finally approached Nnaa with his secret and his plan.

"Nnaa, I like your cousin ChiChi."

Nnaa reacted with little surprise. After all, Baaba was hardly the first to express interest in his beautiful cousin. Nnaa simply looked at Baaba and shook his head. "Don't even think about it. Her father will kill you."

He delivered this judgement with such directness that it caught Baaba completely off guard.

"But, I want to marry her."

Nnaa began to laugh. "What? You want to marry her?" He could not stop laughing.

"Stop," Baaba begged. "Please. I am serious."

Nnaa slowly stopped laughing. "Let's talk about something else," he said simply.

But Baaba insisted. "Please, I want to marry her."

Nnaa viewed his friend critically. "Baaba," he said directly, "you are my friend and I don't want to hurt your feelings, but you must give up your silly notion."

"But …"

Nnaa raised his hand to stop Baaba's protest. "How can you even think about marrying ChiChi. She is in school and wants to go to university to study medicine. You don't go to school. You have no job. You have been idle since you came back from the war. I can tell you right now that she will have absolutely no interest in talking to you," he said.

Baaba was undeterred. "She will talk to me if you arrange it," he replied.

Nnaa stared at his friend as if he'd completely lost his mind. "Haven't you listened to a single thing that I've said? There is no use in it. What's the matter with you, Baaba, are you on a death wish or something?"

Baaba shook his head. "No. I only need your help to arrange a meeting with her outside her father's house."

Nnaa shook his head. "Nope. No way. I am not getting involved. Her father would kill me if he found out I had anything to do with arranging a meeting between her and a boy."

Baaba frowned. "But I thought we were friends. Friends do anything for one another. I would do anything for you," he insisted.

Nnaa made a face. Although Baaba was a good friend and fun to be around, few people really believed he could be counted on in the way that he was suggesting to Nnaa right then.

"Please," Baaba insisted. "All I am asking is that you arrange a meeting. You don't have to say anything to her about me."

Nnaa thought for a moment and then he shrugged his shoulders. "Okay, I can get her outside her house. But that's all," he insisted. "If and when you speak with her, you must tell her I know nothing about your insane suggestion."

Baaba smiled. "Of course."

That business taken care of, it turned out that Nnaa wanted a favour in return. "It turns out you can help me as well," he said. "I am interested in your niece, the one in my school. If you can talk to your niece for me, then I will bring ChiChi to your house."

Baaba felt that was more than fair and was only too happy to agree to the request. They immediately set a date when Nnaa would take her out.

As soon as Baaba went home, he spoke to his niece about Nnaa and it turned out that she was only too happy to meet Nnaa.

It would not be as simple for Nnaa to take care of his end of the bargain.

The policeman's daughter and Nnaa were close. They often studied together in his room. She appreciated the chance to study someplace where she could concentrate. She had three brothers and three sisters and her house was always noisy, so Nnaa's room was where she escaped when she needed to work. Nnaa was also much like her – very studious. He was her senior in secondary school and she looked up to him. They worked together on school assignments. Nnaa was very good at mathematics and she was brilliant in the sciences.

They studied together a couple of times after Nnaa had spoken with Baaba and Nnaa had not said anything. But as the day of the arranged meeting drew closer, he felt that he had to put his plan into motion. So, as he and ChiChi were studying together, he looked at her and said, "I am going to see my auntie tomorrow. Would you like to come along as well? We both need to take a break from the books."

Although the thought of a break from study was appealing, ChiChi was much too dedicated to take time off. "I'd like to but I have to complete my school assignment," she said, concentrating on her book.

Nnaa felt a moment of panic, realizing that he might not be able to keep up his end of the bargain. If that happened, then he would not be able to meet with Baaba's cousin and that would be terrible. So he continued to press his case despite her seeming lack of interest.

"We will only be there for a few minutes," he assured her. "I have to go on an errand for my mother," he added, then, making it sound as if her coming along would be a benefit to him, he went on, "If you come with me, she will not keep me too long." He knew he was lying but he didn't care.

ChiChi considered his request. After a moment, she sighed. "Okay, but you have to help with my maths assignment on Saturday."

He smiled broadly. "Of course I will," he promised.

So it was when they headed to Baaba's compound, Nnaa was more than a little hopeful. ChiChi looked radiant in the new clothes her mother had made for her. Her hair was short and suited her small dark face. Her mother had attended the local home economics centre set up by the colonial masters in her days as a young woman.

Many families sent their daughters to the centre to enable them to learn housekeeping before they became married. They learned the kinds of skills that would help them manage a household successfully.

ChiChi's mother had excelled in dressmaking. Over the years, her skill only improved. She made dresses for her daughters. In fact, she made all their clothes, including their underwear. Not only were her clothes better made than those sold in the market, but making her own clothes saved quite a bit of money for the family – which was always an important consideration with seven children in the family. Even if they were wealthy, which they were not, seven children would have forced her to find ways to economise the family income.

Like most men in the village, her father spent a large part of his salary on alcohol. He loved his drink and was drunk most of the evenings after work. So, to make ends meet, her mother became very industrious. She had a market stall where she sold imported used clothing; not only did she not buy clothes in the market, she earned money from making clothes for other people, especially school uniforms. In addition to the clothes that she made, she sold fruits in her stall and other convenient items.

As they approached the compound, ChiChi turned to Nnaa, "I did not realize this woman was your auntie," she said.

Nnaa smiled and said, "Well, now you know."

ChiChi remained considerate. "I know she was originally from our village but I thought she was from the other clan and not a close relation," she went on in a quiet voice.

Baaba, who had observed their approach, positioned himself at the narrow entryway to the compound, nearly blocking the entrance. He had practised what he would say over and over, and so, when Nnaa and ChiChi arrived, he looked up at them and said in a 'surprised' voice, "Nnaa, what brings you here?"

Nnaa was not expecting to see Baaba at the entryway but he managed to play along as if they'd rehearsed. "My mother asked me to give a message to your mother," he said. Then, almost as an afterthought, he added, "Baaba, this is my cousin, ChiChi. She is the policeman's daughter."

Then he turned to ChiChi. "ChiChi, this is a very good friend of mine, Baaba. You must have seen him around. I'm sure you have seen him when he has come to visit me at my house."

ChiChi eyed Baaba cautiously. "Yes," she acknowledged. "I know who he is. I saw him at the last wake keeping."

Of course she knew who Baaba was. She had noticed Baaba's nice looks and his charming smile, but she had never spoken to him. Her father was very strict and could not tolerate bad behaviour from his daughters. He had four daughters and felt it was his duty to protect them from men. He himself was a notorious womanizer and so did not trust any man around his daughters – he knew only too well what was in their minds and their hearts.

ChiChi had walked past Baaba on a number of occasions but he was always with his friend Emi. The two of them intrigued her. She liked Emi much more than Baaba. Still, she thought that Emi was too arrogant, rough, and abrupt. Unlike Emi, whose personality was defined by his arrogance, Baaba could be funny and charming. She had witnessed this herself when she had attended the wake-keeping ceremony that occurred before a funeral.

She had been sitting not far from his group and she was paying close attention to the group because she admired him. His jokes kept the group laughing all night. He did not talk to her at all that evening. She thought maybe he did not think that she was interesting or worthy of his interest. If only she knew that Baaba was dying to talk to her but could not find the courage.

For his part, he had noticed that she occasionally looked his way during the wake-keeping night. When their eyes met, a quick smile flickered across her beautiful face.

Of course, while Baaba had struggled with his nervousness, Emi had boldly approached her on the very same night. "My name is Emi," he said, introducing himself. "We must meet up sometime."

She was unnerved by his boldness. "Okay," she said, glancing away. His ego was large and this irritated her. "Why must boys always be so loud and bossy?" she had wondered.

Yet, Baaba was none of those things. At least, he wasn't to her.

With all these thoughts swirling in her mind, ChiChi walked behind Nnaa and Baaba as they led the way into the compound.

"Good evening, Ma," ChiChi said politely to Baaba's mother when they approached her in the compound. Baaba's mother looked at ChiChi with delight and surprise. "Oh, dear Lord, my sister is visiting me today." She leaned closer to ChiChi. "You know we are related, don't you? You know me, don't you? I met your father yesterday at the church meeting. My mother came from …" Baaba made a face but it didn't deter his mother. She rattled on and on.

"Please, Mama," Baaba said gently. "This is not the time for your relationship matters. They have come to visit me, not you."

These words confused ChiChi. She glanced over at Nnaa and whispered to him, "But you said …"

He gave her a quick look but she continued.

"… I thought we were visiting your auntie."

"Yes, we are," he insisted quietly.

In fact, Baaba's mother took up the argument – and in a direction that was not pleasing to Baaba. "No, Baaba," she insisted. "She is visiting me as well." Then she turned her attention to ChiChi. "You are welcome, my daughter. I am cooking some soup. You must have some of my food before you leave my house," she said, immediately retiring to her cooking area in order to avoid what she knew to be Baaba's wrath.

After Baaba's mother went to prepare some food, ChiChi looked around the compound and observed that it was organized in a semi-circle. "Why is your compound set up in this manner?" she asked.

Baaba explained that the spaces were for the sons to build their own homes when they earned enough money from the towns.

Like in other families, the expectation was that the children would be educated, earn money, and return to the family compound. In Baaba's family, that meant building modern brick houses in the spaces left in order to complete a full circle.

Unlike her own compound, in which her father's room was at the centre of the compound, Baaba's father lived in a room on the right side of the compound. This spoke of the central place that Baaba's mother held in the compound.

Further emphasizing the point, Baaba's father was sitting quietly outside his room, looking bored and lost – as a child might. He barely noticed the arrival of the visitors or, if he did, he didn't show any indication that he had.

Both Nnaa and ChiChi showed him the respect that he deserved, however, by greeting him warmly. "Good evening, Papa," they both said, smiling at the simple-looking man.

"Evening, my children," he replied. Baaba's father was neither a fool nor a simpleton. However, his role in life had diminished his interest in many things. Still, once engaged, he behaved correctly. "How are your parents?" he asked. "Are they well?"

"Yes, sir," Nnaa and ChiChi replied in unison, bending their knees slightly to demonstrate their respect.

His gaze rested a bit longer on ChiChi. His expression turned a bit sad, as he presumed that she was another one of his son's conquests. It was a constant source of conflict and friction in the compound, particularly between Baaba's mother and father, how Baaba regularly brought girls to his room.

It would only be later that ChiChi would learn of this behaviour.

Baaba's four brothers and two sisters each greeted Nnaa and ChiChi with a simple, "Welcome."

Baaba's mother had given birth to ten children but three of them had died in infancy. Baaba was the fourth child. Two of his brothers and sisters were lingering around the cooking area, obviously waiting for the food.

Baaba's siblings looked at ChiChi curiously. They would have said more to her but they had learned that it was best to speak little to Baaba's friends and girls. They were anxious to avoid the wrath Baaba would show them if they said the wrong thing – not in front of the visitors, of course, but afterwards; after the visitors were gone, all hell would break loose. So they were more than content to sit and watch Baaba and the visitors from a distance.

"Please come into my room," Baaba said, ushering Nnaa and ChiChi into his bedroom.

Baaba's compound was about half a mile from ChiChi's house. It was located more remotely from the main road to the village than ChiChi's house was. ChiChi's house was also closer to the village market. They had different rivers and their farms were located in different areas of the forest.

At the end of the war, ChiChi's father had made some effort to rebuild the family house in the village but he could not afford to complete the reconstruction. As she looked around Baaba's compound, ChiChi noticed that Baaba's house was one of the most dilapidated in the area.

She observed his sisters and brothers looking hungrily at the food their mother was preparing. She took one look at the food and thought, "I should be grateful to God for making life a bit easier in my family."

While life was not easy by any means for her family, there was real poverty in Baaba's household. Her family did live better. They had good food. She felt sorry for Baaba's family and she silently offered a little prayer to God to help them.

Her parents could afford her return to education. She attended a secondary school in one of the most highly regarded educational institutions for high achievers in the Eastern Region before the war. The school was set up and managed by Europeans and run by English missionaries. Admission required the successful completion of an entrance examination. Scholarships were limited so students needed an excellent record and reference from their primary school to be accepted.

None of this had been a problem for ChiChi. She passed the entrance examination with flying colours. No one was more pleased by her academic success than her father. As soon as she was accepted into the school, he declared, "She is going to be a doctor; she must become a doctor." Then he smiled at his daughter. "You are a good girl," he told her. "A very good girl."

He always referred to ChiChi as a 'good girl' whenever he was pleased with her educational achievement. Her father's praise had served to make ChiChi very proud of herself and ever more determined to be the best she was capable of being. She wanted to please her father and by pleasing her father, pleased herself.

The war was a terrible disruption at the school. As soon as the war started, the students were sent home abruptly and the school was closed down. This was a terrible personal consequence of the war for ChiChi. After the war, she attended a secondary school in the nearest town, twelve miles from her village. For the first month, she walked to school. It was only after her mother returned to her trading booth that she was able to afford to have her board at the school.

At the weekends, she came home to collect food and some money to last her for the week.

She was always very clever and was always at the head of her class. Her father doted on her. Everyone liked her. She was a chorister in the village church. At one point, she had been taught opera by one of her teachers because she had such a beautiful voice. She was also a very accomplished athlete. She represented her school in track events, starring in hurdling events.

The future had been bright for her indeed … until the war turned her life upside down in the most negative and drastic manner.

Her future was no longer nearly as rosy. She lived with her parents in the police barracks located in the nearest town to her village, where her father had a two-bedroom apartment. Her father had left Lagos because of the war. He lamented all the time about losing his Yoruba friends and girlfriends. The seven children shared the two rooms with their parents.

In such a small space, it was no wonder that fights and arguments were regular occurrences. The fights were mostly to do with space occupancy and ownership of personal items. Even under those conditions, ChiChi always won any argument or fight. Even in their reduced circumstances – or perhaps because of them – her father was on her side. From his perspective, she could never be wrong.

There was a special bond between father and daughter, one that even the humiliation of war could not diminish. The bond, according to her father, was mystical. In his mind, ChiChi was his grandmother incarnate. He explained he saw her in his dreams when ChiChi's mother was pregnant and she told him that she was coming back to him.

That was what he told.

"Nobody knew how true it was," her siblings argued, "who else was in the dream?" But the argument was to no avail. The story was narrated by their father, who was convinced and determined to take ChiChi's side.

What was more, ChiChi regularly tattled on her siblings. She always told her father the truth and they hated her for this behaviour. The least she could have done was to withhold certain facts from him, if only to allow them to avoid the painful corporal punishment he dished out.

Where her father was stern and imposing, ChiChi's mother was very gentle and caring. She could not have been more different from ChiChi's father. She came from a family of a neighbouring village where her father was the chief.

She was a slim woman, over five and a half feet tall. She was fair in complexion. No matter where she was, people commented on her white teeth and lovely legs. She had lovely long hair; she looked more like a mixed-race person because of her fair colour.

ChiChi's father was tall, over six feet five inches tall and very dark in complexion. Although the two of them together looked a little like beauty and the beast, ChiChi's mother loved him dearly.

And he loved her too, but would not show these feelings to her for fear of being seen as being weak. That is what their world taught – that a man had to be strong, which often meant 'brutal'. In truth, their relationship was not much different than many others. It was the relationship of man and servant. She attended to his every need. She married him when she was in her early teens and had always looked up to him as her master. She did not speak when he did. She waited for him to eat before she did, and she would stay up at night waiting for him to come back from his numerous outings.

He beat her when it suited him. He also flogged her with his police leather belt, but she took it all for the sake of the children.

ChiChi, who was a very bright girl, was sometimes puzzled when he was mean to her mother. Why didn't anyone take any serious action about his behaviour? She could see that wife battering was common but that didn't make it right, did it? She had learned that her grandparents tried in the earliest days of the marriage to reprimand or challenge him. Nevertheless, it all came to nothing because she had children with him and it was taboo for a daughter from their family to consider divorce. That would bring shame to the entire family.

Of course, no one challenged him at home and he enjoyed all the attention from his wife; he kept numerous girlfriends outside his home. He was a well-known womanizer; he liked to befriend women who had lost their husbands. In their bereavement, he would get close to them in pretence of consoling them, gain their trust, and then become their lover. He knew these women were vulnerable during the time of bereavement.

He was like an animal of prey.

ChiChi managed to avoid the worst of her father's behaviour, being the favourite. ChiChi's mother also showed her favouritism because she worked hard and helped her with the household chores. Being very industrious herself, she could see ChiChi taking her place. She constantly reminded her other children, "Your sister will never starve in her lifetime if she continues working hard."

Of course, her mother's feelings added to the jealousy her siblings already felt towards her.

ChiChi helped her mother with her trading when she was home from school. Often, the stuff of the trades ranged from fruit to second-hand clothing. Being a good student, ChiChi also learned how to make clothes from her mother.

A strict disciplinarian, the children only got to know their father when he was drunk and in the mood to tell stories of his life. He had served as a nurse in Burma during the Second World War and once, when he was drunk, he told them the story of how he became a police officer.

It seemed that, upon his return from the war, the British offered the soldiers who had come from the villages two career options – nursing or police work. He had opted for the latter because he liked the uniform.

The colonial masters were still ruling Nigeria then and the uniforms they provided could not help but attract people. The police uniform was well starched and pressed. It had shiny metal buttons religiously polished by Brasso – a brand of metal cleaner.

As she matured, ChiChi often reflected on the curiosity of it, of how her father could have chosen his life career based on nothing more than his liking for the uniform.

It made no sense to her at all. She often viewed the nurses in their bright white uniforms and she loved the way the uniforms looked, but she would never consider becoming a nurse. She was a very sentimental girl and knew she would become too attached to her patients.

And how pretty uniform could convince her to lose sight of who she was and make her do what she didn't think was the right thing.

As it turned out, her father liked police work; he liked it so much that he worked as a police officer all his life and retired from the Police Force. There was even a point where he suggested to ChiChi that she join the police by taking advantage of a graduate programme. By doing so, she would be on a direct and shorter route to becoming an officer.

"You rise quicker through the ranks if you are educated," he told her.

It had taken him years before he rose to the rank of a sergeant, another twenty years before he made inspector grade.

After the war, he began to hope that one day his daughter would become a police commissioner, which was to him, the ultimate achievement for a police officer's daughter.

He was only too aware of the mistakes he had made in his life; he had no desire to allow this brainy child of his to make the same mistakes. Mind you, he encouraged all his children to take their education seriously. It was just that ChiChi was a more gifted student. She was more attentive and studious, and he usually cited her as an example for her siblings to copy.

Of course, this too resulted in envy and jealousy between ChiChi and her siblings. They often – out of their father's earshot – would refer to her as 'father's crying baby'. She was the one always invited to eat from the same plate with their father and given the best pieces of meat in the soup.

It was hard to know if ChiChi was bothered by her siblings' jealousy. She was aware of her father's warm feelings towards her but she did not rely on those to succeed. She was a very hard worker. She often studied by her lantern at night when others were sleeping. She had a mission and she believed that the only way to accomplish it was by studying hard and putting the effort in.

She hated anyone beating her in class or in any of her subjects. Ten years after the fact, she could still remember the one time it happened and she still felt the shame of having come second in an exam. She would never let it happen again.

One thing that could never be said about ChiChi was that she lacked drive and determination. Which made her very different from Baaba. Baaba had only shown any initiative in war – and in trying to become Ogo's intern.

So, it was an interesting trio of people walking into Baaba's room that day – Nnaa and ChiChi and Baaba.

"Please sit down," Baaba said, gesturing towards the bed and the one chair in the room.

ChiChi was very uncomfortable being in Baaba's room – even with Nnaa. At eighteen years old, she was a virgin and had every intention of remaining that way. All her energy had been devoted to achieving her best in school and in her classes. Although she was extremely intelligent, she was not streetwise. Her father's overprotectiveness did not help her. He was like a guard, turning suitors away. It didn't matter to him who they were. Some of them were very rich men who could have helped the family financially. Others were hard workers. He rejected them all – the attractive offers from the rich men and the passionate ones from the hard workers. ChiChi's mother had pleaded with him to let her go so that they could benefit from the men's generosity but he absolutely refused.

So, when Baaba invited them to sit down, she felt very nervous and timid. She chose the chair, leaving Nnaa to sit on the bed. Just sitting on the bed would have felt awkward to her.

Of course, Baaba wished she had taken the bed instead of his friend.

"Why don't you sit on the bed?" he asked her. "It is much more comfortable than the chair."

She averted her eyes and spoke softly. "No, thank you. I prefer the chair. Nnaa can sit on the bed."

Baaba frowned. He had prepared carefully for the visit. He had covered the bed with one of his mother's cotton cloths. Few people had proper bedding – and he and his family were no exception. So, when he had a visitor to his room, he always asked his mother to give him one her 'wrappers' to use as bedding. A wrapper was a piece of cotton that the women used for a variety of purposes. His mother would wash it, use it as her clothing, and then lend it to Baaba when he needed it.

He had also asked his mother for money to buy Fanta for his visitors. Poor, his mother could only afford to give him enough money for a single bottle of

Fanta. It would have to do. Once his guests were in his room, he poured the drink into the plastic cups and offered them to his visitors.

As they sipped the Fanta, Baaba sat beside Nnaa on the bed. They spoke excitedly about the forthcoming annual festival and the costumes they would be wearing for the occasion. They seemed to have forgotten that ChiChi was even there with them.

ChiChi sat quietly, listening to their excitement about the upcoming village festival. She had nothing to contribute to the conversation because she knew very little about the festival. She felt awkward. If only they were discussing school issues … then she would have a lot to say.

Baaba kept up the conversation, watching ChiChi from the corner of his eye. He decided it was time to begin to put his plan into action. He shifted subjects. "I would really like to talk to your sister," he said hesitantly, watching ChiChi's reaction. "Could you leave us alone for a short time so that I can talk to her?"

Nnaa hesitated, not knowing what to say.

"You can play outside with my brother," Baaba added. "I will call you when we are finished talking," he added, winking at Nnaa.

Even though he was part of Baaba's plan, Nnaa felt suddenly uncomfortable. "ChiChi, do you mind?" he asked her.

Of course she did mind but she was too polite to say it like that. Instead, she asked Baaba, "What is it you want to talk about that you don't want Nnaa to listen to?"

He was coy with his answer. "I only want to tell you my plans and see what you think about them."

"Are they your school plans?" she asked. "Because I am only interested in learning about school plans," she continued, glancing over at Nnaa to secure his approval to Baaba's request.

"Yes, of course," Baaba lied.

ChiChi sighed, as if she had no choice then. Nnaa got up and left the room. "Be careful with my sister," he warned Baaba as he was leaving.

As soon as he was gone, Baaba got up from the bed and partly closed the door. He would have preferred to have closed the door completely but he knew that if he did that, she would feel insecure and anxious and that would not serve his purposes at all.

No, he was a strategist. He knew what he wanted and how to get it.

After Nnaa was gone, he sat back down on the bed so that he was facing ChiChi. "ChiChi, I really do like you and I would like to tell you of my plans for the next year," he said, looking deep into ChiChi's eyes.

ChiChi, trying to be polite, encouraged him. "Yes, tell me your plans and I will tell you mine." She was already thinking that she would tell him about her school and the entrance examinations to the university.

"Well," he began. "I am going to Lagos soon, maybe in the next month. When I get there, I will be working with Ogo. I am sure you know him. He is Ochi's

57

uncle, the one that got married a few weeks ago near your village. He has just returned to Lagos after his visit and he is arranging for me to join him in Lagos as soon as he secures a two-room apartment.

"Unfortunately, he is currently living in one room and that would be inconvenient for all of us. This is the only reason I am still in the village." Seeing that ChiChi was listening closely – whether out of politeness or real interest didn't matter to him – encouraged him to go on. "The idea is to have two rooms so that they will have a separate bedroom for privacy.

"He wants to start making babies with his wife and, quite naturally, to do that he needs a separate room. He promised I would sleep in the sitting room."

She blushed, listening to Baaba's narration of his hopes for the future.

"I will be working for Ogo, he has big business in Lagos, and I will make very good money when I get to Lagos." Then he turned his attention to the matter at hand – now that he'd been talking for a while, he seemed to have regained his confidence in speaking with girls. "I want to be your boyfriend, so that when I make money, I will come home and see you."

She sat back, somewhat startled. She was beginning to enjoy Baaba's tale, enjoying the sound of his voice even. But this last bit of information disturbed her. "But I don't want a boyfriend. My father will not be happy. I have to have a husband." She shook her head. "So, you see, it is just impossible. I cannot be your girlfriend." Then she looked away, shy in his presence.

Baaba seemed undeterred. "I have to marry you then," he said simply. Then he sighed. "But your father will not approve until I make money in Lagos. He knows I am from a poor family, you will be educated, and he will not agree to you becoming my wife."

She nodded, recognizing the sense in Baaba's words.

"So, you have to agree first before we talk about your father. If you say yes, the elderly people in my family will deal with all the other issues concerning your father. That is how it works," Baaba said, trying to hide his fear that she would turn him down.

She smiled demurely. "I like you too; but we can't talk about marriage at our age. We should talk about education."

Baaba was encouraged by her attitude. "Yes. But I want to make sure that you don't marry someone else before I am ready."

"I would like to marry you but you have to go school so that we can be both educated. Then my father will not refuse our marriage."

Baaba, with his sixth sense about women, realized that he was in a very good position now. "No, ChiChi," he protested. "I have to go to Lagos and make money first. If you promise to wait for me, then I can go back to school after I have made money. How would I pay the school fees without money?"

She frowned. She was not convinced on this point. So Baaba continued to press his argument. "Look, I would be happy to go back to school if that is your condition to accept me as a husband. In the meantime, you can get as much education as you want and I can pay your fees as long as you agree to be my wife."

Yet, she still didn't seem to understand Baaba's logic. How could one make money without first going to school? "But, Baaba, you cannot make money without going to school. How would you do that, by magic?"

He laughed out loud. "As a matter of fact, yes, by magic, ChiChi. Ogo is a magician and he makes loads of money working on magic to entertain people. They pay him to perform magic and that is how he makes his money." He continued to laugh, delighted by her connection – however tenuous. "He explained everything to me. I know I can be successful if I become his apprentice."

Then, once again, he turned his attention directly to ChiChi. "You are so beautiful. I can't see you waiting for me. I heard you already have suitors and I understand they are rich people."

But she shook her head and frowned, as if she'd tasted something bitter. "I don't want them and I don't like old men. They are almost as old as my father. They have money, of course, but they are too old and I don't like them as much as I like you.

"I do like you, Baaba. You are very handsome. I wanted to talk to you when I saw you at the wake keeping last week, but I was shy." Then she stopped, fearful that she had said too much in this rushed confession. So she added, "Only to say hello as one of the youths in the village, of course. I was hoping we should form a youth club in the village. The club members can help tidy the church ground and the roads, but of course only during the holidays. We can also have a debating club." She smiled at him. "I have already spoken to some of the youths and they are in favour of my suggestions," she said excitedly.

Baaba, who was completely flattered when she said she'd wanted to talk to him, lost her train of thought and could not understand why she was talking about youth clubs and debating clubs. "I am talking about me and you," he insisted, "and you are talking about youths in the village." He leaned forward. "So, I will ask you, will you be my future wife?"

She allowed her eyes to meet his. "I have already answered you," she insisted. "I said yes on the condition that you go to school. I will not marry an illiterate. However, I do like you a lot, especially the way you smile. If we got married, our children would have the same smile," she joked.

Baaba breathed a sigh of relief and confessed, "I was scared that you would reject me, and that would kill me."

ChiChi smiled. "But please, Baaba, don't forget that I agree on the condition that you go to school. No school, no marriage. Okay?"

"Okay, okay," he said agreeably. The truth was, Baaba would have said anything at that point in order to satisfy her. Then he laughed loudly. "You know, I planned with Nnaa to bring you here so that we could have this talk."

She sat rigidly and her expression looked angry – as if she'd been taken advantage of. "I will kill him!" she shrieked. Then she studied Baaba's face. "So, he knows about your feelings towards me?"

"Yes, he knows, and he is outside praying that you accept my proposal because I will give him money when I return from Lagos."

The simple truth was, they were really getting on beautifully even though it was their first proper meeting and the first time they'd ever spoken with one another. They fancied each other. Baaba, of course, was attracted to ChiChi and, as it turned out, ChiChi liked him.

He moved further to the edge of the bed and asked her, "Would you wait for me then?"

She batted her eyes and nodded. "Yes, I like you. I will wait for you." Then her voice became firm. "But don't you go and marry one of those Lagos girls." She shook her finger at him. "They will not allow you to go back to school if you get involved with them. I know this from my father. They used to take all his money and make my mother very unhappy."

Baaba beamed. "Never," he promised." Then he confessed, "I am very happy now. Can I touch your hand?" Baaba moved closer to the edge of the bed.

"Yes," ChiChi said shyly.

Baaba held her hands. He smiled one of his seductive smiles as he looked into her eyes. ChiChi turned her head to the left, avoiding Baaba's eyes. She was fearful of the emotions she felt through her soul, and the way his smile made her feel deep in her stomach.

"Look at me," he encouraged her. "You have such beautiful eyes."

With his encouragement, she turned and faced him. She looked into his eyes lovingly.

Baaba could not believe his good fortune. "You like me, I can see. I am so lucky. I never did think you would give me a second look. I will work hard in Lagos, make money, and buy you whatever you want," he said, overcome with joy.

"But you promise to go to school when you come back," ChiChi said firmly, her eyes serious.

"Okay," he agreed again. "But only for your sake so that you will be my wife."

Baaba asked ChiChi to sit on his bed with him. He made her promise that she would not date any other boy or accept any of the suitors who approached her father. She assured Baaba that her education would keep her too busy to think of misbehaving.

"Are you a virgin?" Baaba asked unexpectedly.

She felt her neck get warm. She lowered her eyes as she nodded her head. "Yes, I am. I want to be a virgin when I get married."

"Can I kiss you?" he asked gently.

Once again, she nodded her head. "Yes, I like you," she said, still gripping his hand.

He leaned in to kiss her. Although he wanted the kiss to be very passionate, she would have none of that. The kiss was very brief. ChiChi pushed Baaba away and reminded him of his promise to wait until they were married. Both enjoyed the closeness and laughed.

After their kiss, they sat talking for nearly two hours. They talked about how the news would be broken to her father and what would be his reaction and how they would deal with any antagonism from him.

It seemed that their entire lives were opening up before them.

They also talked about how many children they would have and how they would live. Most importantly, they talked about caring for each other. They did not want to be like their parents who argued all the time and treated their wives like slaves.

ChiChi was happy. She liked Baaba for his looks. She liked the way he spoke, his eyes, and especially his nose. She also liked the naughty way he smiled. However, the best quality was his height. ChiChi's father was very tall and she grew up hoping that her husband would be as tall as her father. She had a weakness for tall boys and admired them from a distance. She stood five foot nine herself and so would have felt foolish alongside a short man.

Finally, they found themselves with nothing else to discuss. "Can you get Nnaa so we can return home?" she asked. "I don't want my father to become suspicious and angry," she said. The truth was, she liked to return home before he came home from a drinking session.

"Yes, of course," Baaba said. Then he thanked her for accepting his proposal. They agreed that before ChiChi went back to school, they would meet regularly under the Iroko tree outside the village. The tree was located at a secluded corner, away from any footpath. That way, they could have some privacy.

They also arranged for the times to meet. These had to be times when ChiChi left home for her errands. They could not take any chances. They decided that the only confidant would be Nnaa. Baaba had to warn Nnaa to maintain confidentiality.

When Nnaa and ChiChi left, Baaba could not contain his joy. He was happy for his gain and, truth be known, happy that Emi had lost. "Emi has lost this time. He stands no chance with ChiChi. I will tell him tomorrow so he will keep his hands off my future wife."

He was serious about ChiChi and knew that if Emi continued to pursue her, he would end their friendship. In his book of morals, that would be unpardonable. Even amongst thieves there is honour!

Two days later Baaba met ChiChi at the agreed Iroko tree. Both were delighted to be away from the real world and have a world that belonged only to them. They held onto each other and Baaba kissed ChiChi passionately on the lips. ChiChi responded passionately. For Baaba, the experience was made all the better because he genuinely cared about ChiChi.

There was real magic between them.

The next time they met, Baaba suggested that they prove their loyalty and love to one another with blood.

"But how?" she asked.

He described the process of making small cuts in each other's arms and then tasting each other's blood.

Although she was a bit scared at first, she never hesitated. That's how much she had come to love Baaba. So, as ChiChi closed her eyes, Baaba made a small nick in her right thumb and then sucked on the blood.

Then, he had her do the same.

ChiChi also gave Baaba strands of her hair to keep with him; she asked him to keep it on his person at all times for good luck. Baaba reciprocated, pulling out his own hair and giving it to ChiChi. These simple gestures were their assurance that although they would be 600 miles apart, they would think of each other when they looked at the hair. The times they spent together talking and hugging became their private, secret source of happiness until she went back to school.

The only other person who became part of the secret was ChiChi's mother. She had accidentally run into Baaba and ChiChi on her way from the farm. She had taken a short cut to get home quicker. "ChiChi, what are you doing here?" she asked, surprised to see her daughter.

"Nothing, Ma," ChiChi said, acting very nervous. "I am just talking to a friend."

Her mother looked at her suspiciously. "What friend?"

"Baaba," she said.

Her mother nodded her head in a knowing, concerned way. "I know him, he is troublesome." Then the expression on her face shifted and she smiled. "But I like him." She shook her finger at ChiChi. "You had better be careful because if your father finds out what you're about, he will kill the poor boy for nothing."

ChiChi knew that her mother was not just being an alarmist. Her father's temper was legendary. "Okay, Ma, I will be careful."

As she left Baaba and ChiChi, she coughed very loudly. ChiChi smiled, knowing that this was her mother's 'signal' when she suspected trouble. It was her way of warning ChiChi when to be careful.

For her part, ChiChi's mother was calm in the face of her daughter's behaviour. She thought her daughter was growing up and should make her own choices. After all, hadn't she married ChiChi's father at a much younger age?

The liaison became a secret shared by ChiChi and her mother. It had to be because both knew the trouble that would ensue if her father found out about the affair. This was an abomination, he would think, for a mother to condone and encourage her teenage daughter to meet a man secretly.

In later years of their lives, ChiChi's mother suffered severely for keeping this secret.

Chapter 7:
News From Lagos

"**B**AABA, WHERE HAVE YOU BEEN?" Baaba's mother said, stirring the contents of her cooking pot without looking up. "Ochi's mother was here looking for you. She said you had a message from Lagos."

"When did she come here?" Baaba screamed. "What did she say? Did she leave a message for me?"

Before he could continue with more questions, his mother said, "Why don't you go and ask her yourself? Can't you see I am busy?"

Baaba rushed out of the compound, running breathlessly all the way to Ochi's house. When he arrived, he called out to Ochi's mother, "My mother told me that I have a message from Lagos, please tell me what it is."

She smiled. "Ogo sent a letter, but he said I must not give it to any other person but you. That is why I did not give it to your mother," she said, getting up from her seat. As she did, she fumbled around her wrapper on her waist, took out a letter, and handed it to Baaba.

Baaba grabbed the letter, hurried to his favourite bench under the Iroko tree branch, took a big breath, and then took another long look at the envelope. He prayed to God that it was good news from Ogo. He could not handle any rejection now that he had made promises to ChiChi. That would be disastrous.

Calming himself, he opened the letter, peeling the envelope with care to avoid any damage to the letter. He was sweating and his hands were shaking. His expression showed his nervousness, a big frown was etched on his sweaty forehead.

As Baaba read the letter, the frown disappeared slowly and gradually turned into a smile. His heart was light when he called out, "Ochi, Ochi, please come and read this letter! I don't think I am reading it right."

Ochi, hearing Baaba's voice, hurried out from his mother's bedroom and asked Baaba, "What is the matter?"

"Please read this letter and tell me that it says what I think it does!"

Ochi looked at him in a funny way. "Can't you read? You should go to school and learn how to read and write."

"Please. I am not in the mood for nonsense."

Ochi took the letter from Baaba and read it aloud. It summarized the arrangements for Baaba's trip to Lagos. Ogo had given a friend in a neighbouring village money for Baaba's transportation and pocket money for his trip to Lagos. The instructions included Baaba getting himself ready to leave the village with Ogo's friend in five days.

Ochi congratulated him. "Your dream is coming true, my friend."

Baaba looked up in the sky. "Dear Jesus, you are still alive." He sat tight on his favourite bench, took a last glance at the bench, and joked, "We made it, boy, I am sorry I have to leave you behind but I will be back."

Ochi said, "Baaba, I think you have gone mad, how can you be talking to a branch of a tree?"

"Just leave me; I can never forget this bench as long as I live. I have cried so much on this bench and from here God heard my prayers. This bench is my lucky charm."

Shortly after, Emi came to Baaba's house. "I have not seen you for two days, where have you been? We agreed we would see each other every day. The exception was when Ogo was here and you had to spend time with him," he said angrily to Baaba.

Baaba couldn't be bothered with Emi's anger. "I have been very busy. Ogo has fulfilled his promise. I am going to Lagos in five days. He has sent money for my transport. I have spent the last two days collecting the money from Ogo's friend from Lagos. I also had to wash my clothes. I was hoping to see you tonight when I finished packing my bag."

Emi was not moved. "You are not in Lagos yet, but you are behaving like them and ignoring your best friend."

"No, it was nothing like that, you are my best friend, and immediately I can find my way in Lagos, you will be joining me because I can't live in Lagos without you. Who else can I play with?"

Now Emi was a bit appeased. "Okay, you know I will be waiting for you to send for me just like Ogo has sent for you." Emi had agreed that he would stay away from ChiChi after Baaba had spoken to him. His attitude was that there were too many beautiful girls at his disposal, so why would he want to fight his best friend over a particular girl? He knew Baaba was in love with ChiChi. Emi loved his friendship with Baaba and respected Baaba's feelings for her.

No girl was to come between them.

The next days flew. Baaba bid farewell to his mother. She cried all the time and he tried his best to console her. He made her a promise that he would ensure his safety in Lagos. That, of course, was her main concern. She had heard that it was dangerous to live in Lagos, especially for the Igbos who were returning to Lagos after the war.

"I will be fine," he promised.

She packed both cooked and uncooked food items for Baaba. She did not want her son to die of hunger in Lagos. She made him promise that when the food was finished, he should come home because she had heard that people could die of starvation in Lagos. Ochi's mother also brought packets of food for Ogo and Amaka.

"Please find out if Amaka is pregnant when you get to Lagos. If she is having difficulty getting pregnant, she can come back to the village and get local treatment." She also gave him a few herbs and spices for Amaka to help with her conception.

Amaka's mother had nothing for her daughter; she was very poor and had too many children to feed. She gave Baaba a letter she had asked a young girl to write for her. In the letter, she had asked if Amaka was pregnant and demanded that she sent an immediate message home if she was having trouble getting pregnant.

ChiChi had written a letter to Baaba from school. In the letter, she reiterated her promise to wait for him as long as it took. She also asked him to reaffirm his promise of returning to school after his journey to Lagos. She threatened that if he did not fulfil his part of the bargain, she would not marry him because she would not marry an illiterate. She wished him good luck in his endeavours in Lagos and signed the letter 'your wife'. She gave the letter to her mother, who was visiting her in her boarding school, to deliver. Her mother, who guarded their secret carefully, delivered the letter to Baaba.

Baaba read the letter and smiled at its contents. He wrote a quick reply and gave it to ChiChi's mother. He thanked her for delivering it as she tucked it under her folded wrapper and quickly left, before she was seen and people asked questions.

CHAPTER 8:
BAABA'S TRIP TO LAGOS

BAABA LEFT HIS SOBBING MOTHER in the afternoon the day before he would travel to Lagos. From there, he would spend the night in Ogo's friend's house because they had to leave very early in the morning. Baaba and his mother held each other and cried. Then he waved his mother goodbye and promised to bring her nice gifts from Lagos.

"I will pray for you constantly," she promised, already so fearful for his safety that she could hardly stand.

Baaba tossed and turned all that night. There were so many thoughts going through his head. The more he tried to force himself to sleep, the more he tossed and turned. In the end, he gave up the idea of sleeping and just concentrated on his thoughts, on Ogo, Amaka, his mother, and most of all, his sweetheart, ChiChi.

Their meeting had been very brief, but Baaba felt the magic between them. He knew she shared his love and that was very important to him. That meant she would wait for him. "Maybe it was Ogo's magic that made things so easy with ChiChi," he thought.

In the end, Baaba got about an hour's sleep that night. A young girl woke him up the next morning. "Get ready," she said. "We will be leaving soon."

Baaba hurriedly put on his clothes, secured his bag, and sat down waiting for his host to complete the ritual of talking to everyone in the family individually before he went away. Then the bus arrived at about five in the morning; they said their last goodbyes and climbed aboard.

This bus was only a connector bus that would take them to the town where they would take a bigger bus to Lagos. The first bus was full of market women going to the market in the town. They were clutching onto their goods because the ride was very bumpy. Some had infants tied to their backs. Many of the women sold their goods at the bus garage on wholesale. They bought other groceries such as tinned goods, rice, and other items. These items were less expensive in the town. They then brought back the goods to sell to the villagers, earning a nice profit when they resold them. In addition to the women, there were schoolchildren and men who were all heading to the town for other ventures. Some of the villagers worked in the town, especially the civil servants.

Baaba shared a seat with Ogo's friend. The noise from the women and the cries from the children woke him up to the reality around him. His comfortable dreamstate was constantly interrupted by the pushing, shoving, and general chaos in the bus. He hoped the bus trip to Lagos would be better.

Who could travel 600 miles in this unbearable condition?

As the bus went past one of the major roads nearer the town, he thought about how close ChiChi's school was to the road. "I would give anything to see her now," he sighed.

His reverie was interrupted by the voice of the conductor. "Come down, come down now," shouted the bus conductor.

They dutifully disembarked from the bus, collected their luggage, and headed to the area where the buses that went to Lagos parked.

The bus to Lagos was more comfortable. The seats were cushioned, there was more leg room, and most of all it was not noisy. Of course, the comfort cost more but Baaba's companion had a good government job in Lagos, so he travelled with the best. Despite the comfort, if Baaba had a choice, he would have preferred to save his money and travel with the less expensive option. But it was not his money being spent. Ogo had been kind enough to send enough money for him to pay for the luxurious bus.

Most of the roads were in a bad state. Smaller vehicles were stuck in the mud. Passengers of these vehicles had to dismount from the vehicle to push the vehicle through the thick mud or across a pool of rainwater.

Fortunately, the bus ploughed through these obstacles easily. Baaba's bus and the others of the same fleet steered through the water on the road, swaying from side to side, looking like giants on an attack. They stopped at Benin for lunch.

"One hour," the conductor announced in a loud voice. "We will not wait for laggards!"

Baaba and his travelling companion alighted from the bus. There was a lot of noise coming from the women haggling to get customers into their cafes. The women pushed and shoved both the customers and other hawkers, creating a lot of commotion.

Baaba and his companion finally entered one of the cafes and were greeted by a young girl of about fifteen years. "What do you want, sir?" she squawked at the top of her voice, although Baaba and his partner were standing right in front of her.

"Can we sit down first?" asked Baaba's travelling partner.

"Sit there, sir," she pointed. "What do you want? I am in a hurry; madam will kill me today if I do not get enough customers." Glancing at the entrance to see new customers coming in, she was about to lose her patience with Baaba and his mate.

"Do you want *eba* or rice? What soup do you want?"

She hastily took their order, rushed to the service counter, got the food, and rushed back to where they were sitting. She placed the food and two bottles of Fanta beside them and stretched out her hand with her palm open, waiting to be paid. "Hurry up. Hurry up, please," she said, glancing at the entrance.

Another bus had arrived and she would lose other customers if she wasted any more time with Baaba and his companion. She was about to lose her patience when they placed the money in her palm; she quickly counted it, tucked it in her cloth-

67

made purse, and ran to the next bus and shouted for the next potential customer.

They ate the food quickly and Baaba felt very heavy. He liked his mother's food but this was richer with more meat and fish. He also had a choice of soup. His mother could not afford different soups.

He tried to sleep when the bus left Benin but he was too excited and could only take a few short naps. Although he eventually fell into a deep slumber. When he awoke, he awoke with a start. The noise of women and young girls hawking their goods and shouting at the travellers to buy their wares startled him. They walked round the bus with their wares on enamel trays firmly placed on their heads, with a folded cloth to cushion the tray on their head.

"Where is everyone going?" he asked, noticing that the passengers were leaving the bus. He asked his partner if they had arrived in Lagos.

"No, the bus stops here for passengers to ease themselves."

That sounded like a good idea. Baaba disembarked from the bus, stretched his legs, and followed the rest of the passengers to the bush where he urinated. Baaba had not fully recovered from the heavy meal he had at Benin, so he fell asleep immediately the bus resumed the journey and slept the remainder of the trip to Lagos – eight and a half hours on the road.

"Baaba, wake up, we are almost in Lagos. You have to keep awake to see the lights, that's what I enjoy most," said his companion excitedly as he shook the younger man by the shoulder.

Baaba fixed his eyes on the bus window, taking in the scenery: houses, other vehicles, and people milling about as if they were all rushing to somewhere.

He pinched himself. "This is Lagos, I am actually in Lagos." The fact was that Baaba would not have had the opportunity to travel outside his village but for the war. When he joined the Army, his first posting was to Onitsha, a town separated from Nigeria by the River Niger. The Army transferred him from Onitsha to other war fronts before he joined the Air Force. This was the only exposure Baaba had outside the village.

He was now in Lagos, the capital city of Nigeria, and he was here for one reason and one reason only – to make money. He looked up in the sky as he embarked from the bus and silently thanked God for the magical opportunity that had come his way. He remembered being jealous of Ochi a few months back when he returned from Lagos. Now he had arrived in person and it was no dream.

The motor park was the centre for all buses that had travelled from the Eastern Region. From the park, passengers made their way to the town. It was a hectic service point for drivers and the touts who were busy calling out to potential passengers, agreeing travelling prices, and loading passengers' luggage.

Baaba looked around in amazement and marvelled at how busy the motor park was at this late hour of the day. He couldn't help but think what it would be like during the day when people were out and about, doing their businesses?

There were women and young girls hawking their goods by shouting out to the passengers to buy their goods; there were the food sellers who provided cooked meals for the passengers, the drivers, and the touts. How different this was from the village! He was used to quiet during the day and the eerie dead silence of the evening.

He felt alive here in Lagos. One day, he thought, he would like to be one of those hustling to survive in Lagos.

"There they are," a familiar voice shouted.

Baaba turned around. It was none other than Amaka, her voice filled with joy and relief.

"Amaka!" he cried out. He ran towards Amaka and Ogo. He hugged Amaka first and then Ogo.

"Now, you have to believe me when I tell you anything," Ogo said to Baaba, holding his hands with affection.

At the end of the greeting and enquiring about people in the village, Ogo drove them in his Volkswagen Beetle into the town. First, he took his friend to his home, thanked him for helping Baaba, and then drove Baaba and Amaka home.

"Oh my," Baaba sighed, as he looked around the two-bedroom apartment, observing how tidy and clean Ogo kept his home. Everything was in place and orderly. The only time he had ever seen a home this tidy was the local teacher's home in the village – and this was only because the teacher got the students to clean his house and the surroundings as punishment for misbehaviour.

Amaka looked happy and radiant; she had new clothes and had a different hairstyle with a shine to it. She was still shy around Ogo, trying to avoid eye contact when he spoke to her.

"Come in, come in, Mr Village, and put your bag there," Ogo said, pointing to a corner beside the door. Rubbing his palms together and grinning, he continued, "Now you are in Lagos, I will show you one or two things. First things first, Amaka, please get a bucket of water for Baaba's bath. Whilst Baaba is having his bath, start warming up our food."

Amaka took Baaba to the back of the house past the general kitchen area. The occupants of the house used a common cooking area with individual kerosene stoves, carefully stored in allocated corners.

Amaka led Baaba outside to the back of the house outside the main building. She pointed to a corner with buckets of water and said, "When you are ready you can use one of those buckets. Please take the bucket on the right only, the ones on the left belong to our neighbour."

On the adjacent corner was an enclosed bath area made of zinc slats with a narrow entry. Users had to hang a piece of cloth over the wood holding the zinc slats to secure some privacy during their bath. They both walked back, with Amaka asking Baaba about the welfare of her mother in the village. Baaba confirmed she had received the first money Ogo gave to Amaka to send to her mother through a friend.

She thanked Baaba for the part he played in their marriage. She also told

Baaba that Ogo was arranging for her to learn a trade and become a seamstress with a woman friend of his. Sadly, and unknown to her, the so-called woman friend was Ogo's girlfriend.

Baaba asked Ogo where he should leave his bag, which was still beside the door.

"Oh, under that table," Ogo said as he pointed to a bigger table at the left side of the room. There was a smaller table in the middle of the room. There were decks of cards arranged in order on the small table. Baaba thought, "This is all real. Those cards must be for Ogo's magic; I will have to be patient though, and wait and see." Baaba noticed there was a curtain between the bedroom and the sitting room. What he did not realize then was that there was a door behind the curtain leading to the bedroom.

There were two windows in the sitting room. One on either side of the wall, covered with flowery cotton fabric.

"Baaba, you have to take your bath," Ogo said, settling down in a lounge chair in the sitting room.

"Amaka, bring me a bottle of beer whilst Baaba takes his bath."

Obediently, she brought the beer, opened it, and poured him a glassful.

Baaba stared at the couple and thought, "This was the same man who told me that I did not know how to serve drinks to women; how come Amaka is now the one serving him drinks, where are the manners he was preaching to me about?"

He left them to have his bath. He observed Amaka's instructions about the correct bucket, covered the bathing area with a cloth she had given him and washed his body from the bucket.

When he was finished and came back into the apartment, Ogo said, "Let's go to the veranda and talk.

"Amaka, bring a bottle of beer for Baaba. And please hurry with the food."

"The food is coming very soon," Amaka called from the kitchen where she was sweating over the kerosene stove.

"You must be tired," Ogo said, studying Baaba. "You will need a good sleep tonight, but tomorrow we will start work; I will only explain a little bit of the work tonight, but tomorrow, I will explain your role in the whole game."

After a few minutes, Baaba felt a sting on his right arm. He slapped his arm and glanced at his arm to see what had bitten him.

"You will get used to it, there are mosquitoes in Lagos. I will ask Amaka to get one of the mosquito coils. That would keep them away; they hate the fumes from the coil."

Baaba noticed that this was a different Ogo. He was different here in the city. His voice sounded edgy; the confidence Baaba observed when he came to the village was gone. He whispered as he talked to Baaba but spoke to Amaka in a familiar commanding voice.

They talked for a while until Amaka interrupted them to let them know that the food was ready. Both men walked back to the sitting room for their meal.

She put down an enamel tray with a bowl of soup and a plate with the local staple food, *gari*, made from cassava, and disappeared immediately. A couple of minutes later, she was back with a bowl of water for them to wash their hands. She presented the water to Ogo first and then to Baaba. She adjusted the tray on the centre of the table.

All this was so strange and different. The roles had been reversed, with Amaka serving them. "When you finish, call me," she said. Then she went into the bedroom and shut the door, which was when Baaba observed there was a door behind the curtain.

Baaba dipped his fingers in the soup with a ball of *gari* and could not believe the amount of meat and fish in the soup. He thought, "This is the amount of meat my whole family had in one week in the village. Ogo must be making good money to live like this."

"I don't eat much, you know. Eat as much of the meat as you want, I will have just a piece of the meat and some fish," Ogo said encouragingly. He liked fish more, especially the local delicacy – dried cod known as stockfish. An Igbo delicacy, only a few villagers could afford a whole piece. The sellers in the village cut up, bagged, and sold the fish in smaller quantities. The villagers could only afford the smaller portions, however; the soup was so rich and it was apparent that a whole stockfish had been used in the preparation.

At the end of the meal, they talked more about the business. As much as he wanted to listen, Baaba was tired from the journey. He yawned inadvertently and Ogo noticed.

"We must go to bed now, we have a busy day tomorrow," Ogo said when he noticed Baaba yawning. He called out to Amaka, "Bring the mat for Baaba."

Amaka brought a mat rolled up for ease of carriage. She moved the small table at the centre of the sitting room and unrolled the mat, spread it on the floor, and put a pillow and a cotton wrapper on one end.

"Good night, Baaba," she said and walked back to the bedroom. Ogo followed her to the bedroom, wishing Baaba a very good night.

Baaba lay on the mat on his back, folded his arms underneath his head, and went into deep thoughts that shifted from Ogo and Amaka to the people he left behind in the village. He wondered if ChiChi was thinking about him right then. Would she be faithful and keep her promise? Would she be able to resist the amorous interests from potential rich men? He imagined what it would be like living with ChiChi as Ogo was living with Amaka. He closed his eyes and pictured her piercing eyes and imagined his children by ChiChi inheriting those eyes.

With these thoughts swirling around his head, he fell asleep.

While he slept, he dreamed he was back in the village and was meeting ChiChi in their usual hideout. She was crying and begged him not to go to Lagos. A noisy mosquito woke him up. He covered himself with the wrapper Amaka had given him, turned over and went back to sleep.

71

Chapter 9:
Baaba's Early Days in Lagos

He was awakened by the shouting from children and their mothers the next morning. For a moment, he didn't move as he remained on the mat for a moment to recollect all that had happened. Then he got up from the mat, pulled the right side of one of the curtains on the window, and looked outside the window to investigate the noise.

He was startled by the beautiful morning; the sun was shining and the room was getting hotter by the minute. With the windows shut, the air was very stuffy. The aroma of the native *egusi* soup they had the previous night remained in the air. The village air was fresh and the windows left open without fear of mosquitoes.

He saw a queue of women and children standing across the right side of the building. They had buckets and were queuing up to draw water from the tap, known locally as 'the pump'. He was surprised to see Amaka in the queue because that meant Amaka walked past him in the sitting room whilst he was sleeping. A sound was also coming out of the bedroom and it was not a sound from the water fetchers, it was Ogo snoring in a consistent deep tone. Baaba turned from the window, bent down, picked up the mat from the floor, and rolled it into a bundle.

Amaka returned and came into the sitting room from the pump, and said to Baaba, "You need to fetch some water and wash Ogo's car; get an empty bucket from the yard where I showed you last night."

Glad to have some direction, Baaba, who had put on a pair of shorts, flung a shirt over his shoulder and went to accomplish the task.

He joined the queue and waited to fill his bucket. He looked around him in amazement as people rushed around with their chores. Some were having their bath, others were shouting at their children to get ready for school, and men who worked in offices were leaving for work in their suits and ties.

A road stretched out in front of the house. On it, the cars were competing with the buses for space; the bus conductors shouted out their destinations, stopping to pick up passengers by the roadside. Children were already out playing and splashing one another with water from their buckets. Baaba thought, "They are old enough to go to the farm in the village, but here they laze around, playing silly games and eating."

Other children were having their bath outside the open space behind the building and some were getting ready for school. He stared at the children with their school uniforms and promised himself that he would work very hard in Lagos so that his children would one day wear a smart school uniform.

As he dipped the washing cloth into the bucket of water, Baaba suddenly had a terrible worry. "What if I don't make it in Lagos?" He thought about the promises he had made to ChiChi. "What about the money I promised my mother? What about paying my little brother's school fees?"

He quietly made another promise to himself to discipline himself and work hard. He would certainly not spend money on having so much stockfish in his soup.

He had heard that men lose their focus in Lagos, associating themselves with loose women who take all their money. Then the men forget about going back to their villages to help their parents and siblings. He told himself that this would never happen to him. The poor people in the village needed help. If he could make the money, he would make sure they all got help.

As these thoughts went through his mind, Ogo interrupted him. "Baaba, why did you open the curtain in the sitting room? Please do not ever open it again; I don't want the neighbours poking their noses into my business," he warned Baaba. "Now, hurry up with the car so we can get on with the day."

In the meantime, he was going to have his bath and have breakfast.

Baaba finished washing the car and went back to the apartment. There was little natural light in the sitting room because Ogo had shut the curtains. He wondered why Ogo insisted on having the curtains drawn. What was he hiding?

Ogo was in the bedroom dressing up. Amaka had gone to the kitchen area to prepare some breakfast of fried plantain and corn porridge. Baaba rushed to the bath enclosure to have his bath and get ready to go with Ogo.

He was in Lagos now. The world – and the future – spread out before him.

Chapter 10 :
Baaba's Apprenticeship in Fraud

"Thank you, Amaka, that was delicious," Baaba said, licking the groundnut oil from his lips as Amaka got up to clear the breakfast plates from the table.

Ogo asked Baaba to pull a chair from the bigger table and sit at the smaller centre table. He laid out the cards. "The name of the game is, *the more you look, the less you see*." He smiled. "Now watch me shuffle the cards, you have to be fast when you shuffle the cards." He picked up a deck of cards from the table, shuffled it, and asked Baaba to pick a card. Baaba picked the Queen of Hearts. He asked him to put the card back in the deck of cards. Baaba obeyed and put the card back. Ogo instructed him to shuffle the cards himself. He did and gave the deck of cards back to Ogo. Ogo placed the deck of cards on the table and said, "Pick any card from the deck."

Baaba picked a card from the deck, turned it over, and displayed it on the table. It was the Queen of Hearts. Baaba looked at Ogo in amazement, "How did you do that?"

Ogo smiled. "It's called magic." Then he gestured to Baaba. "Come. We are going to the nearest market to do some work. You will watch me very carefully so that you can learn all the tricks of the game. You are a clever boy; I know you will learn very fast."

When they got to the market, Ogo set up his table. He took the deck of cards out of his bag and shouted, "Okay, beautiful women, let's go. Women with beautiful children, come and double your money … Pick a card and win money. If you pick this one, you win. But, if you pick this one, you lose. It's easy!" Ogo was shouting at the top of his voice, standing behind the makeshift working top with a deck of cards in his hand, like a man possessed.

He turned to Baaba. "See that lovely woman. She looks like she could do with more money for her pancake." Pancake was the name for women's face foundation. "Ask her nicely because she is a pretty woman and must have a handsome husband, so treat her gently," he said within the hearing of his potential victim and beckoned her to the makeshift display top.

Baaba took a few steps towards the woman and said nervously, "Come, madam, you will get money."

She looked at him suspiciously, but she moved towards Ogo's table.

Ogo grinned. "Okay, my beautiful woman, if you pick this one you will win, but if you pick his one you lose," Ogo said, shuffling the cards and looking into the woman's eyes.

The woman laid some money on the working top, picked the Eight of Spades from Ogo's hand, and waited in anticipation. Ogo shuffled the deck of cards again and asked her to pick out a card. She nervously picked a card and screamed in delight when it showed to be the Eight of Spades.

"You win," Ogo said as he returned her money and took an equivalent of the amount, raised his hand to the air so that the other women standing around could see the amount, and shouted, "You unbelievers, now you see how easy it is to win money. Come on and win some money." He handed the money to the woman even as he continued shouting his anthem, "If you take this you win, but if you take this you lose."

Baaba didn't understand. He wondered why he was giving money away when they were supposed to be making money. He found out the reason soon enough. Ogo's 'losing' the first hand convinced the other women to at least try it. "Raise your hands if you want to play," Ogo commanded the women. A good number of the women raised their hands to show their willingness to participate in the 'game'. He turned to Baaba, who was now mesmerised by the whole game and said, "Collect money from these beautiful women, let's double their money." Baaba picked up a bowl Ogo had brought with him and passed it round the women, who dropped their money into the bowl.

Ogo quickly took the bowl from Baaba, emptied the contents into his pocket, shuffled the cards, and asked each woman to pick up a card. The cards were all coming up wrong, and that meant they lost their money. Ogo leaned to Baaba and whispered, "Start packing up the bag."

Baaba put back the bowl into Ogo's working bag together with a few other working tools, including a locally made fan that was supposed to be used to attract the customers.

When they were on their way to the market Ogo told Baaba that he got the fan from a native doctor or 'JuJu man'. Ogo believed the fan helped to attract the women to his game. He told Baaba that a woman was not supposed to touch the fan. "I have specific instructions from the JuJu man to make sure that a woman never touches it.

"If she does, the fan will lose its power."

He confided in Baaba that Amaka knew this secret and dared not touch the fan because she understood that he played the card game for their living. What Baaba couldn't understand was how Amaka, an innocent village girl, had come to be an accomplice in crime in such a short period with Ogo.

"Money is devilish, it can change anybody quite easily," he thought.

Baaba's thoughts were jarred back to the present when Ogo nervously asked, "Are you ready? Get ready to go." The women were shouting at Ogo to give them back their money, as they had not won. Ogo shouted back at them, saying that he was not responsible for their losses. They picked the cards. It was their own fault to have picked the wrong cards. He shrugged. They picked the cards not him.

He winked at Baaba, put the deck of cards in his pocket, pulled the plastic cover from the working top, turned his back to the irate women, and walked away with the women shouting abuse at him. Baaba followed quickly after him, with the women booing and calling them names.

He had an arrangement with another stall owner to store his table until later. He paid him for this favour.

Ogo did not seem to mind the abuse from the women. He hardly heard them. But Baaba was stunned by it.

"Hurry," he said to Baaba. He didn't want any further problems. "It's important to move quickly." He confessed that, on one occasion, the women had beaten him. During that incident, the women not only took their money but also his personal money.

He could not allow that to happen a second time.

He also warned Baaba that sometimes they call the police. "Not to worry," he added. Though the police could arrest them he assured Baaba that usually the police do not take serious action. "They usually detain you in the police cell and then release you when you offer them a bribe."

They visited one other market on that day and trade was good. They encountered no problems from the women there.

The day's business done, they headed home. Once there, Ogo emptied his pockets on the small centre table and asked Baaba to count their loot. He requested a bottle of beer from Amaka and eased himself into the lounge chair.

Baaba completed his task, looked at Ogo, and told him the amount they made. "How much did we have in our pockets this morning?" he asked. Baaba answered. "And how much have we got now?" he asked with a self-satisfied smile.

It had been a good day.

Ogo took the money from Baaba and called out to Amaka. Then he counted some money and offered it to Baaba. "This is your share. Every time we work, I will give you some money to save towards people in the village. You must not squander it or I will stop giving you any money."

Baaba happily accepted the money and the instructions. "Thank you very much, Ogo. God will bless you." He went to the bag he arrived with and took it from the corner of the sitting room, tucked his money into the bag carefully, and put the bag back in its original spot.

Then Ogo turned to Amaka. "Amaka, this is your food money and this one you will put in the jar of money for home people," he said, handing Amaka two piles of money from his earnings.

He put the rest of the money in his pocket for his beer, rent, and other household expenses. He had no bank account, so he managed his money the way he saw fit, under his mattress. The money was to go towards his new Zinc house in the village. He wanted to earn the respect of the villagers and his dead parents, who would be proud of him if he maintained the family line.

Baaba worked with Ogo a few more months, gaining enough experience and confidence. He did not need any prompting when it was time to escape from the irate women. His skill – and his savings – was growing. He was not spending his money carelessly. He took Ogo's advice about saving his money for the home people to heart. He updated his wardrobe and bought himself a watch. His skin was shiny and healthy due to Amaka's cooking.

During all this time, neither Amaka nor Ogo asked him to contribute to his room or board. It was all free.

One morning, Ogo approached Baaba with a smile. "Baaba, today is your day, you will play my part today at the market." He winked at Baaba. "I think you are ready."

Far from being nervous, Baaba was excited. "I was hoping you would ask me one day. I am very ready."

"Now, remember to make sure you ask the women for their money before you start. If not, they will not play the game if one of them loses. But if they hand their money over all at the same time, then we already have their money so they have to play and lose."

The advice was unnecessary. Baaba already knew the workings of the game and could not wait to show Ogo his newly acquired skills. Baaba took over immediately they got to the market, shouting the anthem, "You take this you win, you take this you lose."

Ogo was impressed with Baaba's charm on the women and how they flocked to admire his charisma. He handled and shuffled the cards in an innovative way. He captivated his audience with his gesticulations.

He was quite the showman.

On counting the loot at the end of that day, they had made more money than usual. Ogo said to Baaba, "You see, I told you, you will be a natural in this game. I can relax now because you can go out there and make us money."

After a few months, Ogo told Baaba that someone was going to the village on holiday. He was going to give him the money for the village people and he would like Baaba to send money to his mother.

Baaba wrote a letter to his mother and ChiChi, stating he was getting on very well in Lagos and was well. He also told them how Ogo and Amaka were looking after him. He promised both women that he would return to the village in a short while on a brief visit.

He asked for ChiChi's response to his letter through the bearer to confirm that she was still waiting for him. He inserted money in each envelope and gave them to Ogo for delivery by his friend.

Chapter 11:
Baaba Qualifies in Wayo

Not much later, Ogo became sick with malaria. He was running a high fever. He arranged for a neighbour's son, Oji, to go to the market with Baaba. Sadly, Oji was not an impressive young man. He was a truant who loitered aimlessly throughout the day. His parents had given up on him after bailing him out of police cells on several occasions. He frequently got into trouble, fighting and causing grievous bodily harm, picking women's pockets from the local market. He was also known to have close contact with known criminals.

Oji was notorious in the neighbourhood for his idleness and troublemaking.

Of course, he jumped at the offer from Ogo; he had always wondered how Ogo made his money to live in a nice house and own a Volkswagen car. He had always admired Ogo's sharp dressing and cleanliness.

And so, the chance to learn Ogo's secret just presented itself on a plate. His own intention was less to help Ogo than to learn his trade and set up his own trade copying Ogo.

Ogo, needing the help, did not bother obtaining any permission from Oji's parents. They did not know where he was half of the time, so his parents would not miss him. For his part, Baaba was delighted with the decision. To his mind, it meant Ogo trusted him and believed that Baaba could handle the game by himself.

If Ogo believed in him, he was determined to make a success of the opportunity to prove his gratitude to Ogo.

That night, Ogo decided which of the markets would be suitable for a starter like Baaba. He made his decision in selecting the specific market from his experience; the women in this particular market were easy to deal with because they were well-to-do and would not miss a small amount of money. They call you a 'Wayo man', meaning a trickster, and would move on to their business in the market. But the women from some of the other markets would get irate because they were poor, and losing even a small amount of money meant trouble.

Ogo went through the crucial aspects to assure Baaba's success the next day in the market. For her part, Amaka was fussing over Ogo, offering him malaria tablets, and feeding him with hot 'pepper soup' because Ogo had lost his appetite and her mother had told Amaka that hot pepper soup helped in the recovery of lost appetites.

"You have to finish your talk with Baaba quickly so that you can have your steam and bath with the herb-infused malaria cure," she told Ogo. He had to inhale the steam from the herb-infused boiling water and then have his bath with the water. The herbs washed off the grease from the body and left the skin free to breath. This was the local way of treating malaria.

Amaka had earlier boiled the concoction of leaves and roots for hours for the infusion to take place. It smelled awful and sickly but it seemed to do the job.

Baaba had little sleep that night. Despite his confidence, he was anxious. This would be his first job with no supervision from Ogo. Not only was he a bit nervous, he was sweating because he had wrapped the cloth around him to prevent mosquito bites. He certainly did not want malaria.

So, although Ogo had a table fan, he took it to the bedroom at night for the couple's comfort. Despite his promise to buy another fan for the sitting room, Ogo had not yet done so. So the sitting room was very hot at night. The walls seemed to release all the heat trapped from the sun during the day. One could feel the heat radiating from the walls at night. There was no outlet for the odour from the food. The room always had a stuffy smell. The chairs equally had a particular smell, having absorbed the smell from the food. It was like the odour from a pet's sleeping bag.

After a few weeks, Baaba had gotten used to the smell, but not the heat. And he dared not open any of the windows for two reasons; one, to avoid the neighbours 'poking their noses' into Ogo's business and, two, to avoid mosquitoes coming in to feed on him. He could not afford to be ill; he had a mission, and being sick with malaria would prevent him from attending the market.

Baaba turned and tossed on his mat and finally fell asleep sometime after midnight. He dreamt of ChiChi congratulating him on his success at the market. He told her he was scared and nervous, and she held him close and assured him of his success. The dream was so real to Baaba that when he woke up, he concluded that God was telling him through ChiChi that the day would end successfully.

He took extra care choosing his clothes for the day. He put on one of his latest collections. Looked at his reflection in the mirror in the sitting room and smiled. "I wish ChiChi could see me now," he grinned to himself. "She would be proud of me." He just knew it. He looked closely at his image again in the mirror and noticed that even his dark-skinned complexion was shiny. His hair had been jelled and brushed back in Ogo's style. He had new shoes and a new watch. He brushed his bushy eyebrows, which he had inherited from his father, with his wet fingers moistened with his saliva.

"Have you got everything in the bag?" Ogo asked Baaba.

"Yes, I have," replied Baaba.

"Come here then."

Baaba moved towards Ogo's chair. Ogo asked him to kneel down so he could reach his head. He knelt down and Ogo blessed him, saying, "May the God of our fathers lead and guide you today. May you return with good money and not get into any trouble. May my luck be with you, I pray in Jesus' name." He concluded with, "Amen."

Baaba, who had his eyes shut for the prayer, answered, "Amen."

Amaka, who was also standing by the door, added, "Amen."

Oji reported for duty a few minutes later.

"Baaba, please explain to Oji what he is to do on your way to the market. I have explained a bit to him but you need to instruct him, especially when it is time to leave the spot."

Baaba nodded.

"Good luck and I will be praying for you," Ogo concluded, touching Baaba on the shoulder.

On their way to the market, Baaba explained the game to Oji. "You must watch me all the time," he said. "Sometimes I have to speak to you without a word. It is important that you watch my eyes and my reactions all the time. That way we can communicate without the women knowing."

"I understand. Trust me," Oji boasted. "I am expert in fooling people."

After that, they were silent. Baaba mentally rehearsed the anthem and the act. He tried to remember Ogo's mannerisms with the women to attract them to play the game. His thoughts concentrated on the correct use of the magical fan and remembering the angles that Ogo had told him gave the most positive result. He assured himself he could do it but he was still nervous. He motivated himself, "Today is the day you should use your charm to the utmost; you have what it takes, so flaunt it today.

"After all, you get along easily with women."

On arrival at the market, Baaba noticed that there was a gathering of women opposite the spot which Ogo had used on their last trip to this particular market. He asked Oji to find out what was attracting the women's attention. Oji came back and informed him that a woman was selling second-hand clothing at cheap prices.

Baaba thought, "Good luck! I have to use my creativity to attract the women away from the clothes seller."

He hurriedly set up his pitch, unwrapped the magical fan, and shouted out the anthem. Rather than shouting out the anthem, he made a song out of it. He bellowed this song as loudly as he could, adding a bit more to it with, "Come on, you beautiful women, why are you buying second-hand clothing when you can afford new clothes with my money. You can double your money and buy new clothes instead of leftovers from the white man."

His singing attracted the women on the second-hand pitch. Baaba had surprised himself. He did not know he could sing with such an enticing voice. He had never tried singing to an audience before, but he attracted the women. He sang the anthem louder, gesticulating with his hands. He also turned the fan, facing it towards the second-hand stall where most of the women gathered. He was hoping the black magic on the fan would help.

Two women who were standing on the second-hand pitch, on hearing Baaba's song, left the second-hand stall and switched places to Baaba's pitch.

He welcomed them. "My beautiful ladies, you are the sensible ones; you do not want to buy second-hand clothing. You need brand new clothes." He smiled. "Play your cards right and you could win enough money to buy food and new clothes, instead of second-hand clothing," he sang.

"Go on, show us then."

"Patience, patience, we have to wait for the others; don't you want them to be like you and win money? I have enough money for everybody today and I am feeling generous. Just put your money in the bowl and you will see me double it for you."

More women switched over from the used-clothing stall and this got Baaba more excited. He sang louder to attract the rest of the women. He asked Oji to go over to the second-hand pitch and get the women to come to their pitch instead. He warned Oji, "Make sure the woman who sells the second-hand clothing does not notice you talking to the women. You have to be discreet. If she found out that you are taking her customers, she will get angry."

Oji nodded and casually walked over to the woman's pitch and spoke quietly to some of the women.

After a few minutes, the women were leaving the used-clothing pitch for Baaba's table. He rubbed his hands together and raised his voice even more, "You beautiful angels, what do you want to do with second-hand clothing; come here, and double your money so that you can afford new clothes."

The second-hand clothing seller this time overheard Baaba and, having lost most of her customers to Baaba, walked straight to Baaba's pitch angrily, "What do you think you are doing? You do not think I don't know you are a Wayo man."

Baaba panicked. He had to stop this woman before the women caught on to the trick. He decided to use a soft approach and go on the charm offensive. He held her hand and said in a whisper, "You are such a beautiful creature, please let's work together. I need the money to eat."

The woman pulled her hand away and said, "What about me? I have to eat too, and you have taken my customers."

"Madam, my customers will walk away if you don't stop. I need money to send to my mother in the village. I will buy six dresses from you for my wife at the end of today."

She relented and said, "I will keep quiet for now, but if you do not buy the dresses, I will make sure you never come to this market again to play your *wayo*."

Baaba apologised again and accepted her conditions. He did not intend to buy any clothes but, for now, he could do without her interruptions. He would not buy second-hand clothing for his ChiChi. She was worth more than that. He would make sure she *never* wore second-hand clothing.

The woman left him alone and he resumed his performance. He made sure he held the fan in the correct angles just like Ogo had shown him. He fanned, sang, and gesticulated with his arms. The women were putting their money in the bowl that Oji presented to them.

Meanwhile, Baaba noticed a woman standing in the front row. "Isn't she a beauty?" he thought to himself. To his eyes, she looked like ChiChi and had the same features, like the pointed nose and nice eyes. "What is your name, beautiful one?" he asked her, breaking the first rule of the game.

Ogo had warned him to never get into a personal relationship with the customers. They can tell the other women from the market if they find out where you live and can invite the police if you break off the relationship with them. Was he about to break the first rule of the game?

"My name is Agnes," she said.

"Are you married, Agnes?"

"No," she said.

Baaba was now being distracted from his job.

For a minute, he imagined he saw ChiChi's figure standing in front of him, saying, "What are you doing? Is this why you are in Lagos?"

Getting the better of himself, Baaba cautioned himself immediately and looked away from Agnes. He turned to the women and said, "How many of you would like to buy new clothes for your children? Who would like to show off new clothes to their husbands or boyfriends?"

He tried to generalise the statement so that Agnes would not think he fancied her. He could not break his promise to ChiChi. This was temptation because Agnes was the type of girl Baaba would go for. He liked tall, dark women, but mostly he liked his women to have what he referred to as 'piercing lovely eyes'.

The women screamed, "What about the magic? You are taking too long, if you will not do the magic, please give us our money back." But Baaba had patience. He was a good apprentice; he used delaying tactics to get more money into the bowl.

When he felt he had collected enough money, he took the bowl from Oji, which he noticed had more money than usual, emptied it in his pocket and started the act of card shuffling, and repeatedly said, "Take this you win and pick this you lose." Still, he was uncomfortable because he could not keep his eyes off Agnes.

"Would ChiChi find out if I dated Agnes?" he wondered. He shook his head. "No. I will not do that to ChiChi. She has agreed to marry me so why mess it up?"

He knew that if he got involved with another woman, the village people who lived in Lagos would take the story back home and that would be the end of him and ChiChi. They gossiped a lot and seemed to know whatever was going on amongst their tribe's men. He decided it was not worth it, and Ogo had issued serious warnings to him about getting close to any of their customers.

Yet, all through his card act, these thoughts occupied his mind.

Meanwhile, his apprentice, Oji, had also let his thoughts wander from the task at hand. He observed that the women concentrated so much on the card act that they ignored the security of their bags and purses. He thought, "This is a pickpocket's paradise."

He could pick as many bags and pockets as he wanted because they were more interested in making extra money than taking care of the money they had. Of course, the temptation got the better of him, so he moved from where he was standing behind the table into the midst of the women. Baaba looked up, trying to find Oji, his apprentice, but he was nowhere in sight. He was busy targeting which bags to pick. Baaba shouted his name out, and he answered and went back to the position he should have been in the first place.

In a hushed voice, Baaba said angrily, "What is the matter with you? What were you doing over there instead of watching me as I said to you earlier?"

"Nothing, I was only trying to attract more customers," he lied.

"But we have finished with attracting customers; you are supposed to start getting ready as I was finishing the act so that we can disappear before we get into trouble."

"I am sorry, Baaba," Oji apologised.

"Get ready, we are leaving. You follow me when I take the first step. If you don't, then it is your problem because I am not getting into trouble because of your lousy attitude."

At the first protest from the women, Baaba pretended he needed to get some more money from his boss for any wins on the cards. The women demanded their money before he went but he assured them he would be gone for a very short while. He was sweating profusely, not only from the heat but also the aggravation from the second-hand clothes seller who was all the time watching him from her pitch.

"Why are you taking your bag if you are only going to get some money from your boss?" one of the women called out.

"If I leave the bag here, the magic will be gone; I am the only one who can touch the bag." Then he added, "You all need to wait here until I get back." With that, he winked at Oji and they left in a hurry, leaving the women waiting for their money.

Baaba looked behind him to make sure none of the women had followed them. He then slowed his pace and relaxed a bit but he remained troubled. "Oji, what were you doing in the midst of the women?"

Now Oji told him the truth. "I was doing a recky job," he said. 'Recky' was the slang for reconnaissance. The soldiers used recky instead of the full word during the war. The civilians overheard the soldiers using the word and copied it.

"What recky job?" Baaba asked.

"Didn't you notice there were so many bags I could have picked today?" Oji asked in surprise. "The women did not care about their personal belongings during your act, so it would be a good opportunity to pick their pockets and bags."

"What?!" Baaba asked incredulously. "Are you mad? That is not the kind of job Ogo has sent us to do; that is stealing."

Oji shrugged his shoulders. "So? What are you doing if not stealing? You take their money too."

"If we were in the village I would slap you because you cannot talk to me that way," Baaba said indignantly. "I am not stealing. I am doing magic for the women, and it was their choice to play or not, not steal their money!"

"Okay, okay. I am sorry but please don't tell Ogo, so that I can come with you again. I enjoyed your performance so much today."

"Sure, you enjoyed … because you were not working but looking at women's bags to pick," Baaba replied angrily.

"No, I promise; that will never happen again." Then Oji smiled. "By the way, I saw you looking at the young woman standing in the front row. I know you liked her."

"I don't want to talk about such nonsense. There were so many women and I couldn't tell which one you mean. I have a girlfriend in the village and when next I go to the village, I will bring her photo to show you. She is the most beautiful girl you will ever see in your life."

Oji smiled knowingly. "Sounds serious. Will you marry her?"

"Yes," Baaba responded.

Realizing that he might have overstepped, Oji's expression grew serious. "Please remember not to tell Ogo about my pickpocket habit so that he would let me come to the market with you again. I really want to learn the trade."

"It is difficult to take you seriously," Baaba said.

"Please. One more chance. If I misbehave, then tell Ogo not to let me come to the market with you," Oji pleaded.

"All right," Baaba said, promising him that he would not tell Ogo of his pickpocket tendencies.

Ogo breathed a sigh of relief when they arrived home. "Thank God you are back. I was worried as it was your first day. Oji has never been to the game before. I don't really care how much you made; I was more worried about your safety because if anything happened to you, your mother would kill me. The village people will say that I have sold you to a JuJu man to make money."

"Well, Ogo, you are worrying for nothing. I had everything under control," Baaba assured him, even if that wasn't quite the truth. Then, he sat down to count their day's earnings. When he was finished, he passed the money to Ogo.

Ogo was shocked. "I can't believe how much you made today!" he exclaimed. "You made more money than me. How did you do that?"

"My charm," Baaba said with a confident smile. He knew that the earnings proved that Ogo could trust him even more and let him into his other secrets. He had overheard Ogo talking to one of his friends about a deal they wanted to engage in which had nothing to do with the game. However, it was all very quiet and secret.

But Baaba had patience. He would let Ogo tell him at the right time, no rush.

He was happy with his present job.

Ogo shared the money as usual and gave Oji his due. He gave Baaba his share with the usual warning about keeping it for the people in the village.

As Oji counted his share, he looked up at Ogo, "Can I go with Baaba another day?"

Before he answered, Ogo turned to Baaba, "How did he do today? Was he good with calling the women?"

Baaba hesitated and then he replied, "Yes. He was very good and I would like him to go with me again."

Ogo nodded. "All right, Oji, you have passed the test. You can go with Baaba on his next job."

Oji was thrilled that Baaba kept his promise and kept his pickpocket tendencies quiet. For this reason, and this reason alone, he decided he would behave himself, learn the trade, and set up his own card game business.

Meanwhile, Baaba had no plans of setting up his own business just yet. He had promised Ogo he would work for him until Ogo released him from the apprenticeship. Of course, he hoped that would not be too much longer, as he did not want ChiChi to wait for too long and be tempted by other suitors.

ChiChi had sent him a letter through Ogo's friend, assuring him that she would wait for him. She thanked him for the money he sent to her and told him she used it to buy some of the books she needed for school.

When he was reading the letter, he thought, "What a girl; instead of using the money to buy clothes like other girls, all she talked about was school and books." He realized just how fortunate he was. He decided he would send her more money for her school, books, and her mother's needs. Whenever the time came for him to return to the village, he would buy her the type of clothes he would like his future wife to wear. He had seen nice dresses in the shops and he would use some of his savings to buy her nice clothes, shoes, and jewellery.

His savings grew rapidly from the game. It wouldn't be long before he could afford a Volkswagen Beetle. He imagined what it would be like to have ChiChi sitting beside him in his car. He could not forget that Emi was still in the village and could still go after ChiChi. Therefore, in his next letter, he enquired from ChiChi if Emi had made any advances to her.

Although he knew how lucky he was ... he couldn't help but feel a little jealous.

Chapter 12:
Ogo Bites Off More Than He Can Chew

THE GAME WAS BRINGING IN more money than they could imagine and everyone was happy. They were sending money to the village on a regular basis and keeping plenty for themselves.

"I am going to buy a new car soon. I like the new Passat," Ogo announced one evening while they were having their evening meal.

"I thought you were saving money to renovate your parents' house or build a new house on your parents' land," Baaba said, concerned that Ogo was going to behave like Lagos people and forget where he came from. His Beetle ran well. He did not need a new one.

Ogo nodded his head. "Oh yes, I will have enough money for the building and the car," he replied cheerfully and confidently. "I also think we need to move to a bigger house so that our new child will have more space."

Baaba's mouth dropped open. He stared at Ogo and then looked at Amaka, who looked away. She was embarrassed at the way Ogo announced her pregnancy to Baaba. But then she smiled, and said, "Yes, Baaba. I am going to be a mother soon." She giggled at the look on his face. "Ogo asked me not to tell you and look at what he has done; he's made it look like I am the one who did not want to tell you."

Ogo, in good humour, laughed. "She is going to the village to have the baby," he said. "Lagos is not a nice place for a young girl to have a baby. She needs her mother and her siblings to help and support her during her pregnancy, birth, and nursing the child. I have no time to do that for her in Lagos, so Amaka will go home next month."

Despite his happiness at the news, Baaba could not help but feel betrayed that Ogo had been keeping secrets from him. "I have trusted him and told him about ChiChi. Why didn't he tell me about Amaka's pregnancy earlier?"

Whatever Baaba or Ogo felt about the pregnancy, it would not have remained secret much longer. Amaka was constantly sick in the mornings and could not wait to return to the village. She knew she needed her mother, as this was her first pregnancy and birth. She stopped cooking because she felt sick whenever she went into the kitchen, so Baaba took over the job of cooking for the three of them. He had no idea how to cook but Amaka sat at the central cooking area, instructing him throughout the process. After a few meals, Baaba perfected his cooking skills.

He made nice meals that were almost as good as those that Amaka made. Which was just as well, because when Amaka went back to the village, they would have to eat and someone would have to cook. It definitely was not going to be Ogo; he was the master of the house.

Which got Baaba wondering how Ogo used to eat when he was living in Lagos alone before the arrival of Amaka and himself. He could not resist but asked Ogo, "How did you eat before our arrival?"

"I had a woman who sells food and she used to bring food for me to buy. She cooks very well and her food was cheap."

This made Baaba even more curious. Why had Ogo trusted a strange woman to cook for him? She could put JuJu in his food. He knew this from the stories he had heard about Lagos women. However, there wasn't much time to consider these things. The month went by very quickly, and the game business was still booming. Baaba had introduced other innovative ways of attracting the customers. His card-shuffling skills quickly became more refined than Ogo's.

The night before she was to return home, Amaka spoke to Baaba. "I only agreed to go home because I was confident that you would take care of Ogo. Please talk him out of buying a new car and moving to a bigger place. We don't need it; I will be having the baby in the village anyway, so we don't need any more space. We need to save money to build our own house in the village. He likes you and will listen to your advice." She eyed him seriously. "And make sure no woman comes into this house to take Ogo from me. I am scared of Lagos women. You must also remain loyal to ChiChi, if not you will miss a good-looking girl who is your wife-to-be." She left other instructions for Baaba about keeping the house clean and feeding Ogo.

Baaba wrote a letter to ChiChi, telling her how much he missed her and that he would soon be home to see her. He slipped some money into the envelope and gave it to Amaka. He also gave Amaka some money as a gift and thanked her for being a good friend and contributing to his coming to Lagos. He promised he would never disappoint her and would take care of Ogo.

For the first week after Amaka left for the village, all was well. Then, soon after, upon returning from the market, Ogo announced that he would like Baaba to take over the game business. A friend was introducing a new business to him and he would be spending his time on that.

"A new business?" Baaba asked. "How long will you be engaged in this other business?"

Baaba was surprised that Ogo was abandoning the card game. The card game was bringing enough income for their everyday needs. They had savings. He felt Ogo was getting his priorities wrong, but there was not much he could do about it. It was Ogo's life and Ogo's decision.

Meanwhile, Ogo never told him what type of business his friend had introduced to him.

Baaba had taken over the card game business as Ogo was absent most of the time anyway. When Baaba asked him where he went when he wasn't working the game, he replied, "It is my business, but I will let you know when it materialises and then I will bring you into the business. However, for now I am only trying it for the first time. I am sworn to secrecy so I cannot tell you; I will tell you at the right time."

Baaba was making money with the card game, but Ogo seemed not to care any more about all his plans to build a house in the village. He was coming back home late every day. On some nights, he would not come back to the house to take his share of the card game. He continually boasted of what he would do with the money he was expecting from his new business.

"Baaba," he said, "if I succeed in this new business, we may not need to be doing the card game any more because this one is more lucrative and there will be no women involved."

In truth, Ogo detested the fact that he took their money. He felt that the new business would be more prestigious.

"But the card game is giving us the money we need," Baaba argued. "If we can go to different markets each day, we would make even more money. With you in one market and me in the other we would be making a good amount each day."

But Ogo was unmoved. "No, Baaba. I have made up my mind, the card game is not for me any more. You have to stick with Oji as your apprentice. I have given you all the training, skills, and tools to carry out the card game, so you don't need me."

Baaba saw no sense in his explanations. "What business would yield more money than the card game?" he wondered. He wished Amaka were in Lagos to talk to Ogo. He had promised Amaka that he would take care of Ogo in her absence but Ogo was ignoring his advice. Ogo was determined to abandon the card game.

Baaba felt dejected and thought, "Where is this devil coming from? Ogo was well into the card game before I came to Lagos to live with him; why is he abandoning the source of our income?"

He was unable to answer his questions so he prayed to God for answers and solutions.

A couple of months later, Baaba came back from the market with Oji. They were counting the earnings they had made when they heard a knock on the door. Baaba quickly hid the money under the chair and told Oji to find out who was at the door.

As Oji opened the door, two policemen pushed their way into the apartment, enquired whom they were and said they had a warrant to search Ogo's house. He had been involved in a criminal offence. Baaba told the policemen his name and was very nervous. The money he had made for the day was still underneath the chair and if the police got hold of it, he would have done all that work for nothing.

They demanded to know who owned the apartment and Baaba confirmed that it belonged to Ogo. He also confirmed to the police that Ogo had not been home for two days and he did not know what had happened to him.

"Are you saying you don't know where he is right now?" the policeman demanded.

"That is correct. I don't," he replied. He continued, "I have been worried that he has not come home for two days. Though I am used to him not returning home on some days, he told me he stayed with his friend on those nights, but I don't know who the friend is either."

"Do you know what business he does?" the policeman asked.

Baaba shrugged. "I think he is into importing and exporting." In fact, he had no such idea. But Ogo had rehearsed him to give this answer in case of police trouble.

"What products does he import and export?"

Baaba was struck dumb. He had no idea. Ogo had not rehearsed him to be ready for the next question. "I think he imports sugar, sir," he said.

"Do you know where his warehouse is located because we would like to go there for our investigations?"

"I don't know, sir; I have not long ago arrived from the village. I am new here and he does not tell me what he does. I am his servant, and I help him with the chores in the house."

"And who is this person?" the policeman asked, gesturing to Oji who was starting to shake, so scared that he would end up in the police cells. He had been in police cells several times before and he was prepared to do anything to avoid another detention, especially now he was earning money through the card game. Although there were still times, when Baaba wasn't looking, when he picked pockets as well.

"He is our neighbour's son," Baaba said. "He comes here to play with me because I am alone most of the time and sometimes I need to talk someone."

"What do you do, young man?" the police asked Oji.

"I help my mother in her stall in the market. She allows me to rest some days, this is why I am with Baaba to play and chat today, as this is my rest day."

"So you two are not involved in Ogo's business?"

"No, we are not; I don't even know what business you are talking about," Baaba said.

"Do you know his friend Ebi?"

Baaba furrowed his brow. It was a genuine expression. He did not know him. "No, we don't know him and have never met him."

"We need to search the house to see if he kept any of the contraband in here."

"He does not keep anything in this house, you can check," Baaba said nervously, thinking of the money under the lounge chair. Thinking seriously about how to get the money out of the house without the police finding it, he came up with a plan. Winking at Oji and directing his attention to the money, he then rushed into the bedroom and beckoned to the police to come into the bedroom. "I know he kept some of his things in this box," he said, pointing to Amaka's jewellery box.

A classic distraction. Oji understood immediately and almost instinctively slowed down behind the men as they went into the bedroom. As soon as their backs were turned, Oji quickly picked up the money and hid it under his shirt, securing it with his belt.

Baaba showed the policemen a small jewellery box that belonged to Amaka. She had taken the valuable items to the village; Ogo sometimes kept his jewellery in the box too.

The policeman shook his head. "No. What we are looking for is bigger than this. It cannot fit into this box."

Baaba shrugged. "Oh well …, that is the only hiding place I know.

After their search, the police found nothing incriminating except the decks of cards. When they asked him about the cards, Baaba claimed Ogo and his friends liked to play cards. "But they sometimes left their cards after a game; especially if they were drunk," he explained.

Baaba breathed a sigh of relief when the police left. He did ask them what crime Ogo had committed, but they would not give him the information because the police said their investigations were not completed. Until the investigation was completed, they kept the details secret. The police did say that Ogo was in a police cell and would be there for quite some time.

"Which police station, sir?" Baaba asked.

The policeman shook his head. "Sorry, young man. We cannot tell you that either." And with that, the policemen left.

Baaba and Oji looked at one another and just about collapsed on the floor from their relief. The stress of the visit – and the happy ending – left them giddy. They both started talking at once and continued talking about the incident until late in the evening. They just could not stop talking about it. They wondered what Ogo had done. Baaba told Oji how Ogo boasted of making big money soon. He told him about his plans to buy a new Passat and move to a bigger house.

Oji, with his knowledge of crime, suggested that it must be a big business then. He feared Ogo had taken on more than he could handle and this time was in real trouble.

At least Baaba had told the police the truth – he had no idea who the friend who introduced Ogo to the new business was. He knew nothing.

With a card game, the police were generally more lenient. A warning after a few hours in the cell; and then, after some bribery and some negotiation, a release. They always blamed the women who were stupid enough to spend their food money on a money-doubling game.

So the fact that Ogo was still in the cell suggested that something more serious was going on.

However, there was nothing to do about that but to finish their business. So Oji gave Baaba the money. Baaba thanked him for hiding the money. He also expressed his gratitude for his understanding of his non-verbal instructions.

"I was tempted to take the money and run, you know, but I don't know what stopped me," Oji joked.

Baaba looked at him with a curious expression. Then they decided to eat their dinner. Baaba pleaded with Oji to stay with him. In truth, he was scared to be on his own. The police visit had shaken him. He did not know whom Ogo was dealing with; they may be big criminals and may come to the house.

He did not want to be the victim of an affair or business he knew nothing about. If Ogo had gotten himself in a bigger criminal activity, he did not want to be the one to suffer the consequences.

Oji, knowing no one would miss him at home, was happy to stay on through the night. Lying on the mat in the early hours of the morning, they talked about the events of the previous night.

"Oji, do you think we should continue the market game with Ogo in police custody?"

"This is now our game. If Ogo has put himself in trouble, that has nothing to do with us. Whatever he has done has nothing to do with the market. Can't you see? If the two events were connected, the police would have arrested us. Stop worrying about him."

"But I am. I can't help it. He brought me to Lagos and if anything happened to him, then I am in trouble."

"Did he tell you what he was doing?"

"No, he did not."

"Then my advice is that we continue the game business and wait for his fate. If he goes to jail, you will have to pay the rent and feed yourself. He wouldn't do that from the jail, would he?"

"I know, but I am really worried."

"Worry will not feed you nor make money to send to your mother and ChiChi."

At the mention of ChiChi's name, Baaba's thinking shifted. If he were to end up in a police cell, would she still marry him? ChiChi would be an educated woman; she would not marry a common criminal who had a prison record. He put both hands under his head and stared at the ceiling. "What are we going to do?" he asked again, as if he hadn't heard Oji's answer already. "What are we going to do?"

Baaba couldn't get over the fact that Ogo was in trouble. "If I knew which police station Ogo was being held in, I would go and try to help him."

"Well, you don't know so stop thinking about it," Oji said impatiently.

That wasn't so easy for Baaba. He thought about Amaka and the baby. He had sworn to her that he would look after Ogo. Should he write to her and tell her what was going on? Would Ogo want him to?

But what if Amaka found out through other village people? Could she ever forgive him for not being the one to tell her? Baaba shook his head as if to free his mind of all these pesky concerns. There were so many questions but no easy answers.

He drew a deep breath and said out loud, "My ChiChi, where are you? I need your advice now. I know you would know what's best in this situation."

Oji let out a soft sneer. "Well, your ChiChi is not here. So, can we concentrate on the matter at hand? There is trouble and you are talking about a woman," he said with mild disgust.

"Oji, you fool, you do not understand how much I love that girl. I am in Lagos for that girl and I will make it for her sake. I made promises to her ..."

Before he could say another word, Oji interrupted him. "Are we going to the market or not?"

Chapter 13:
Ogo's Jail Sentence

EVENTUALLY, THE POLICE REVEALED THE cell where Ogo was being held and said he was allowed a visit. So Baaba went to see him. It was then that Baaba learned that Ogo was charged with possession of Class A drugs. The court refused bail and the judge remanded him in KiriKiri prison until his hearing.

Ogo received a seven-year sentence for possession and intent to export cocaine to America.

Hearing the sentence, Ogo broke down in tears. So did Baaba. And now he would have to write to Amaka to tell her what had happened to her husband. At least, now he knew Ogo wanted him to tell her. He had discussed the subject during his visits.

However, there was simply no good or easy way to break the news. When she learned of the situation, Amaka was distressed and wondered how she could bring up the baby on her own. In his letter, Baaba promised to look after her and the baby. For he had made a promise to Ogo to care for his family. He would send money regularly to Amaka. This was to show his gratitude for their kindness.

Besides, Amaka was a kind girl. She had not forgotten Baaba when she left the village with Ogo. She had kept her promise and encouraged Ogo to bring Baaba to Lagos. And, while she had been in Lagos, she also looked after Baaba, cooking, washing his clothes, and taking care of him.

So, even after Amaka gave birth to a little girl, Baaba kept his promise and continued to send money to her.

The child was two years old when Amaka met a man who was visiting the village from London. His sole intention for the visit was to find and marry a girl before his return to England, where he lived in London and worked as a pharmacist.

He fell in love with Amaka. Despite the entreaties of his family and relations who tried to dissuade him, he could not give up his feelings. Yes, it was true, Amaka had a child already and the child was an extra responsibility.

"You will be raising another man's child," his mother warned him.

They also wanted him to marry a girl who had not been married before. But he ignored all the advice and proposed to Amaka. She said yes.

He married her and took her to England with Ogo's daughter.

In Lagos, Baaba visited Ogo regularly, keeping him informed of events in Lagos and in the village. Ogo had asked that Amaka bring his daughter to the prison so that he could see her but Amaka flatly refused.

When Baaba informed him of Amaka's marriage and her trip to London, he was completely heartbroken.

Chapter 14:
Baaba Ends Up on the Street

Despite Oji's arguments, Baaba could not continue the card game. He did not want to end up in prison like Ogo. Even Ogo, when Baaba came to visit him in jail, tried to persuade him to continue the card game, but he refused. He looked at Ogo in jail and thought, "A man has no powers if he loses his independence."

To compound his fears, the police, whilst investigating Ogo's case, found out that Ogo was a market trickster. For this reason alone, Baaba could not go to the market. Fear of imprisonment made the decision easy. If he got into trouble, Oji, the truant, would abandon him and he would end up losing ChiChi as well.

He used up the savings he had and could not pay the rent for Ogo's flat. He sold the furniture and whatever was of value left in the apartment just to survive but life got too difficult. He considered going back to the village but when he thought of the poverty he faced in the village, he decided to tough it out in Lagos. "I am not going to steal, but God will definitely find something for me," he told himself.

The landlord evicted him for failure to pay the rent and he found himself on the streets. He had no friends and no relations. No one from his village would accommodate him. They all knew he was trouble. His association with Ogo was another hindrance. They all knew Ogo was a Wayo man.

He walked the streets during the day and found corners to sleep at night.

He visited women who hawked food on the streets and begged to work for them in return for food. Some of them obliged and some were hostile. "You should go to your mother and ask her to look after you or send you to school, not beg for food," the hostile ones shouted at him.

He went into a food stall one day, and the owner liked him and offered him a job. She paid him with food. He was grateful to her. At least now he knew he would get a daily meal. He slept outside her stall at night. She promised to pay him wages if he worked hard and her customers liked him. He was on a probationary period.

Whilst working in her food stall one day, two police officers in uniform came to the stall. They walked to one of the benches where the customers sat and waited to order their lunch. Other customers were also waiting for their meals or having their meals.

"Baaba, please leave washing up and serve the customers," the owner called out to him.

"Yes, Ma," Baaba replied and hurriedly wiped his hands on a towel.

He rushed over to the woman.

"Take the bowl of water to the policemen to wash their hands and ask them what they would like for lunch," she ordered.

Baaba took the bowl of water to the policemen. He stopped and gave a loud scream, "Oke, what are you doing here?"

One of the policemen jumped up and hugged him. "What are you doing here yourself?"

"It's a long story."

Oke introduced his colleague and said, "Please meet my friend from my village; I have not seen him since I left the village." He looked back at Baaba, "Why are you so thin? Do you have no food to eat? You used to be very muscular."

"Well, that's life," Baaba muttered.

"What is wrong, Baaba? This is not you. This is not the Baaba I know."

Baaba shrugged. "I need to talk to you but not here, not with all these people."

"All right, tell Madam to serve you food as well so that we can talk."

"Madam will be angry. It is better you give me the money so that I can eat later."

"I will talk to Madam then."

"No, please, don't. I will tell you when you finish eating."

"So, what are you really doing here?"

"I have told you that we will talk later but for now, Madam wants to know what you would like to have for your lunch."

"Okay, tell Madam we want our usual, *eba* with assorted meat."

Oke watched Baaba go back to Madam and give her their order. It was then he realized that Baaba was working for the woman. He was shocked and said to his friend, "That boy is one of the show-offs we had in the village. He was an army officer during the war and, after the war, he refused to go back to school. He played with all the girls in the village and we envied him because he was very handsome." He shook his head. "Life can be cruel and unpredictable. I can't believe that he is serving a woman who sells food on the roadside for a living. He was so lazy; he could not help his own mother with any chores."

And it was true. That was Baaba's life story told in a few minutes.

When they finished eating, Oke spoke to Baaba briefly, giving him his address and inviting him to visit him at his home.

"Have you got money to pay for your transport to my house?" he asked Baaba.

"No, but I can walk."

Oke put his hand in his pocket, gave Baaba some money, and said, "Make sure you come because I really want to speak to you."

That evening, when Baaba finished his job with Madam, he headed to the address Oke gave him. He knocked on the door and waited. Oke opened the door wearing a T-shirt and pyjama bottoms.

"Come in, come in, Baaba. I was hoping you would come."

Baaba looked around Oke's apartment in amazement. It was spotlessly clean. Everything was in order. The apartment was well furnished. Although it was a one-bedroom apartment, it was well looked after. He had nice romantic music playing in the background and the book he was reading before Baaba arrived was on the bedside table.

"Sit down and make yourself comfortable."

Baaba was hesitant to sit. He felt dirty and ordinary. But with Oke's encouragement, he sat on the edge of one of the cushioned chairs.

"Listen, my friend, you must relax. This is your home, so help yourself to beer in the fridge." Oke then laughed. "You have to help yourself; I am not your wife to serve you."

Baaba then gave a smile, got up, and took a bottle of beer from the fridge. He sat back on the chair, opened the bottle, poured some in a glass, and said to Oke, "Your friend is in trouble."

Oke didn't answer directly. "Would you like something to eat?" he asked.

"No, I ate at Madam's *bukka*." This is the term for a roadside food stall.

"Then just tell me what is going on and, if you get hungry later, I have some food in the kitchen."

Baaba narrated his plight to him. He carefully omitted that he was involved in the card game with Ogo. He told Oke that he was living with Ogo before he got into trouble and ended up in prison.

Oke said he was not surprised that Ogo ended up in jail because he had heard about the drug deal from his police friends who were involved in the investigation. Meanwhile, Oke was very sympathetic to his old friend and asked Baaba to stay with him instead of living on the street. He informed Baaba that there was a recruitment drive by the Lagos police. "They are looking for new recruits. With your height and your experience in the Army, you will be accepted into the Police Force. You are tall and muscular."

"But I don't have any qualifications like you. You have the school certificate," Baaba said, worried about his lack of education.

"They are not looking for education for new recruits, only if you are applying for officer grade. They just want young men who are healthy and strong."

Oke asked him to have his bath and rest for the night and not worry about his problems. "If you are accepted in the Police Force, you will get your salary at the end of every month. You can then take care of yourself and have your own accommodation. Meanwhile, you can stay here as long as you want. I live alone but my girlfriend visits me occasionally. She is a nice girl and you will meet her on her next visit."

Chapter 15:
Baaba's Luck Changes

OKE LEFT FOR WORK THE next morning with instructions that Baaba should not go back to Madam. He gave him some money to go to the local market and buy some food to cook. He also gave him money to go and have a haircut.

Baaba could not believe his good fortune. God, he thought, had sent Oke to him. "I know you will not abandon me, God, please make this work," he prayed that night. He thought about ChiChi. Would she marry a policeman? He had doubts, but he could not worry about that for the moment. The immediate problem was survival. She would certainly not marry a homeless man. If he could survive this period, he could look for a better job in the future.

Oke came back from work the next day and announced that he had arranged for them to meet with his superior officer who was in charge of recruitment.

He took Baaba to the police recruitment officer who gave them all the documentation needed for Baaba to complete. Baaba attended the recruitment day event. He passed the initial selection. They offered him an interview date.

Oke told Baaba that the interview stage of the recruitment was the most difficult to get through. He coached him every night on the questions that he may face at the interview. Even though he was nervous, he felt he was ready when the day came.

"When did you come to Lagos from your village?" the officer asked at the interview.

"I have been in Lagos for a few months," he replied.

"What have you been doing in Lagos?"

"Working with my brother," Baaba said, trying to mask his nervousness.

"So, what did you do for your brother?"

"I helped him in his shop selling water," he lied.

Despite his lies and nervousness, he managed to pass the interview.

CHAPTER 16:
BAABA JOINS THE POLICE FORCE

EVENTUALLY, BAABA WAS POSTED TO Ajengule police station. On his first day, Baaba walked into the police station looking very smart and handsome in his newly starched uniform. As soon as he arrived, the female officers commented on his appearance.

"Where did this one come from?" a female officer joked.

"He should be a doctor or a lawyer, not here in Ajengule with us," another officer said, laughing.

Baaba ignored all the taunting and concentrated on learning new instructions and orders from his superiors.

"Baaba, this is Sergeant Ade. You will work with him so that he can teach you all you need to know," the police inspector said.

"Yes, sir," Baaba responded eagerly.

The inspector continued, "Sergeant Ade is one of our best Criminal Investigation Department officers. He will guide you on investigations, interviewing skills, and report writing. You are fortunate to be recommended to train as a CID officer without walking the streets first. You must have the gods on your side as the force has only just changed the rules on training. Years ago, recruits had to walk the streets for a good number of years before becoming investigating officers."

"Yes, sir," was all Baaba could manage.

Sergeant Ade looked very professional and spoke well as he studied Baaba. "My name is Sergeant Ade. You are to be my boy, yes?"

"Yes, sir."

Baaba worked with Sergeant Ade for one month. At the end of the month he received his first salary and thought, "This will not be enough for me to live on, what about sending money to ChiChi?"

When he got home that evening, he told Oke he had received his first salary. He thanked him for his kindness, especially for providing accommodation for him.

"What are friends for? One day I might need your help too," he said.

"I will make sure I pay you for your kindness one day," he promised Oke.

Baaba was happy to have an income even if it was much less than what he earned at the market. Still, his low wage continued to trouble him.

"How does one live on such a meagre salary?" he joked in the morning when he was going out with Sergeant Ade.

The Sergeant looked at him closely. "We have to subsidise with other means."

"Other means?" Baaba asked.

"You will find out," Sergeant Ade replied.

Baaba needed to supplement his income. He worried that ChiChi would not marry him with such a low income. All he did was for ChiChi and he had to find a job that would ensure she was comfortable when they were married.

On arrival at work one day, Sergeant Ade said to him, "Please go to the man we visited yesterday and ask him to give you 'my envelope'."

"What envelope, sir?" Baaba asked naively.

"Just ask him for the envelope; do not say anything else to him."

"Yes, sir," Baaba responded with a salute.

So Baaba went to the man's house. The man handed him an envelope. "You must not open this envelope," the man said.

He left the house but the temptation to open the envelope was overbearing. He fought with his conscience for a while and then decided to open the envelope and find out what it contained.

Baaba was surprised to find that the envelope contained money. He was confused. What was this money for? Why was the man giving money to Sergeant Ade? He was an accused. When did Sergeant Ade arrange this because he had always visited this man with Sergeant Ade? They had never discussed money.

He had no answers to any of these questions. He handed the envelope to Sergeant Ade, who opened the envelope, counted the money, and handed him some of the money. "Baaba, this is yours, now you can send money to your ChiChi."

Baaba counted the money and realized it was more than his monthly salary; he knelt down and thanked Sergeant Ade. Now he had money not only for ChiChi but also enough to pay for accommodation and move from Oke's house.

He would like to have his own place because ChiChi had to come to Lagos to live with him. He also had enough money for his mother and his sibling's school fees.

Baaba said, "So this is the other means of subsidising our salary. Now I know the way, thank you, Sergeant Ade."

"You do not let any other officer know about this, we all do our own thing and there is a lot of jealousy amongst us."

"Not me, sir, I will never tell anybody."

When he got home, Baaba recounted the money and believed he was in luck *again*. Then he had an astonishing thought. It was possible to be a police officer and a criminal at the same time. He informed Oke that he would like to secure a place. He thanked him for his kindness, help, and tolerance.

"How will you pay for accommodation? Why don't you wait a few months so that you can save enough money to pay for your rent," Oke advised him.

"I can manage; you need the space. Your girlfriend has been tolerant. If I have a problem with my rent, I can move back," he joked.

Baaba used part of the bribery to pay for a room and sent some of the money to ChiChi and his mother. He looked back on his life on the street and he knelt down and prayed to his God. Baaba believed he had his own special God that looked after him. He had a relationship with his God, which he could not share even with ChiChi.

CHAPTER 17 :
BAABA APPREHENDED FOR BRIBERY

ONE DAY, SERGEANT ADE SAID, "I want to try you on a case. You will have no assistance from me but you must report every step to me." He pointed to a man who was standing at the police desk and said, "You need to interview that man, obtain a statement from him, and follow up with a visit to the accused's premises."

Baaba, who was still nervous with all the new skills and knowledge he was supposed to learn, said, "Yes, sir." He walked up to the man and said, "Come with me to the interview room."

The complainant, Mr Ajayi, followed him to the interview room.

"I have this case with the son of our Chief," the complainant told Baaba. "He thinks that because he is the Chief's son, he can do what he likes."

The man then went on to narrate his problems in the past with the Chief's son; the argument was about land ownership.

"The land belonged to my great-grandfather, but the Chief's family took it away from my father because he owed them money. Now, I want to pay them the money he owed but they refuse. They claim he sold the land, but it was leased, not sold. My great-grandfather leased the land to them." He ended his story with, "I am prepared to fight them until my last breath."

Having obtained all the information, Baaba's next step was to visit the Chief's son. He arranged to pay him a visit the next day.

Although the accused was the one that usually offered bribery, Mr Ajayi was desperate and needed the police on his side. He gave Baaba some money after his interview. He said it was for Baaba's transportation to the Chief's house.

That night, Baaba could barely sleep. He was tossing and turning, thinking of how he could approach the Chief's son and earn his own supplement for his salary.

"I am looking for the Chief's son," he announced on arrival.

"I am his wife, can I help you?" a woman asked.

"I am here to see your husband, madam," Baaba replied.

"Hold on, I will tell him."

"Good morning, are you looking for the master?" a man asked as he entered the room.

"I am a police officer from Ajengule police station; somebody has made a complaint about your master. I need to see him."

"What's the complaint about? Who is the man?"

"I am sorry, sir, but your master has to come to the station to give a statement."

The man excused himself. "Give me a few minutes and I will find out where my master is."

"My master said that I should deal with it," the man announced on his return.

"Why can't I see him?"

"He said I should represent him."

Baaba felt that because he was from the Chief's family he avoided certain duties because he had servants to carry out his bidding. He would have to make do with the messenger. Which was his first mistake. Sergeant Ade would have insisted on dealing with the Chief's son, not his messenger.

"You will have to come to the station with me then," Baaba told him.

On arrival at the police station, Baaba took him to the interview room and informed him who the complainant was. He also gave him details of the complaint. "I knew it was him. He can't let go. The land belongs to us not him; he is always harassing my master, but we will deal with him."

"Do you want me to deal with this man so that he can leave you in peace?"

"Yes, anything you can do to get this man off my master's back," he replied. "The land belonged to his family but they sold it to our family, and now he feels he has money and wants to turn the clock back."

"I am asking you again, do you want me to deal with this man so that he can leave you alone?" Baaba asked impatiently.

"Yes, I said, anything."

"It will cost you and your master something," Baaba nervously told him.

"How much will it cost?" the man inquired.

"Five thousand naira."

"That is no problem; I will tell my master and come back to see you."

Baaba gave him his address and told him to come back with the money in two days.

Two days later, the man did come to Baaba's room.

"Did you speak to your master?" Baaba asked him.

"Yes, I did, and he has authorised our agreement."

"Good, where is the money?" Baaba asked nervously.

"My master would like to hand the money personally to you. He does not trust anyone with his money. He wants to see you in person to confirm that you would get rid of this man."

"Okay, when would he like to see me?" Baaba asked. Which was his second mistake. He should have asked his boss to come to him.

"In two days' time," replied the messenger.

So it was arranged. When he left, Baaba lay down on his bed. "I wonder how much the Sergeant will give me?" he thought. The Sergeant would surely give him two thousand naira out of the total amount. "If I got two thousand naira,

I will send five hundred naira to ChiChi, five hundred naira to my mother and siblings for their school fees and feeding ..." he thought, already spending the money he did not have. "And, if I crack this first bribe on my own, the sky is the limit, because I would ask for bribery from other complainants and accused. I would have to have a strategy whereby I can take bribery from the complainant and the accused; this will make it more lucrative, playing one against the other."

In his thinking, his criminal training with Ogo could really pay off.

"Welcome, my boy," said the messenger on Baaba's arrival at the house.

"I am here to conclude our agreement," Baaba said, trying to hide his nervousness.

"Your money is ready."

"I am in a hurry. I have other responsibilities. And I need to get back to the office quickly."

"Okay, hold on a minute so that I can get the money for you," said the messenger calmly.

He left Baaba in the sitting room.

Sitting alone in the sitting room, Baaba looked at the luxury around him. He wondered what it would be like to afford all this luxury for ChiChi. That would make ChiChi very happy and he would be very proud of himself for fulfilling his promises to her. She would not insist on him going back to school if she was comfortable.

Baaba waited for about half an hour and still there was no sign of the messenger. He wondered why he was taking so long, he knew of the appointment and should have made sure that the money was available. He felt very uncomfortable. Nobody seemed to be around for him to talk to or ask any questions. Where could he have gone to?

After forty-five minutes, Baaba got up, left the room, and saw a woman preparing the evening meal. "Have you seen the Chief's messenger?" he asked.

"Yes, he has gone to get the money," she replied.

Baaba got suspicious and wondered why this woman should know about his arrangement; it was supposed to be very confidential.

Maybe she is his wife, and some men confided such matters to their wife.

"Go inside and wait for him, he will be here soon; have patience," said the women with sympathy for his long wait. "Would you like something to drink?"

"No, madam, I am all right."

He went back to the sitting room and sat down.

The messenger returned and handed Baaba an envelope. "Here is the money, but you have to count it to make sure it is correct."

Baaba opened the envelope and began to count the money. Which was his third mistake. One should never count the money upon receipt. Sergeant Ade had coached him. Had he not been listening?

As he counted the money, two uniformed police officers walked into the room.

"Is this the man?" one of them asked the messenger.

"Yes, that's him."

"You are under arrest, we are from Agege police station, and we received a report that you are trying to bribe the Chief's son."

Baaba stared at the messenger, who laughed. "Yes, I am the Chief's son, not his messenger, you greedy policeman."

Although surprised, Baaba feigned ignorance. "What bribe?"

"The one in your hands," replied the officer sarcastically.

The Chief's son said, "I am fed up of this man sending policemen to my house to demand bribes because of a piece of land that does not belong to him."

They led Baaba out of the compound and took him to the police headquarters in Ikeja, where they locked him up in the cells. He could not sleep, there were giant mosquitoes waiting to suck his blood if he dared fall asleep. Apart from the mosquitoes, how would he explain this to ChiChi if he ended up in prison? She would not marry an ex-convict; she would have other suitors who were not criminals.

He thought about his mother and the family's reputation in the village. He thought about Ogo in KiriKiri prison. "I wonder how he spent his time." He prayed to God that he did not end up like Ogo and lose ChiChi. He realized that his police career had also ended.

It was in the early hours of the morning that he fell asleep.

"Get up, the Sergeant wants to see you," shouted a policeman opening the cell door.

Baaba got up and followed him to the Sergeant's office.

"So you call yourself a police officer," the Sergeant sneered. "When did you join the force?"

Baaba took one look at him and knew he was in serious trouble. This man looked all business and there was a permanent frown on his face. He was an officer from the police complaints unit.

"Nine months ago, sir," replied Baaba in a low voice.

"So you, a new recruit, think you can start taking bribes without even learning the ropes of the job." He shook his head in disgust, "When I joined the force, it took you several years before you were allowed to conduct an investigation on your own. These days, they come out of school and the only reason they join the force is to collect bribes."

CHAPTER 18:
BAABA IS SAVED BY SECTION 419 OF THE CRIMINAL CODE

"YOU ARE IN SERIOUS TROUBLE; didn't you know who the Chief was?" the Sergeant asked in disgust. "I will take a statement from you and you will be charged to appear in court."

He was released on police bail, pending the court case after one week. He went home determined that whatever it took, he was not going to prison. He thought about running away back to the village. But what would he tell ChiChi?

In the end, he decided to talk to a lawyer, who was from his village, to ask him to represent him in court. He still had some savings from his salary, so he paid the lawyer with his savings.

He kept this to himself; he could not afford to let ChiChi know about his criminal activities and he was ashamed to talk to Oke, the friend who had helped him join the Police Force.

"My Lord, this is a case of obtaining under false pretences," said Baaba's lawyer during the hearing. "Under Section 419 of the Criminal Code, this crime does not warrant a prison sentence."

Baaba listened in astonishment to his attorney's argument. How could it be so simple? And yet, this argument stood, and Baba was fined and discharged from the Police Force but with no prison sentence.

Baaba could not believe his luck as he left the court. "God heard my prayers; I can't believe I am free."

CHAPTER 19:
BAABA INVENTS A NEW LINE OF WAYO

REE BUT NOW UNEMPLOYED AND with more time on his hands than money, he went back and reinvented the card game with Oji. He dreaded the thought of going to prison. He knew he had responsibilities towards ChiChi, his mother and siblings. Although the card game brought in good income, it was a dangerous game, but it was all he knew.

Oji was very greedy and always wanted easy money, so he was a good partner, if less cautious.

"We can't be doing this in the market," Baaba said to Oji. "We might get caught; I would not like the police to apprehend me in the market.

"I have been in the Police Force and now I understand how they operate, if you can't afford their bribery, then they will make sure you end up in prison."

"Yes, of course there must be other ways to make money," Oji replied. He then told Baaba about his mother's friend. "You know that Yoruba madam who owns the shop down our street, she is seriously looking for a baby. The husband is very rich but she cannot have a baby." He paused. "She would do anything to have a baby, maybe we can help her."

"Are you out of your mind? How can we help her get pregnant?"

"We will tell her that we have JuJu from our village that helps barren women have children."

"Yes ...?"

Oji went on, "She is a friend to my mother, and they talk about these things. She has told my mother, she would do whatever it takes for her to get pregnant because she is scared her husband would go for another wife who can give him an offspring."

"How did you find out about all this?"

"I happened to overhear their conversation."

"You Mr Clever, how on earth would we get her pregnant?"

"This is my plan," Oji whispered excitedly to Baaba. "I will tell my mother that I can find a man who can help our neighbour get pregnant."

"Then what do we do after that, Mr Clever Oji?"

"We will ask her to pay us so that we can invite the JuJu man, we will tell her that this JuJu man has helped so many women get pregnant."

"And if she agreed to this proposal?"

"We will then ask her to visit us in the night; we will tell her that the JuJu man cannot be seen in daylight.

"He only sends 'angels' to visit his women clients at night," Oji continued.

"What angel?" Baaba asked, exasperated. "Have you gone mad, boy?"

Oji shook his head. "No. I have not gone mad." He smiled as he continued, "We will put her in your bedroom, with no lights on; we will ask her to undress and wait for an angel to visit her. We will then go into the room and sleep with her in turns. I assure you that by the time we have finished with her throughout the night she would be pregnant," he said, rubbing his palms together in delight.

Baaba rolled his eyes. "Now, I know you are completely crazy."

"No, I am not. You want to make money. This is just another way to get money from women." He shrugged his shoulders. "You're the one who doesn't want to go to the market."

"Oji, pregnancy does not occur as a result of the number of men or the number of times you sleep with a woman. If she is barren, we cannot get her pregnant!"

"But there is no harm in trying, is there? You are the one who said you don't want to continue with the card game." Still trying to convince Baaba, Oji said, "If this works, we will have a large client base because I do know a number of my mother's friends who cannot have children."

"And if it fails?"

Oji shrugged. "If it fails, we will try another scheme. If we don't try, we will never know if it would work."

Baaba really felt Oji was talking foolishness, but Oji insisted, "If you let me do the planning, you will see that it will work."

Baaba felt like he was caught between a rock and a hard place. He reluctantly said to Oji, "Okay, you talk to your mother, see what she thinks, and we will take it from there, but I can't see it working."

"It will work, I promise you. You want money, don't you? What about sending money to ChiChi?" Oji knew that the mention of ChiChi's name would convince Baaba to give it a try. "Either that or you come pickpocketing with me."

"God forbid," Baaba replied. "Just talk to your mother. She might refuse to talk to her friend."

Baaba knew that the idea was ridiculous. He knew he was better continuing with the cards. He had perfected the market card game but it was becoming very risky because the police now had his name on record from the bribery case. So he decided to go along with Oji's madness.

Two days went by and Oji still had not spoken to his mother. Baaba was getting impatient. He needed money to pay his rent and send home. His landlord was a tough man who could not tolerate late payment of his rent.

He certainly didn't want to go back to the streets. That life was tough. He would not let that happen the second time. Oke was God-sent. He knew he wouldn't be so lucky next time.

Baaba had witnessed his landlord evict a tenant previously and take possession of his belongings, including his new television. That was a major loss to the tenant. He had to make money and if Oji's way was the way forward, then he was up for it.

"Why have you not spoken to your mother?" he asked Oji impatiently.

"She has been fighting with my father and is very upset. I need to get her in a good mood or else she will dismiss me with her usual wave of hand."

"Okay, try and talk to her tonight, so we can start the business."

Oji smiled. "I thought you were not interested. You said it would not work."

"Please stop joking and talk to your mother tonight, whatever mood she is in," Baaba insisted.

That night, Oji spoke to his mother. The next morning, he announced ecstatically, "You see, I told you that Madam has a serious problem and would pay to have a child."

"Right, okay, so what's the next plan?"

"My mother promised to speak to her tonight; we will then find out if she is interested in the deal."

Oji's mother came home late that night, having spent the evening waiting for her friend to close up her shop. She had already told her that she had an important matter to discuss with her.

The madam asked Oji's mother what it was about, but she kept her in suspense and told her, "It is a very confidential matter; we need to sit down and talk."

This got the woman worried because Oji's mother sounded serious. "I hope she has not seen my husband with another woman."

Madam's husband was unhappy with her for her inability to conceive. There were rumours about girlfriends. He also turned to drinking to drown the sorrows of a childless life. His mates and others in the village, including his family, taunted him because he could not produce an offspring.

So Madam closed her shop early and sat down with Oji's mother.

"You know how we are really worried that you should get pregnant so that your husband does not marry another woman?"

"Yes, and you know this is a problem I cannot solve. I have tried everything from going to spiritual churches to *baba alawos*," she said sadly. "All to no avail."

"This is why, as a friend, if I can find a solution, I would not hesitate to pursue it for your sake."

"What do you mean?" the woman queried.

"My son knows a JuJu man who can help you get pregnant."

The woman made a face. "Are you joking? Oji, to help me? Your son needs to help himself first before he can help somebody else."

"Oji has a friend whose mother had the same problem and this man helped her have twins. What is wrong with trying all avenues to resolve your problem?" Oji's mother asked her friend.

Madam looked doubtful. "I cannot let my husband know about this, he has spent a lot of money on spiritual healers and JuJu men. He has just about given up. I would like to surprise him though, if I can find a way."

She continued sadly, "He has promised that he would not take another wife but his family is on his case. He is the only son in the family and they would like him to have an offspring to sustain the family name." She shrugged. "Who would inherit his riches?"

She was silent for a few minutes. "How much does the man charge?"

"I am not sure, but I can find out from Oji and let you know by tomorrow."

Oji's mother confirmed to Oji that the woman was interested but wanted to find out the cost of the treatment.

"I will ask my friend how much the man charges," Oji told his mother.

Oji could not wait to tell Baaba the good news. The night dragged on and on, with him anxious for the coming morning.

It seemed that every other night was short but this one went on forever; Oji only wanted to see Baaba's reaction to the good news.

Chapter 20:
Baaba Exploits Women

OJI GOT TO BAABA'S APARTMENT before 6 a.m. He pounded on the door and shouted out, "Why are you still sleeping when I was awake all night, thinking about our new business?"

Baaba, on hearing the ruckus, got up, still half asleep, and opened his front door.

Oji stood there grinning. "Baaba, we are made. Madam has agreed to pay for the treatment." He rubbed his hands together. "We need a plan of action today."

Baaba was astonished. "Tell me more," Baaba pleaded.

"She wants to know how much the bill is."

"How much do you think she can afford?" Baaba asked Oji.

"Madam's husband is rich and she owns a shop, so she can afford to pay any amount we ask her."

"In that case, let's ask ten thousand naira. If she refuses to pay that amount we will haggle with her. We'll tell her that we are middlemen for the spiritual healer and would also want our introductory fees. You would have to invite her to my house, where we can talk to her."

"I will go to her shop tomorrow and ask her to come here with me."

Baaba looked around his apartment and thought, "If this woman is that rich, she must be living in a very good house compared to this tiny apartment." He shook his head. "No, we cannot invite her here. We will have to invite her to the local hotel, it is only a mile away from here."

Oji decided he was not going back home to his mother but would stay with Baaba. "It will be better if I stayed with you during the course of this business so that we can be in control," he said to Baaba.

"I don't really like to live with anyone because I am waiting to bring ChiChi to Lagos, but for now you can stay until the business is over."

Oji was pleased with this arrangement and left to tell his mother that he would be staying in Baaba's house for a while. The following day, Oji went to the madam.

"Oji, your mother told me that you know a JuJu man who can help me conceive."

Oji nodded. "This man is very good. He helped my friend's mother have twins after she had tried for many years."

Madam made a face. "I don't trust you. I have known you since you were very young and you have not achieved anything, but you are always in trouble."

Oji did not take offence. "I know, madam. But I like you and would like to help you."

"How much does he charge and when can he do it?"

"I have spoken to my friend and he would represent the JuJu man, but you have to meet with him first."

"Why can't I meet the JuJu man in person? Why go through your friend?"

"Because you can only see the JuJu man at night; if he met you during the day before your treatment his medicine will not work on you. Children are made at night; this is why he must only meet you at night-time."

That seemed to make sense to her. "I am still not sure about this, but your mother is a very good friend and wants to help me. She knows my pain about not having a baby."

"Your husband will marry another woman if you don't give him a child; I have personally seen him with other women, is that what you want?" Oji said, trying to trouble her. It was, of course, a lie, but he was interested in scaring and blackmailing the woman.

It did the trick. "All right, arrange the meeting with your friend tomorrow."

"We have to have the meeting at a hotel because we don't want neighbours to see you visiting my friend. Someone might tell your husband."

"Which hotel?"

Oji told her the hotel where the meeting would take place and the time.

With that, he went back to Baaba to deliver the good news.

The next day the three met at the hotel. Baaba thought the woman was pretty and could not understand why she could not conceive, as if beauty was the key to conceiving. "I can understand why the rich man married her. It was for her beauty."

Baaba introduced himself as Oji's friend. He explained to the woman that this JuJu man helped his mother to conceive.

"Madam, he has helped so many other women. He is well known in my village; if you don't get pregnant in two months, he will give you the money back, so you have nothing to lose," Baaba said, to convince her to part with the money.

"How much does he want?" she asked Baaba.

"If ten thousand naira will buy a child for you, wouldn't you pay?"

"I would pay that amount if there is a chance that it would work, but I am not sure of this."

"Oji told me you have tried other JuJu men, so why can't you try this one?"

Somehow, she found that convincing. "Okay, I will try him, but like I told Oji's mother, I do not want my husband to know that I am going to another JuJu man. The last one took much money from us and we never got any positive results. My husband has warned me that he would rather be childless than engage the services of these unscrupulous JuJu men.

"I am taking a chance and hope that he doesn't find out."

The meeting ended after an hour with Madam promising to get the money within the week. "I will tell your mother when the money is ready," she said, turning to Oji.

Still, she had a very worried look on her face. She thought she might be lucky with this JuJu man but she worried about her husband finding out. "If my husband finds out, he will have a reason to get rid of me and marry another woman, but I have to take a risk to solve this problem …" With these thoughts swirling in her head, she paid for the hotel room and left.

When she had gone, Baaba and Oji looked at each other and were speechless for a few minutes, trying to take it all in.

"Did you hear that?" Oji said, pretending to be calm. "She will pay the money. We are made." He jumped up from his seat in the hotel room, raised his hands, and looked up to the ceiling. "Thank you, God, you heard my prayer, I know I will make big money one day."

"Please, Oji, stop counting your chickens before they are hatched," Baaba warned him. "Madam may change her mind or even tell her husband." He shook his head. "After my police case with the Chief's son, I don't trust anybody until I see the goods. The Chief's son deceived me and I never want to fall into such a trap again."

"Do you want to bet that she will pay?" Oji asked Baaba, stretching out his right palm.

"It's not the paying I am worried about; it's the result. How on earth are we going to get her pregnant?"

"You have to invite your friend, the one that likes women a lot; he has to be part of this," Oji said unexpectedly. "I am sure if the three of us slept with that woman several times during the night, she would get pregnant."

"Are you nuts? She would definitely know who we are," Baaba said with a frown on his face. "She has met us."

"You don't believe in God, do you?" Oji asked Baaba.

"How can you be mentioning God? He does not like evil, we are trying to cheat Madam and you think God should intervene," Baaba said, shaking his head in disbelief.

Chapter 21:
Baaba's Devious Act

MADAM INFORMED OJI'S MOTHER THREE days later that she had the money and would like Oji to come to the shop and collect it. As soon as he heard the message, Oji rushed round to Madam's shop. "Thank you, madam, Saturday night then," Oji said on collecting the money from the madam.

Baaba and Oji counted the money several times. They were speechless. They stood looking at the money on the table and then looking at each other in silence.

After a few minutes Baaba sighed and said, "Okay, now we have the money, what about the pregnancy?"

But Oji's thoughts were still on the money. "Where should we hide the money?"

"Inside the mattress, we will not spend it because if we fail, Madam would want her money back. I am not comfortable about this business. So, what do we do now?"

"How can we have money under the mattress and be living like paupers? Why make money if you can't spend it? I need to buy the bike I have wanted for a long time," Oji argued.

"And you think that Madam would not notice? She will definitely know that you are spending her money. I insist we do not touch the money until we have a concrete plan. You are not buying any bike with this money. This money is hot, we need to allow it to cool down before we touch it," Baaba said firmly.

"I have been running around for this business and now you don't want me to spend the money?" Oji asked, exasperated. Oji was not pleased with Baaba's decision, but he went along anyway, and they hid the money under the mattress.

"I told Madam that she would meet the JuJu man on Saturday night."

Baaba laughed ruefully. "So where is the JuJu man then?"

"We need to talk to your friend who likes women a lot. He is strong and three of us can handle Madam. There is no way Madam will not get pregnant after we have all slept with her."

Baaba agreed to invite his friend on Saturday night. His friend was another loafer who had no job but went around living off women. He told Baaba and Oji about his prowess in bed. It did not take much persuasion to convince him to join the plot.

Keeping to their instructions, Madam arrived late on Saturday night. She had lied to her husband that she was visiting her sister in Ibadan. She arrived to find the three men waiting for her. The only light in the house was a candle at the entrance and even this was shaded.

"Welcome, madam. Sit down on that chair," Baaba said, pointing to a chair specifically placed with its back to the bedroom door. It was eerily quiet.

"The man will be ready in a few minutes. He is praying before the event so that it can work," Baaba told her.

Baaba blindfolded her. He told her that this was to prevent her from seeing the healer. If she saw the healer, the JuJu will not work. Then Baaba led her into the bedroom that was dark with the curtains drawn.

The three men dressed in flowing white gowns and slept with her in turns until the early hours of the morning. Then they told her the JuJu man had to leave so that she would not see him.

Madam did not leave right away. She waited until her husband went to work. He usually left for work about 9 a.m. Exhausted from her experience, she sneaked in from the back door into her bedroom and fell asleep immediately on her bed.

Although Baaba was wise not to want to touch the money, it was that very day that he changed his mind about it. He needed money and there was the constant aggravation from Oji. He got the money out of his mattress, gave Oji two thousand naira and his friend one thousand naira.

Baaba carefully hid his share in his mattress, deciding that he would only pay his rent from the money. He would wait and see what happened with Madam.

Oji, on the other hand, could not wait to spend his loot. He bought new shirts and shoes to match and a bike. He had his eyes on a girl who lived on his street. He could not approach her earlier. Now he had money, it would be easier to court her. He waited for her on her usual route to the market. He had one of his new suits on and, posing on his new bike, he courted her. She could not resist his new look and his transformation and agreed to date him.

Three months went by and, to keep himself busy, Baaba went to different markets to play the odd card game with Oji. He was very cautious and left at the first sign of trouble from any of the women. He also bribed the police on the odd occasion when the women reported his activity.

He also maintained his visits to Ogo in jail. He brought him toiletries and cigarettes. Ogo did not smoke but he needed cigarettes as an exchange for protection from the rough prisoners.

But mostly, those days, he worried about Madam's condition. But then Oji's mother told her son that Madam was pregnant. "The doctor has confirmed it," she announced.

"What?"

"Madam is pregnant and her husband is sending her abroad to have the baby, he is overjoyed."

"You are sure?"

"Of course. She told me today when I visited her shop. She said I must tell you immediately. Madam also requested to see you so that she would demonstrate her gratitude; you should go and see her."

Oji ran out of the house like a man possessed, going first to find Baaba. "Baaba, can you believe what I have just been told by my mother? Madam is pregnant and her doctor has confirmed it, she wants to thank us."

"What?"

"Yes, she is pregnant, she is going abroad to have the baby."

"Say it again."

Oji laughed. "It must be the husband who has a problem, not Madam." He laughed again. "Our business worked, she is pregnant."

"Whose baby is it? Mine? Yours? My friend's?" Baaba asked, bewildered.

"You worry and analyse things too much, you should start thinking of all the other women we could help and make serious money in the process," Oji said, ignoring Baaba's concern about the paternity of the child. "It is the man's child, full stop," he said.

Oji went to visit Madam for the 'thank you' present the next day. Seeing him, Madam stood up from her chair and gave Oji a big hug.

"Careful, madam, don't squeeze me too much. Think of the baby."

She handed him an envelope.

Madam's friend, who was sitting with her, asked, "Isn't that Rose's son, what's in the envelope?"

"It is for his mother, I owe her some money," Madam lied, winking at Oji.

Oji left with the envelope unopened because Madam's friend was too inquisitive.

On his way to Baaba's house, he opened the envelope and counted the money and it was two and half thousand naira. He held the money in his hand and thought, "I could tell Baaba that it was two thousand naira and keep the five hundred; but Baaba might see the madam again and ask how much she gave to Oji. If Baaba found out he would not trust me any more. There are potential clients, why spoil it ..." Despite his greedy nature, his better judgement kicked in.

He placed the money back in the envelope and went to Baaba's apartment.

Baaba gave him one thousand naira and kept one thousand, five hundred naira. They decided not to give any of the money to their friend. After all, they did the hard part of the work in convincing Madam to part with the money in the first place.

"Baaba, I think he is the father of the child."

"I don't want to think about it any more, the thought was doing my head in."

Of course, Baaba now felt happy to spend the money. Madam was pregnant and only God Almighty knew how that happened. As it happened, Madam went abroad and had a baby boy, brought him back to Nigeria, and had a big party. She cordoned off part of the street to accommodate the large number of guests. The dancing and spraying of money went on all night.

Baaba and Oji were special guests at her party. She instructed that they receive special food and drink.

The madam later introduced her friends who could not have children to Baaba and Oji. Word quickly spread about the JuJu man who could help women conceive. Some of the women consulted Oji's mother directly.

However, most of the women lost their money and Baaba's excuse was that they did not keep to the JuJu man's rules. The women kept their night visits a secret. Only the participants knew the activities of the nights. They could not disclose their experience to anyone, including their husbands. Baaba recruited another friend to join in the night ritual but the success rate was very poor.

Despite that, he was taking the women's money on a regular basis. He moved to a bigger apartment in a newly constructed building where civil servants lived. He was moving up in the world.

CHAPTER 22:
BAABA VISITS THE VILLAGE

BAABA FINALLY DECIDED TO VISIT the village. His timing coincided with the end of the school academic year – July. ChiChi had informed him that she completed her school certificate examinations in June and he had promised to visit the village when her examinations were completed.

Honda had introduced a new product in Nigeria only a few months earlier – the Honda 350. It was a biker's ultimate dream machine. Baaba saw the advertisement and fell in love with it. He debated on the decision of buying a car or the bike. A Volkswagen car cost a little more than the bike and he could afford a car. However, he fancied himself as the man that Honda used for the advert. He was macho and looked like every girl's dream with the muscles on his arms crying to burst out. His manly desires got the better of him in the end and he bought the bike. He decorated it with many extras and accessories. He also paid for a customised horn for the bike.

He went on a shopping spree, sparing no expense. He bought clothes, shoes, and jewellery for ChiChi, and clothes for his mother and siblings. He also bought new clothes, shoes, and a gold watch for himself. He needed to show off to ChiChi and the village people. They had condemned him, made nasty remarks about him, and said he had no future. He also wanted to prove to his father that he could be an achiever without education.

Most importantly, he wanted his mother to be proud of him.

His plan included bringing ChiChi to Lagos. He reasoned that she could apply for admission into Lagos University. He would buy a small car for her so that she could attend university from home. His wife would not live in the university hostel. That was risky because other men would be attracted to her. He was sure that he could convince her to come to Lagos with him. He needed her in Lagos. He had been alone for too long. His wealth had attracted girls, including the women who came for the fertility business. One of them had fallen for him and pestered him to become her lover. He resisted their entreaties. He had made promises to ChiChi and did not want to disappoint her.

Oji, who had moved out of his parent's home, had a few girlfriends. He had tempted Baaba to date one of his girlfriends' mates by bringing them to his house, but Baaba rejected all advances from the girls.

"Baaba, what is wrong with you? Are you a man?" Oji taunted him when Baaba turned down a pretty girl brought to his house.

"Oji, please stop bringing women to my house. I am not interested. My girl is in the village and she is the only girl I want."

"But she is not here to know what you do. I can't understand the way you think."

"Thank you, Oji, but we made a pact with blood."

"That girl has used JuJu on you."

Baaba made a face. "Stop talking nonsense."

"Well, I know Igbo girls. She has put a spell on you so you cannot admire another woman."

"Thank you. It's my choice and I like the JuJu she has put on me."

Two days before his departure, he transported the bike in a hired van for delivery at the nearest town to his village.

He asked Oji to keep a watch on his apartment. "Don't you bring women here," he warned him.

"But the place is very nice and I will be tempted."

"I know how I am leaving this place. If you dare bring your women here, I will kill you when I get back. I've got it ready for ChiChi, so don't mess it up."

This, at least, cheered Oji. "At last, I will see this 'Queen ChiChi'. I hope Lagos men don't grab her from you if she is as beautiful as you say."

"If I wasn't used to your rubbish talk, I would slap your face for having such filthy thoughts."

Oji smiled. "Okay, good luck, Mr ChiChi's husband."

Baaba didn't keep his money under the mattress any more. He now had a bank account and he withdrew a large sum of cash from his deposit account. He had progressed from the days of Ogo's way of thinking.

On arrival at the town, he paid for the transport and storage of his bike. He booked into a nearby hotel, had a bath and a change of clothing. He wanted to look his best for ChiChi.

He glanced at a mirror in the hotel room and smiled, "Ogo didn't look this nice and expensive when he came to the village. Life could be so very unpredictable. Ogo was now in prison and he was the one coming to show off in the village. Another boy in the village might want to be his 'houseboy'. He had a white, long-sleeved shirt that was more expensive than Ogo's shirt. He had more money to spend in the village. He also had a prospective wife, unlike Ogo who had to ask him to speak to Amaka – a task he was glad to accomplish and which changed his own life.

He paid a taxi to take his luggage – his gifts. He rode the bike behind the taxi and made a grand entry into the village. On arrival outside his father's compound, he blew the special horn on the bike and the villagers rushed out of their homes to investigate the strange noise.

Without question, his arrival caused a stir in the village. The villagers gathered at his father's compound to admire his bike. They gasped in amazement that this troublesome and lazy boy could make enough money to purchase such a huge motorbike.

His mother, who didn't know of his visit, ran out of the compound, and screamed, "Is this my son? ... No. I am dreaming!" She called out to Baaba's father, "Come out of your room, your son has arrived. He has got an aeroplane!" She hugged Baaba tightly and would not let go.

However, Baaba's father remained in his room and this made her angry. She marched into his room and shouted at him to get outside. He reluctantly obliged ... he could not stand any trouble. He was happy alone in his room, which was his sanctuary from her madness. He stood at the entrance, detached from the crowd that had gathered around Baaba.

"Go and greet your son," his wife said, dragging him to Baaba.

"Welcome, Baaba," he said, stretching his right hand to him. His face remained blank, showing no emotions.

"Papa, how are you?" Baaba asked, shaking his father's hand.

"I am fine. How are Lagos people?"

"They are fine."

He then walked back to the compound and sat quietly on a bench, watching the hubbub. More villagers and children gathered to admire Baaba's bike.

"Is it an aeroplane or a motor cycle?" they asked each other.

One of the women asked Baaba how much he paid for it. Before he could answer, the woman said, "The money for your bike could build your mother a nice brick house ..."

Baaba interrupted her, "I have enough money to build my mother a brick house, don't you worry."

Baaba's mother held his hand and pulled him towards the compound.

Baaba implored the villagers to return to the house in the evening for a celebration of his arrival.

He asked his younger brother to go to the local shop and buy drinks and food for the villagers. The women were jealous of Baaba's mother. Her son had made it in Lagos. That meant she would now be out of poverty, he would give her a lot of money.

The celebration of Baaba's return started early in the evening and lasted for about three hours. The news of his arrival travelled fast to other villagers, including ChiChi's village.

The old men poured drinks for libations, blessing him and calling on their gods to give him more money in Lagos. "May God give you more riches ... Let our gods keep the door open ... more will come from where this has come from."

Baaba gave them money because the next day was the local market day. Of course, the villagers had no clue as to the source of the money and, even if they knew, it would not matter.

All that mattered was that one of their sons had made it in Lagos.

Later that night Baaba zoomed into ChiChi's compound on his motorbike, showing off his shiny bike and his riding skills. The noise from the bike woke the family and their neighbours.

All the men, women, and children ran out of their huts to admire the visitor, some of them barely awake. ChiChi's sister shouted, "Baaba is back. He has a new motorbike."

ChiChi ran out of her room.

Baaba lifted ChiChi off the ground, swirling her around in a full circle; he stopped to look at her, put her down, and said, "Let me look at you, my wife."

"I am not your wife yet," ChiChi replied shyly.

Baaba said confidently, "You will soon be my wife, you will see."

ChiChi was full of admiration for Baaba's new look, but at the same time she was shy to show her emotions. Showing her emotions could mean that she was desperate. Her parents brought her up to respect herself. A girl needed to be reserved and let the men desire her.

She looked at Baaba and felt a rush of blood through her body. "Wow, he is really handsome," she thought as she admired his white shirt and expensive trousers. If he could afford all that, he must surely be capable of looking after her as a wife. He had promised to spoil her when he made money.

Baaba held her hand and would not let go. Admiring her beauty, he whispered in her ears, "You are so beautiful, not like those ugly Lagos girls. I will make you look even more beautiful when we are married."

"I like you," she whispered demurely.

This statement was all Baaba needed to confirm that his waiting had not been in vain.

He looked at her again, full of lust, and thought, "She is definitely coming to Lagos with me. I can't live without her any more … Her father can kick up all the fuss he wants … God himself has already ordained this marriage."

Baaba gave ChiChi's mother money and the gifts he had bought for her. He also bought gifts for her siblings. Everyone was happy and they talked into the night. He requested if he could take ChiChi to his house, with the excuse that he had left her presents at home. Her mother agreed and Baaba took ChiChi on his bike. As they left, the young people admired Baaba and were jealous of ChiChi.

When they got to Baaba's compound, he gave ChiChi her presents – clothes, shoes, jewellery, and a ring. He told her that the ring was for her engagement. They spent the night discussing their future together. Baaba wanted ChiChi to come to Lagos with him. He had enough money to take care of her.

She wondered how he came to earn so much money in a short time in Lagos. "You told me you were in the Police Force," she said. But she knew policemen didn't earn so much money. Her father had been a police officer for years and could not afford more than the basic needs of his family.

"I left the police and I am now a businessman."

"What type of business do you do?" she asked him.

"When we get to Lagos, you will see the type of business. For now, you have to get ready because I am not going back to Lagos without you."

"My father will kill us if I go to Lagos with you; do you know he has been posted to Obalende police station in Lagos?" she asked anxiously.

"Yes, I know," he said. "I will talk to him 'man to man' when we get to Lagos."

"My father wants me to continue my education to university. He would go mad if I went with you because he wants me to become a doctor, so that I can help the poor people in our village. He said that would make the village people respect him."

"But that's all right," Baaba assured her. "You will still get all the education you want. I want my wife to be a doctor and I will be 'the doctor's husband'. Don't you realize that a man is whatever his wife is? People will approach me when they need your help because I am your husband."

He smiled. "Of course you will go to school; we will tell your father that the marriage will not stop you from going to school." He squeezed her hand tighter. "I don't want to live in Lagos without you any longer. I get so lonely and I miss you all the time. Reading your letters is not the same as being with you. I have enough money for us to live on. I can pay your school fees and then I will continue working hard to make more money. I will buy you a car and then we will have children."

"But if I start having babies then I can't go to school," ChiChi said with apprehension.

"When you have children, we will get a maid to look after them while you go to school. You will have to go to school from the house; you can't live in the school like other students because you will be a married woman."

ChiChi was doubtful. "I am still not sure how to convince my Papa; all he wants is for me to go to school. He wants me to be a medical doctor."

"You will become whatever you want; I have no problem with that."

Baaba spent the rest of his time in the village in ChiChi's company.

She stayed at Baaba's compound. His mother was very happy with this arrangement.

ChiChi had promised she would let him make love to her after her school certificate examinations.

Having waited patiently as promised, Baaba asked ChiChi, "Can I make love to you?"

She hesitated. "But I will get pregnant," she said timidly.

"No, I will make sure you don't get pregnant."

"You promised to wait until I finish my education," ChiChi replied, wondering how he would prevent her getting pregnant.

"Yes, until your school certificate examinations. But university takes years and we can't wait that long."

Baaba's mother, who wanted ChiChi as much as her son, tidied Baaba's room and changed the bedding Baaba had brought from Lagos for the young lovers. She was praying that Baaba would get ChiChi pregnant, that way she will be married to him. No other man would accept her with a child. That was not their cultural practice. People frowned on such marriages. She would be considered 'used property'.

And worthless.

Chapter 23:
Baaba Takes His Love to Lagos

The two weeks Baaba spent in the village flew by. ChiChi had agreed to go to Lagos with him. How could she resist? Her father could not afford the university fees on a policeman's salary. There were six other children to care for in the family.

ChiChi was the third child; the first son was her mother's priority. She spent all she had on him. She paid his school fees and spoilt him.

Baaba lay down on the bed with ChiChi and wondered how he would explain his line of business to ChiChi when they got to Lagos. "I wonder how she would react when she finds out that I dupe women." How could he explain that he slept with the women in group sessions to help them? He dismissed the thought immediately. That must wait for now. He would cross that hurdle when he got there. The important thing was to get her to Lagos.

"Baaba, you have to talk to my father when we get to Lagos."

"I will do that immediately when we get to Lagos. I will ask the old man from my village to talk to him. They are friends. He will listen to the old man because he respects him.

"We will then come home to the village and do the marriage ceremony," Baaba assured ChiChi.

Baaba did not forget his promise to his best friend, Emi. He brought him presents from Lagos. He also gave him money.

On one of his visits to Baaba in the village, Emi asked him, "What about the promise you made to me? You promised to take me to Lagos like Ogo did."

"No. I have not forgotten my promise but I have to speak to ChiChi first."

"Why do you have to speak to her first? Do you need her permission before you can help your friend?" Emi snapped.

"Emi, she will be my wife. I tell her everything; after all, we will all be living in my house. She needs to agree to my decisions."

He promised to talk to ChiChi and obtain her approval – "That would be easy; she likes me and she would do anything I ask her, but I have to respect her."

Baaba told ChiChi about his decision to take Emi to Lagos. He asked ChiChi if he could invite Emi to Lagos with them. ChiChi did not object. She had come to respect the close bond between these two friends. She would not come between them. She also felt sorry for Emi who was now loitering about in the village and looked dejected whenever she met him. He paid her visits to enquire about his friend, Baaba. Emi felt Baaba was his only gateway out of the dark village, where he had no future. He prayed that his friend would succeed in Lagos.

He also hoped that he would not forget his promise.

He was overjoyed when Baaba told him that ChiChi did not object to his proposal. He remembered how Ogo had left Baaba in the village because of Amaka. He could not compete with Baaba's love for ChiChi. It was a different kind of love; he knew that, from the moment Baaba got ChiChi's attention. He had shown from his behaviour who was 'number one' in his heart. Although Emi was not happy about competing for Baaba's love with ChiChi, he had to respect his friend's feelings because he needed him.

Baaba hired a van to take them to Lagos; this was because of his bike. He could not ride his bike back to Lagos. That was a 600-mile journey.

The couple took their seats in the front of the van, while Emi hopped in at the back.

ChiChi's mother was aware of and agreed to the relationship. She liked Baaba a lot and looked forward to his being her son-in-law. Tall, handsome, and now he had made money. She was happy for him to be ChiChi's husband. She did not care any more about the repercussions from the father. She knew what punishment ChiChi's father would dish out to her if he found out she collaborated with the couple.

"You will make sure she goes to school; if not the father will go crazy," she warned Baaba.

"I promise with all my heart; my wife will be a doctor," he assured her.

After all the emotional farewells and crying by both mothers, they left for Lagos. During the journey, Baaba held ChiChi very close to him in the van. He kept reassuring her that he would take good care of her.

ChiChi fell asleep in his arms during the trip, and Baaba spent his time looking at her and admiring her. His life dream was coming true. He was deep in thoughts about how to handle her father. He knew he was very stubborn and troublesome. He thought, "I will do whatever it takes; the father will not stop my love for this girl."

They arrived in Lagos very late at night with ChiChi feeling extremely tired from the journey.

Baaba welcomed her into his home, "Come in, my dear. You are home." He lifted her off her feet and carried her into the one-bedroom apartment. He had watched an English film where the bridegroom did the same to his new wife and had quietly said, "I will do that to ChiChi when she gets to Lagos."

He took her round the apartment and showed her where the kitchen and bathroom were located at the end of the building. He boiled water and led her to the bathroom to have her bath. He left her in the bathroom, came back, sat on a chair, and breathed a sigh of relief.

"Baaba, you are now a man, you now have a wife, and you have to be responsible." He uttered a quiet prayer, "Please, God, don't let me disappoint ChiChi, you know how much I love her. I don't want any other man around her;

and I want our marriage to be the best."

He was still lost in these thoughts when ChiChi said, "Do you have any cream for my body?"

"I will buy some for you tomorrow," he promised. "Men don't use cream."

They had their dinner and ChiChi retired to bed. Baaba brought two bottles of beer and sat down with Emi outside the apartment. The fresh air was a welcome relief from the stuffiness inside. It was only when you came outside that you realized the heaviness of the air in the apartment.

They talked for hours into the night. Baaba had to tell Emi all about the business he was doing and explain the details of his participation in the process. As he did, he felt as if he was reliving his experience with Ogo – only from the other perspective.

He promised him a good share of the proceeds and coached him on the dos and don'ts of the business. He also emphasized that Emi understood the technicalities of dealing with the police.

Emi was fascinated. He listened carefully, following every word Baaba spoke with a nod of the head to show his understanding. Still, Baaba worried. He needed Emi to really understand. Speed of understanding was a requirement for success in his line of business.

"When we have done a few of these sessions, you will fully understand," he assured Emi, who was still trying to grasp how the business worked.

Both men went to bed in the early hours of the morning. Emi slept in the sitting room. Before taking his place on the sofa, Emi thanked him for his kindness and promised to follow his lead.

Baaba switched on the bedroom light. ChiChi was asleep. He stood near the bed, watching her breathing. "What a beautiful creature," he thought. She was even prettier asleep than awake.

"I love you, girl," he whispered and then he joined her in bed.

CHAPTER 24:
CHICHI SETTLES WITH BAABA IN LAGOS

ChiChi settled quickly in her new home. Baaba cared for her as he promised. He treated her like his queen, offering to help her with the housework. Their culture demanded that the man of the house does not handle house chores but Baaba did not care. He loved his girl and that was all that mattered to him. If people found out he helped her with the chores, they would call him 'woman wrapper' – meaning he was a fool to a woman.

'Proper men' neither performed nor helped their wives in the kitchen; that was a woman's job. Nevertheless, this was his queen, he did not want her to suffer and sweat because she had no help.

"I will get you a house girl; we have to ask your mother to look for a girl in the village. I don't want you to suffer with housework," he told ChiChi when she was washing their clothes and sweating.

"Okay, we will tell Mama," she replied.

Meanwhile, Baaba continued his business with Oji, but had to secure a two-room apartment for Oji. He needed to move the business base away from his home because of ChiChi. He had to shield her from the nastiness of his work.

The business was progressing very well. Oji sourced most of the clients. Only a handful of the clients got pregnant and Baaba always had a reason to dismiss the other women, emphasizing that they did not stick with the rules of the rituals. He also threatened to tell their husbands if they became uncooperative.

At the end of her second month in Lagos, ChiChi got very ill. In a panic, Baaba feared she had malaria. He bought malaria tablets for her but she did not get better. She was vomiting in the mornings. The beautiful smile that Baaba loved had vanished from his girl. She lost her appetite and only wanted pepper soup with no meat, only fish.

"That girl is pregnant," announced the neighbour knowingly one morning when ChiChi was being sick in the compound.

ChiChi looked up, perplexed, "How do you know?"

"I have five children of my own, and you are asking me how I know?" She laughed. "You are glowing … you have early morning sickness; what other symptoms do you need?"

ChiChi could not wait to tell Baaba. Still, she felt bad. "My education is gone; I can't go to school with pregnancy. I feel so sick, how can I go to school feeling this sick and vomiting or feeling nauseated constantly?"

That evening, she looked at Baaba. "Baaba, you promised not to get me pregnant."

"Yes. I promised," he said confidently.

"Well, I am pregnant. Our neighbour, Oke's mother, told me this morning that I am pregnant."

"But she is not a doctor, how can she tell?"

"She said my illness showed all the signs of pregnancy."

Troubled but unperturbed, Baaba said, "We have to go and see a doctor to confirm this; but I always tried my best to make sure I don't get you pregnant."

Of course, the doctor confirmed that ChiChi was pregnant.

ChiChi could not understand her fate. "How can I be pregnant when I was a virgin two months ago? I thought it would take much longer to get pregnant. This has ruined everything; my father will kill us both."

Although he feigned being distressed, Baaba was mischievously pleased with the outcome. If ChiChi had a baby for him, it meant she was then officially his and there was nothing the father could do to stop them being parents to the child. Certainly, he would not want his daughter to have a 'bastard' child. That was a taboo in the village. Any girl who had a child without a 'proper father' was loose. It was also difficult for her to marry. In exceptional circumstances, only civilised men who had lived in towns or who had broken the cultural barriers married such women.

ChiChi was physically miserable most of the time. Baaba tried his best to comfort her. He bought her presents to cheer her up and reassured her that everything would turn out fine. She lost weight and looked sickly. Baaba felt he was to blame for her condition. "How can my ChiChi suffer so much because I got her pregnant?" This was his fault. She was not fun to be with any longer. They used to play and run around the house like children. Now she lay sick in bed and was not interested in his jokes. He found it unbearable to leave the house and attend to his business.

He missed his appointments with Oji and the women clients because he was caring for ChiChi.

Oji was angry. "You see, I told you not to mix business with woman. You should have left her in the village. We were making good money. Now she keeps you at home and you do not turn up for our business. What will she eat if you do not come here and make money?"

But then, things improved. From the fourth month of the pregnancy, ChiChi got better and once again became her usual self: cheerful and vibrant. Baaba remarked that she looked more beautiful with the passing months. She was glowing but her hips were spreading with her bulging stomach. He liked the curves she developed. She was very thin before the pregnancy but now she looked like a fully developed woman.

ChiChi complained about the increase in her weight, "Baaba, I am getting too fat; this is the bit I hate about this pregnancy."

THE 419 CODE

"You are not fat; you are developing as a woman."

He narrated one of the stories Ogo told him, about a tribe in the South-Eastern State of Nigeria – the Ibibios. To this tribe, fat meant beauty – the men liked flesh on their women. When a girl reached marrying age, she went into a special 'fattening room'. Female elders attended to her every wish. She spent weeks or months piling on the pounds. The girl was gorged on high-calorie foods. During the whole time, the women hid the girl from the prying eyes of men.

Once the girl was fat enough – to their standard – she was presented to admiring suitors.

ChiChi laughed, "Well, we don't need a fattening room. Still, I feel like an elephant."

Baaba told ChiChi such stories he heard from Ogo and it seemed like there was a story for every event. The stories made her laugh and he used them to cheer her up. He was happy that she was laughing again and that she was fun to be with.

CHAPTER 25:
CHICHI'S ENLIGHTENMENT

As time went on, ChiChi was desperate to know about Baaba's business. She had pleaded with Baaba to explain his disappearance on some nights. After making up stories initially, Baaba decided to tell her about his business to stop her nagging at him all the time. He also wanted to make sure that ChiChi was aware of his activities in case there was police trouble.

He thought long and hard about how to tell ChiChi that he did *wayo* for a living. The girl's father is a policeman after all. She had been brought up in a home where crime was seriously frowned upon. She might decide to leave him. After all, she wants to become a doctor. A doctor could not marry a criminal. He kept her away from his business discussions with Emi and Oji. He locked the door to the sitting room when they had meetings. Her duty was to serve them food on request. She respected Baaba and did not ask too many questions, but insisted on knowing the general profile of his business.

Her nagging could not go on; he had to tell her, but how would he do this? He was in a dilemma.

The benefits of telling ChiChi far outweighed the fear that she would leave. Most importantly, she could compromise his position if the police came to his house and asked questions. She could say the wrong thing that would incriminate Baaba. He sought Emi's advice; and he too was of the opinion that she should know.

So Baaba set about planning the best way to tell her.

He bought a new watch from one of the shops in Lagos Island. He also bought some clothes and shoes. He booked a hotel room for the weekend. He knew that she relaxed in a hotel environment because there was no stress of housework. He knew this from the change he observed from her behaviour at previous times when he had taken her away to hotels for weekends. He did that occasionally to give her a treat and a break from the housework.

He told her that he had booked a hotel in Badagry for the weekend just for the two of them. She was overjoyed that they were going away to break the monotony of cooking and housework. She liked every opportunity to spend time alone with Baaba because she could talk to him without the constant interruptions from his business friends.

Baaba booked one of the best rooms in the hotel. The healing business was fetching good money and he thought the least he could do was to spend some of it on his girl. He knew some of his friends who only took their girlfriends to hotels: never their wives. They felt it was not right for a married woman to go to a hotel. Only single girls go to hotels. However, it was different with ChiChi. She was his friend. They could talk for hours uninterrupted in the hotel. On their last visit to a hotel, they talked past midnight and continued the next morning until lunchtime. They talked about everything and everyone. They talked about their plans for the future, their marriage ceremony, the number of children they would have and their names. ChiChi's education was another topic they often discussed. They planned about how to get her father on their side. The topics were endless and they switched from one to the other. It was fun for both of them.

At dinner in the hotel on their first night, Baaba held ChiChi's hand, looked deeply into her eyes, and said, "Do you know how much I care about you?"

ChiChi smiled and replied, "Very much, you always ask me that." She held his hand tightly and asked, "Do you know how much I like you?"

"Very much," Baaba replied.

This was a game they played regularly to affirm their love for each other.

Then, he became serious. "I ... don't know where to start ... I want to tell you something, but now I don't know how to say it."

"That means you are hiding something from me."

"No, I *want* to tell you."

"Go on then, tell me. I am listening."

Baaba held her hand; looking into her eyes, he gave her the full details of his business. He went as far back as Ogo's business, his police trouble, and his healing business. He explained that it was necessary she knew because he wanted to be open. She also needed to be aware of the downfalls of the business with the police getting involved. He coached her on the correct language to use during police interrogations. He was not educated and could not get a decent job.

When he stopped talking, ChiChi breathed deeply and said, "I knew it. I have been suspecting that you were not doing good business, the way you whisper and lock the room with your friends; did you think I am stupid?

"I am going to be a doctor, and you think my husband will be a criminal?" she asked, her voice flaring with anger. "Have you thought of my father's reaction when he finds out? Is this why you refused to go to school, so that you can become a criminal? You told me you were doing import and export business, and that the presents you gave me were from the ship!"

He begged her not to raise her voice until they retired into their hotel room. She went completely quiet, withdrawing her hands from his hold, and said, "Let's go to the room, I want to sleep."

Baaba spent the night trying to pacify ChiChi. He knew his girl and it did not take long for him to calm her down. He convinced her that this was the only way for him to make money to pay for her university education. This was blackmail, but he knew ChiChi would fall for it.

She needed to go to school to satisfy her father. After all, her father could not afford her university fees. He wanted her to apply for a scholarship, but that was taking a gamble. There were so many applicants and some of them were from rich families who had people in high places. These families offered bribery to the university authorities to secure admission for their children, so what chance did she stand against them?

She thought long and hard about her new discovery about Baaba's business. If she left Baaba, who would pay for her university education? Her father's salary could not pay her fees. She had no one apart from Baaba, so if this were the only way, she felt she had no choice. After all, on top of everything else, she was pregnant.

"As soon as you make enough money, you have to stop the *wayo* business, okay?"

He nodded.

She pressed the issue, making Baaba promise that he would stop the illegal business once he made money. She could earn enough money as a doctor to look after the children and Baaba. The only qualified doctor in her village lived like a royal, in a large house, and had two cars. His children were in good schools and people respected him.

Baaba was relieved of this burden; he told ChiChi that he loved her even more and always knew she was the right girl for him.

Chapter 26:
A Father's Wrath

ChiChi's father, who spent most of his evenings in a beer parlour, happened to meet up with an old friend who said to him, "You did not tell me that your daughter is now married to Baaba. When was the wedding ceremony? Moreover, why was I not invited? I thought we were good friends …"

ChiChi's father was confused. "What are you talking about?"

"I saw ChiChi with Baaba in Ajengule market. They were holding hands. He told me he was living with her in Lagos."

"My daughter in Lagos? You are a joker. Which daughter?"

"I am not lying. I saw them with my own eyes."

"You must have seen my other daughter, who is already married and living in Lagos."

"No, I know your daughters – four of them. I am talking about ChiChi, the one in secondary school."

Well, his evening in the beer parlour had been ruined. He asked his friend a few more questions to make sure he was not referring to his other daughter. But the friend was sure it was ChiChi.

ChiChi's father could not sleep that night. "It's impossible. She had only just completed her school certificate examinations." If this story was true and his daughter was in Lagos with Baaba … he could not imagine a worse insult.

He reasoned that Baaba must have used 'charm' or local black magic to trick his daughter to go with him to Lagos. She knew how much he wanted her to go to university and qualify as a doctor.

He shook his head. No. It couldn't be true.

In the end, he decided he would use the Police Force to deal with Baaba if the story was true, but he prayed it was not.

His friend had given him Baaba's address. He could not go to the address on that day because he had been booked on a special training course for investigating officers. He decided that he would take time off work the next day and pay Baaba a visit. So, the following morning, he travelled to the address. He took a decision that if he found his daughter with Baaba, he would take her away and get rid of whatever spell he had put on her. He wanted to do that before it was too late.

Meanwhile, Baaba had held off from speaking to ChiChi's father. Upon their arrival in Lagos, Baaba had decided that ChiChi should hide from her father until he was ready to approach him. They had planned not to let the old man know that ChiChi was with him in Lagos until Baaba had the time to get his uncles to go to him on his behalf. This was the tradition; he could not go to her father on his own. He was too young to deal with such issues; in their culture, it was an insult to make a direct approach to the girl's father.

A loud knock on the door woke Baaba and ChiChi from bed. "Open this door quickly, I know you are in there," a voice shouted from outside the apartment.

Baaba looked outside through the apartment window, and there was ChiChi's father standing with his hands on his waist, looking very angry.

He shouted again, threatening to break down the door.

ChiChi joined Baaba at the window, saw her father through the blind, and panicked. She immediately left the apartment through the back door to hide in the next building.

"Come in, sir," Baaba said as he opened the door.

"Where is my daughter? I want to know where she is! Tell me. Where is she? Tell me it's a lie."

"She is not here, sir," Baaba said, spreading out his hand and inviting him in. "You can search the place if you'd like." Baaba opened the door to the bedroom and left the door wide open. "She is not here, sir."

"I was told she was living with you. Where is she?"

"She is not here, sir," Baaba said, only telling the truth in the most literal sense. For she *wasn't* there just then.

"I am warning you. If you are lying, I will certainly find out. I don't need to tell you what the consequence will be. I will make sure you are locked up for a long time."

"Would you like to sit down and have a bottle of beer?" Baaba asked calmly.

"I don't want your drink. If I find you are lying to me, I will lock you up in the police cells and make sure you go to jail for kidnapping," he said angrily and stormed out.

Baaba called out to ChiChi to return to the apartment.

"What do we do now?" ChiChi asked Baaba. She felt her heart beating very fast. She looked up at Baaba with tears in her eyes.

"Don't worry. I will talk to my uncle this week. He will sort it out with him." He reassured her. "He will sort it out, trust me. Your father is my uncle's close friend."

ChiChi was crying. He comforted her and promised he would deal with the matter as quickly as he could.

Even though ChiChi wasn't in the apartment, her father did not believe Baaba. He did not trust him. He enquired if anyone was going to the village shortly. He needed confirmation from the village. Finally, his enquiry led him to a man from his village. He was going to the village on the weekend.

He visited the man's house and implored him to visit his home in the village. He instructed him to ask his wife the whereabouts of his daughter.

He waited for another week before the man came back from the village.

"Your daughter, ChiChi, is not in the village."

"Did the mother tell you where she was?"

"She is in Lagos. I visited Baaba's mother as well. She confirmed that her son was in Lagos with ChiChi. She said they were getting married."

"What did my wife say?"

"She said your daughter is with you in Lagos."

"I see. This boy has taken on more than he can chew."

The next morning at work, he booked an appointment to see his friend, the Assistant Police Commissioner. He could talk to him in confidence. He needed his support to deal with Baaba. He wanted Baaba jailed for abduction. "No punishment is severe enough for this boy."

For ChiChi's father, everything seemed to fall apart. The behaviour of this boy was major disrespect and an insult. He was a respectable man. He had dreams for his daughter.

As he considered the situation, he reviewed his own life and remembered an incident that happened years ago. He had gotten an eighteen-year-old girl pregnant. "This must be punishment from God. I have messed women up in my life. Please, God, forgive me! I need you to save my daughter."

But this was not just about ChiChi. Baaba's lies were a direct challenge to him. He had to fight for his honour. He must rescue his daughter; it was his job as her father.

The Assistant Police Commissioner shared a love of Yoruba women and the music of Ebenezer Obe with ChiChi's father. He was a Yoruba musician, so they frequently had nights out to listen to his music. Because he was a lower-ranked policeman, ChiChi's father dealt with more cases on a daily basis than his friend did. He had daily contacts with women complainants and accused. Some of them offered their bodies for favours.

The Assistant Commissioner handled only specially referred cases, he had limited access to the public.

As such, ChiChi's father regularly introduced some of the women to him. The Assistant Commissioner could not otherwise meet the women. He owed him a favour or two.

ChiChi's father thought, "He is my friend and now I need him. He should use his high-ranking position to deal with Baaba. He would demand that Baaba is locked up in jail for abduction."

When they met, his friend invited him into his office. "Sit down, my friend. What's wrong? You look troubled. And, it is very unusual for you to book an appointment officially to see me. I thought we were meeting tomorrow at Mama Bode's house, not in the office."

ChiChi's father slumped into a chair in his office.

"I am finished," wiping a tear from his eyes.

"Is the family all right? Talk to me, my friend!"

ChiChi's father could not utter a word.

"Has someone died?"

"No, that may be more bearable than what has happened."

"What is the problem? We can solve it, whatever it is. That's why we are friends. Go on, tell me all about it. As long as it is not death or blindness, we can deal with it."

ChiChi's father then told him about Baaba and the story he had heard from his friend. "And I want this girl to be a doctor. She is so intelligent. She had distinction in her secondary school exams. All my hopes are ruined. I am finished," he cried out.

"No, you are not finished. This is a small matter we can deal with, easy." The Assistant Commissioner rang a bell on his desk and a policeman came into his office.

"I want you to tell the sergeant on duty to go and arrest a man. My friend will give you the details of his address. I want him in my office on Friday morning. I want to deal with him personally when you bring him in."

"Yes, sir," responded the policeman.

The two men spent time in the Assistant Commissioner's office talking about the ills of society. They talked about how the world was changing. Children had no respect for their parents as they did. A short while later, ChiChi's father went back to his office for the day's work, but could not concentrate and excused himself, and left work early.

On the Friday morning – as promised by the Assistant Commissioner – two policemen visited Baaba's house to arrest him.

"What have I done? Have I committed any crime?" he demanded of the policemen. "I know my rights. I have been in the force, and I know you cannot ask me to come to the station without a warrant. I also have a right to see the warrant."

"It's the girl's father who reported you to the Assistant Police Commissioner. I know they are friends. I would advise you to come with us and sort it out as a family problem. You need the Assistant Commissioner to hear your side of the story. The girl's father is alleging kidnapping, which is a serious offence."

Baaba turned to ChiChi and asked, "Did I kidnap you?"

"No, he did not kidnap me. I am his wife, and Papa does not want him to marry me. It's not kidnapping," she said.

"He still needs to come with us to the station. The Assistant Commissioner wants to see him. If he resists arrest, we will have no choice but to use force."

"Please, Baaba, we will have to go with them and tell the Assistant Commissioner that we like each other," ChiChi pleaded with Baaba.

Baaba agreed with her and relented.

ChiChi's father was in the Assistant Commissioner's office when they arrived. He immediately started shouting abuse at Baaba, calling him a 'destroyer'.

"I've known you from child hood; you have been nothing but trouble for your parents and everybody else. Why do you want to destroy my daughter? She is supposed to be in the university." He was beside himself with rage. "You want to waste my daughter's life like you have wasted yours!

"The police booted you out of the force after nine months due to your bad ways. I don't want my daughter near a man like you."

The Assistant Commissioner asked ChiChi's father to calm down. He wanted to talk to the couple.

The Assistant Commissioner turned to ChiChi and asked, "When did you come to Lagos?"

"Last year, sir."

"Where do you live?"

"With Baaba, sir."

"Does your father know you are living with Baaba in Lagos?"

"No, sir."

"So what are you doing in Baaba's house?"

"He wants to marry me, sir."

"Did your father approve of this marriage?"

"No, sir, but Baaba is making arrangements to send his uncle to him, sir."

"Has he paid your dowry to your father?"

"No, sir; but he will pay."

"What about your education?"

"I will still go to school, sir."

"How can you be married and still go to school, my daughter?"

"Baaba will get a house girl, sir."

"Do you know our tradition? Your father has to agree to your marriage before you start living with the man."

"But my father does not like Baaba, so he will not agree, sir."

"Do you not agree with him?"

"No, sir; Baaba is a nice man and he likes me, sir."

The Assistant Commissioner asked her a few more questions, and asked them to wait outside his office whilst he conferred with ChiChi's father. Strangely, he paid no attention to Baaba and did not ask him any questions.

Baaba held ChiChi's hand whilst they sat outside the office. He gave her a kiss on the cheek and assured her that it will all end well with time.

"He doesn't even know I am pregnant, I think he will kill us if he finds out." ChiChi looked up at Baaba with tears in her eyes. She knew her father. He did not believe in defeat. He was a very determined man. He would hunt Baaba down and would not relent until he left ChiChi alone.

"He will calm down once you are in university; we must make sure you apply for a place in the university," he said.

The Assistant Commissioner's office door swung open and a policeman ushered them back into the office.

The Assistant Commissioner asked them to sit down. ChiChi's father was sitting in a corner, still looking very angry.

The Assistant Commissioner said to the couple, "My dear children, there are ways we do things in our culture. You need to go to a girl's father and ask for her hand in marriage. You have to pay the dowry and fulfil the necessary marriage custom." He continued, "My friend is unhappy because he thought his daughter was in the village after finishing her secondary school exams and getting ready for the university entrance.

"Do you think he is wrong to be angry?" he asked them.

"No, sir," both responded.

"So, why have you behaved in this disgraceful manner?"

"Sir, I will do the right thing, but for now he needs to calm down. ChiChi is going back to school and I will make sure she gets her proper education. This is what he wants; he cannot marry his own daughter. I will take very good care of her; he will not regret my association with her. I like her a lot and we are already living together." Baaba spoke for the first time, pleading with the Assistant Commissioner.

ChiChi's father said angrily, "How do you intend to maintain a wife when you have no job?" He balled his fists angrily. "I know you are into dubious activities. I have been a policeman since returning from the Second World War. I have maintained a very good record as a citizen. I do not want my daughter married to a criminal. It is a disgrace that I will never allow to happen," he said, banging his fist on the Assistant Commissioner's desk.

"I am not a criminal, sir … You may not agree with what I do, it is called business and I help people who need my services." He took a breath. "Must everyone be a policeman to be a good citizen?" Baaba asked, directing the question to the Assistant Commissioner.

"No, my son, but people get into criminal activities calling it business." He sighed. "Anyway, I am not here to judge anyone or discuss what you do. We need to sort this problem out with my friend. I have known this man for twenty-three years; I have never seen anything affect him the way this has. He is very angry and wants his daughter to go back to the village."

ChiChi interrupted the Assistant Commissioner, "I am not going back to the village. I am staying with Baaba in Lagos. My father said the problem was my education. Baaba has promised that I would go to the university at the next semester." ChiChi knew that by next semester, she would have had the baby.

The Assistant Commissioner turned to ChiChi's father and said, "My friend, you heard your daughter. She has promised to go to school. She does not want to go back to the village. Why don't you give them a chance and monitor that she goes to school next semester?"

Now ChiChi's father turned his anger towards his wife. "That woman is responsible for all that is happening. How can she allow you to leave the village without letting me know? She is a bad woman. She wants to ruin all my children." He vowed to take revenge on her mother.

ChiChi knew that he would take it out on her poor mother, so she quickly said to her father, "Mama did not know when we left. We deceived her; she knew nothing about our plans, so please keep her out of this."

ChiChi's father always blamed her mother for anything that went wrong in the family. It was always her fault. She had tried in the past to ignore his blame on her mother for every negative event. This time she had to speak up on her behalf. She added, "Please don't direct any of your anger at Mama. She is innocent of all our movements. We deceived her, and she warned us about your reaction if we tried anything funny."

"You can defend your mother but you were supposed to be in her care in the village; does this make her a good mother?"

"Let's forget the woman in the village and deal with the issue at hand," the Assistant Commissioner interrupted the argument between ChiChi and her father. He realized he was equally guilty of the offence. He blamed his wife for any misbehaviour from his children as well. It is the tradition. The mother's job was to bring up the children; so she should be blamed if they go wrong. "You can sort that out later. Your daughter has reaffirmed that she wants to live with Baaba. She is nineteen years old so she is not underage. Your wife was only fifteen years old when you married her. You should help them settle down and make sure that ChiChi goes to school. Education seems to be the major problem. He has promised to send her to school at the next semester. I think we should give them a chance; he seems an intelligent boy, and he cares for your daughter."

The Assistant Commissioner told them about his own daughter who got pregnant at seventeen years and could not identify the father. "At least you know who your daughter is living with. If you harass them, they might decide to keep away from you. It is better you stay close to them so that you can advise and monitor what they do. You cannot send him to prison for marrying a grown-up girl."

ChiChi's father listened to the Assistant Commissioner without interruptions or further argument. When the Assistant Commissioner ended his speech, ChiChi's father held his hands to his head in resignation and said, "But the boy is too irresponsible to marry anybody. He will turn this girl into a thief, just like he is."

"My friend, you are a policeman and you know you cannot accuse anybody of a crime until proven guilty.

"If this boy decides to undertake criminal activities, he will suffer the consequences. He will end up in jail; but he looks very intelligent.

"He will lose her if that happens. He will take care of her. Let's give them a chance."

Turning to Baaba and ChiChi, he said, "You will have to go and beg your father's forgiveness. You also have to keep in touch with him to seek his advice, when you have problems. He is your father, and he is angry because he wants the best for you."

The meeting ended with a forced handshake by the parties, ordered by the Assistant Commissioner.

"These children sometimes don't know how we feel about them; please, my friend, forgive them. They may surprise you, they have a life together, let them make something out of it," he said to ChiChi's father as the couple left his office.

ChiChi's father was still not convinced, but he respected his friend's opinion.

He had never liked Baaba. His mother was his relative and had left his village to marry Baaba's father from another village. He knew when Baaba was born. He had always been troublesome. He did not respect anybody including his own father.

"I will have to talk to his mother, who is my relation. There must be a way to make these children see sense."

What he did not know was that the two mothers in the village had agreed to the affair, and sanctioned the couple's trip to Lagos.

"Thank God, my tummy is still flat, can you imagine what he would have done if my tummy was bulging with pregnancy?" ChiChi said, breathing a sigh of relief as they left the Assistant Commissioner's office.

As he left the Assistant Commissioner's office, ChiChi's father looked out through the fourth floor office window and watched them leave the building. He was shocked to see ChiChi mount Baaba's motorbike whilst Baaba sped off, screeching the tyres to show off to the policemen watching them through the windows.

"She is really ruined but I will not give up on her," he promised himself.

A short time later, her father heard about the pregnancy – again from a friend but this time decided to keep away from them. He would have nothing to do with the couple. He had to find a way to forget her. It would be very painful because he loved her. After all, she was his favourite child and he had always accorded her special treatment. Her siblings were always jealous of his special affection for her.

Baaba, just like that, had destroyed all his love and affection for his daughter. He was sure she was beyond saving. Thanks to Baaba, his hope of her becoming a medical doctor was lost.

Years had passed and ChiChi had another child. She also went to Lagos University and the Teaching Hospital to study medical science.

With two children and the third one on the way, she could not go for a medical degree. The couple decided it was not an option, as she had to live in the university. However, with medical sciences, she could attend university from home. She spent four years in the university and got her diploma with flying colours.

She had servants and Baaba bought her a nice sports car – an Opel. She also had a personal driver.

They had moved to a detached house and she had all the amenities to herself. She was not sharing with neighbours any more. Their love grew stronger.

The normal progress for ChiChi was to apply for jobs after her National Youth Corps service. Baaba decided that she should be a full-time housewife. He was making enough money to sustain them. He had met new business people;

they introduced him to other types of business, including people handling stolen goods from the ports.

Through it all, he remained a very jealous man. He did not want her exposed to the attention of other men.

She tried in vain to persuade him that his feelings were foolish, but he refused to be swayed. He promised to look after her and make sure she was comfortable financially.

CHAPTER 27:
BAABA PREACHES 419

BAABA CAME HOME ONE DAY and found Emi sitting with a man he did not recognise.

"Hello," he said cautiously. He knew that the man could be the police in civilian clothes; he was not taking any chances.

"Baaba, this is Henry, my friend. He is from Calabar but lives in Lagos. He would like to talk to you."

"Hello, Mr Henry," Baaba said, stretching out his right hand for a handshake.

"Good afternoon, sir," the man replied, shaking Baaba's hand nervously.

"My friend, what can I do for you? I have just come home, and I want to have my lunch. I am very hungry," he said impatiently, still suspicious of the visitor.

"I am a businessman," the man said nervously.

Emi had already warned the stranger that Baaba could dismiss him, if he did not present his business effectively.

"What type of business does he do?" Baaba asked Emi, settling down in the lounge chair.

Then he turned to the stranger, "What type of business do you do, my friend? Are you a policeman?" He prided himself that his police training made him able to recognise them. He could detect them whatever disguise they had. And these included the women police officers who threw themselves at you as a means of penetrating your organization. He knew all their tricks.

"Do I look like a policeman?" Henry asked, hitting his right fist to his chest to drive his point home. "I am looking for something to eat like you, how can I be a policeman?" He sat upright in the chair and continued, "I met your brother and we became friends. I like your brother; he is a gentle man. He bought food for me this afternoon. I came here because I want to repay his kindness. I am a businessman but I need someone who can understand my type of business."

Baaba asked again, impatiently, "I said, what type of business do you do?"

"My business partner went back to the village; I can't operate alone with nobody to watch my back."

"Well, if you will not tell me the type of business you do, I am sorry but I would have to ask you to leave my house. I am hungry …" With that, he called out to ChiChi, "Is my lunch ready or do I have to shout to get my lunch?"

Henry replied with a cynical smile, "I do all sorts of business I come across. I have one now and I need a partner. Your brother has told me you are fearless and can handle any type of business."

Baaba, still apprehensive, asked Henry, "Where do you live?"

"I live in Ikorodu."

"Do you know who I am?"

"I have heard about you from a friend .Your brother has told me a bit of what you do. I told your brother a bit about the business, and he assured me that you are capable of handling it."

Sitting back comfortably on his lounge chair, Baaba again said, "Okay, Mr Henry, tell me about this business of yours." Baaba was sitting on his special chair. This chair was isolated from the guests' sitting area. It was placed on a higher level than the rest of the chairs in the sitting area. Baaba preferred this arrangement so that he could look down, and impose himself on his guests. This boosted his confidence when he was dealing with potential clients. Only Baaba sat on it. Everyone else in the household knew to keep away from the chair.

He called out again to ChiChi, "Bring us some beer and prepare food for us."

ChiChi always found herself in the kitchen cooking to meet Baaba's demands. His concerns and fears meant that no one else in the household prepared nor served his food. Not even the house girl. He did not trust any one with the safety of his meals, and secondly, only ChiChi could get the taste right. He loved her culinary skills and she knew exactly what and how he liked his meals.

The house girl concentrated on the children's needs.

He ordered ChiChi to feed his numerous friends and visitors. He expected her to have sufficient food in the house at all times. He had previously told her, "A hungry man is an angry man; feeding my clients is part of customer care.

"Food relaxes people and encourages trust. You must not be upset when I ask you to cook for my friends."

ChiChi spent a lot of her time in the kitchen, sweating from the kitchen heat. The kitchen provided a place of solace for her. It became her sanctuary, where she could sit and think about the world around her. She wondered how long Baaba could go on with his *wayo* business. "If he ended up in jail, how will I cope with bringing up the children?"

Baaba sat back on his chair to be more comfortable, lit a cigarette, and offered a stick to Henry. "Okay, tell me about this your business."

"Thank you, sir," Henry said, accepting the cigarette with gratitude.

Henry lit the cigarette and exhaled the smoke through his nostrils. He enjoyed smoking but could not afford a complete pack. He bought individual sticks of cigarettes from his local shop. He could only buy his cigarettes from this particular shop. The owner knew him and sometimes would give him sticks of cigarettes on credit.

He slowly and carefully explained the details of the business to Baaba and Emi. He stopped occasionally to acknowledge his listeners' understanding. "I think you understand me," he would say at the end of the various stages of the business.

The idea was to make someone believe that they would print fake naira notes. They would tell the victim that he/she was lucky to come across the business.

They would tell the victim that they have secured negatives for printing money from the Central Bank. These were condemned notes authorised for disposal. Their job was to convince the victim that they needed some capital to sponsor the production costs of the counterfeit notes. They had 'connections' in the Central Bank to exchange the fake notes.

Baaba interrupted, "But which bank will take fake notes?"

"It does not get to that. If you wait, I will explain the rest of the business."

He continued patiently, "Firstly, we ask the *mugu*, our victim, to pay for the purchase of the paper negatives.

"We cut up plain white paper into the size of naira notes. We stain the notes with iodine. We prepare a chemical solution which will wash off the iodine. We use talcum powder as the drying agent.

"At each stage, we give him a new 'bill' for each of the items that is needed to convert the negatives to the fake notes.

"The next stages of the business and the bill would be determined by how rich the victim was, and his reaction at each stage." Henry chuckled, "It is an unending cycle. It is marriage without divorce."

Baaba and Emi listened intensively, soaking up every detail.

He went on to explain that they would load the cut-up paper in a box; and layer the top of the box with a few genuine naira notes for the demonstration. The initial deceit was to make the victim believe that the entire box contained real money. They would use a 'palming' technique, which simply meant covering up.

Baaba interrupted again, "If you stained the money with iodine, how do you wash it off?"

"It will wash off because before we stain the notes, we will mask it with corn meal which will block the iodine from staining the notes."

Baaba didn't look convinced.

"Don't worry," he assured them, "I will demonstrate it to you and train you very well. I have done it a few times with my friend and it works." With another chuckle he said, "The main trick here is 'the more you look, the less you see'. People have been doing this business from time immemorial. It is nothing new, only that we have modernized it."

The process seemed complicated to Baaba so he asked that Henry should give them a practical demonstration. "It sounds interesting but I still need to see it performed," he said when Henry stopped talking.

"I need money to buy the paper, iodine, *ogi* – or corn meal cereal – the local bleach, and talcum powder," he requested.

Baaba, still not convinced, gave Henry and Emi money to buy all he needed to give a practical demonstration.

Returning from the shop, Henry asked that they have a role play. Baaba would be the victim and Emi would be Henry's assistant. Henry explained, "To distract the victim, an assistant is needed." He explained that this was the reason magicians used assistants when they performed. It was to distract the audience.

Henry asked for a small basin and requested that ChiChi make the *ogi* into a starchy form. Boiling water turned the wet cornflour into a starchy, glue like substance.

Baaba again called out to ChiChi, who came from the kitchen. "Yes, Baaba," she responded, opening the lounge door.

"Boil some water, take this, and make *ogi* for me," he said, handing the raw cornflour to her.

"When you come back, bring that small white basin with the *ogi*."

She left the men and went back to the kitchen to carry out her husband's instructions. She dared not ask any questions when Baaba gave instructions during his business meetings.

With Baaba and Emi watching carefully, Henry dyed the real clean and fresh naira notes he had obtained from the bank.

He told Baaba and Emi that the notes had to be new and clean, because they were supposed to be new fake notes.

Like an artisan, he coated the notes with the *ogi*. He waited for the *ogi* to dry on the notes. He then stained the notes with the iodine.

Again, he waited for the notes to dry. As they waited, the three men drank beer, chatting about the potential of this new business.

Baaba assured the two men, "This business is obtaining under false pretences. We could always use Section 419 of the Criminal Code to get away if the client decides to make trouble," he said, rubbing his hands together, excitedly.

He ordered ChiChi to serve them more beer. Henry deserved more beer. He saw that this business had the potential to yield more money than all the other illegal businesses that he was familiar with previously, including the pregnancy trick.

One box could contain at least a million naira; their bills for the processing would run into thousands of naira. You had to be very rich and greedy to fall for this.

Henry reassured them, "You will find that once the victims have invested the initial amount, they find it difficult to stop. They focus on completion rather than their investment."

Baaba came up with another idea. He said to his two accomplices, "I will coach my policemen. If any of the victims reported the business, the police would have a ready question for them. The question is 'How did you think that somebody can print money for you? Is he the Central Bank that prints money?' The victim would hopefully see the futility of the venture and walk away."

The role play completed, Henry slowly and carefully went through the details again, stressing the important stages of the business.

"Okay, let's talk money. I always like to be upfront about sharing the loot. What will be your contribution to the business and what would be mine?" Baaba asked Henry.

"There is the cost of buying the box, the paper, cutting up the paper at the printers, uniforms – white coats – entertaining the victim …

"I have no money to sponsor the business but I will 'catch' the victims while you pay for the materials for the job. You will also present the deal to the client; because you have a good personality, anyone would believe you," Henry replied.

In their language, Henry was termed 'the catcher' and Baaba, 'the executor'. Emi remained the assistant.

"In that case, I will sponsor the business. I will take 80 per cent of any money paid and you will get 20 per cent."

Mr Henry frowned. "Come on, Baaba, what about 30 per cent? It is difficult to convince a *mugu*. Without a *mugu*, there will be no execution, you know."

Baaba shook his head. "No, Henry. You seem to forget that when police get involved, I have to pay them to destroy the case with 419."

"Okay, Baaba, sir. I did not think of that. If you will take care of the police, then I can't argue; but Emi's share as an assistant has to come from you."

Baaba agreed that he would take care of Emi. They also agreed that if Emi got a client directly, then the situation would change. In such an instance, Emi and Henry get 15 per cent each.

"ChiChi, where is the food?" Baaba shouted.

ChiChi came from the kitchen, opened the lounge door, and asked, "Are you ready to eat now?"

"Yes," Baaba replied. "And bring some more beer."

ChiChi brought the food to the sitting room, accompanied by the house girl.

Baaba looked into the sauce bowl and frowned. "Is that all the meat you have? Please bring more meat for my visitor."

As the men ate, Henry confided that he had a client whom he had earlier approached with his previous partner. He said that the man was ready to go ahead with the business. He had met with him on three occasions in the last month. He had delayed the transaction because he could not afford the cost of the processing materials. He told them that they were God-sent.

"And this 419 … this is the first I've heard of it …"

Baaba told him how he used this term in court to get away with his crimes. Henry was pleased he had won Baaba's confidence. The sky was the limit, armed with Baaba's police knowledge.

When asked how he would secure the clients, he replied, "I know rich men. Some of them are so greedy they would fall for any scheme to make more money. It is insane."

Baaba told them he would not spare anyone, including his rich uncles and relatives. He planned to approach them through their wives, girlfriends, employees, and mothers. The meeting ended with arrangements made to prepare the materials for the first victim.

Henry advised that they must have materials with or without a client. This, he explained, was because he could 'catch' a client any time. Once a client is attracted, he/she could not be given the time to think about the proposal. His clients also included rich women who had market stalls on the Lagos Island.

CHAPTER 28:
BAABA TRANSFORMS 419

BAABA, HENRY, AND EMI AGREED to buy and prepare the materials the day after their meeting.

Henry was overjoyed. "This is what I like; you are ready with the money for the materials." He made a face. "Other people I approached only told me fanciful stories; they could not perform when it came to spending money. They don't understand that you need to spend money to make more money. They always worry about losing their money; it was always the same question, 'What if the client does not pay? How do I get my money back?'"

"I will get my money back, all right," Baaba said confidently. "No client would come in here without paying me at least the cost of the materials.

"You will see the real Baaba in action when you bring in the first client. They don't call me the 'Boss of Wayo' for nothing."

The meeting concluded. The three men, who were already slightly drunk, continued drinking until late afternoon. They talked about the potential of the business. They fantasized about what they would spend their money on when the business started yielding money.

Later in the evening, Baaba volunteered to take Henry home. In the guise of a kind gesture, he needed to know where he lived if they were to be partners.

Henry lived in a very poor area of Lagos. Poverty was evident in these areas as you approached the neighbourhood. To gain access to Henry's one-room apartment, they walked through the back of the house, stepping over dirty gutters.

His room was bare with no furniture but a single wooden chair. He had his cooking utensils in the room, opposite his single bed. The only window in the house was shaded with a dirty rag. There was a stench from the gutters outside. He also had a kerosene stove tucked in a corner of the room.

Baaba's house was a palace compared to Henry's place.

Henry immediately apologised to Baaba for his poor living standards.

"Have you never made money from your business?" Baaba asked.

"Things went wrong for me and I lost all my money."

"No client will like to come here. It is filthy. You can never make money in this place," Baaba said.

"This is why I need you to perform the magic, so that I can move from this place."

Baaba assured him that as long as he got the right clients, he would perform and achieve good results. Baaba and Emi left immediately. The only place for them to sit was on the dirty bed. Henry had no food or drink to offer them.

Two days later, Henry came back to Baaba's house ready to go to the printers.

They all went to the printing shop. Baaba took over the conversation on arrival. He needed to know the source of the materials. He wanted to meet Henry's printer. He wanted to know how the material was prepared. He could not rely on Henry. After all, he might want to branch out on his own in the future. Henry could be another Oji, who became uncontrollable in the presence of money.

"Mr Printer, I am Henry's friend and I am here to spend money, so you have to give me your best service," Baaba said authoritatively.

The printer welcomed them to his shop and thanked them for choosing him. It turned out that he was from the same village as Henry, who had earlier explained to him the reason for their requirements.

He did not care what they did with the cut-up paper, as long as they paid him for his services.

They discussed prices and Baaba paid him. They agreed on the collection day. The men left and went to the market to buy the rest of the ingredients.

Baaba spoke to ChiChi that night about the new scheme. She laughed and said, "Who will believe that you will print money for them? Who will fall for such nonsense?"

"Oh," Baaba smiled, knowing how easily people were fooled, "Where is your faith, woman? Wait until the money starts rolling in, then you will know who."

Henry came to Baaba's house on the paper delivery day. After they received the delivery from the printer, he left to pay a visit to their first client.

He returned later in the evening. He told Baaba and Emi that the man had agreed to come for the business at the weekend. He was expecting the arrival of his goods from abroad. He did not have time until the weekend.

On the day of the man's arrival, they prepared the notes. They coated the notes with the thick *ogi* starch and left them to dry. They then stained the dried notes with iodine, and again left them to dry. To mask all the characters on the notes, they stained them a second time. The characters on the notes could not be visible to the victim.

Henry arrived with his first victim on Saturday morning. He was a rich man who owned building materials shops. His aim was to get richer than his stepbrother. He was from a polygamous home, and there was a lot of competition between the children. He needed to increase his stock and open more branches. He was a perfect candidate for the business.

Henry had initially approached him through one of his staff. He could not resist the temptation of easy money; especially since no one would know the source of his wealth.

Baaba was dressed in one of his best native outfits and really looked the part. Emi was acting the part of an assistant from the Central Bank and had to look corporate, so he wore a suit. He was representing his 'boss', who had a high

145

position in the bank, responsible for the eventual reintroduction of the money into the system.

They all sat down in the sitting room; Baaba offered the man a beer. He declined with the excuse that he liked to remain sober during the working hours.

Baaba went to work immediately, explaining the potential of the business. "If I had enough money to sponsor this business, I would not involve anybody else. It is a once-in-a-lifetime business; at the end of this business, you would have the capital to inject into your business and have more branches."

He put on a white overall and covered his nostrils with a handkerchief. He handed the others handkerchiefs, asking that they too cover their noses. He explained that the chemical was very dangerous and could be poisonous. This added authenticity to the demonstration. Henry was impressed with Baaba's performance. He had not only grasped the concept of the business, but was now fine-tuning the process.

"We have to perform a ritual of secrecy because a lot of money is involved, and greed could turn friends against each other. This would be our oath of trust. We have to make sure we trust each other to the end.

"We have to keep this business secret; and I am not taking any chances. No one can talk about this business to any person outside this room, including wives." Of course, this was a blatant lie as he had already told ChiChi about the business and the man's visit. However, the oath was to ensure complete secrecy. If the man did not talk to anyone about the business, they had more chance with him. He would also be reluctant to involve the police.

He got a razor blade and asked that they made snips on their arms. Each of them had to taste the blood from each other. Baaba was shocked that the man did not object to this. That meant his initial speech had impressed the *mugu*.

The three men performed the secrecy ritual in silence. Baaba warned the victim that if he ever mentioned the business to anyone, including his wife, the 'money spirit' would ruin the business. He concocted some local calcium powder with the blood; they all dipped their thumb in the blood concoction and licked the mixture from their thumb.

Confidentiality assured, Baaba started the demonstration.

He drew the curtains in the sitting room. The room was dark. He lit a candle and told them that light had an adverse effect on the paper. But, of course, this was to reduce visibility.

He took a few notes from the box, making sure he only removed the genuine notes. He immediately shut the box, explaining that the air must not get into the box. Otherwise, the preservation material on the paper would wear off. "No air must be allowed into the box, otherwise we are finished," he whispered.

The notes were jet black in colour from the iodine stain. He acted professionally, like a scientist working in a laboratory. He poured the bleach onto a flat plate with hot water. The hot water was to melt the *ogi* starch. He placed the genuine notes in the bleach solution. He left the notes in the mixture for a few minutes while they waited. After a few minutes, the stain on the black notes started wearing off. Baaba used metal tongs to turn them over, warning the men to cover their noses properly with their handkerchiefs. He also adjusted the handkerchief he had over his nose. The notes initially changed to brown and then the characters of the notes gradually appeared.

He rinsed the notes with clean cold water. He then asked Henry to turn the lights on.

This was the only time any of the men spoke. Throughout his demonstration, everybody maintained absolute silence.

Baaba sat down and asked them to remove the handkerchiefs from their noses.

He then covered the plate with a lid. Using a hot pressing iron, he dried the notes. This part of the act, again, was new to Henry.

He thought, "This man is really the *oga* of *wayo*." He had only demonstrated the basics of the business; and here was Baaba adding other interesting slants to it.

Baaba watched the expression on the victim's face intently.

What Henry and Emi did not know was that Baaba had had a trial run with ChiChi, privately, in their bedroom the previous night.

Baaba asked the three men to touch and feel the notes. More talk from Baaba convinced the man that the business had potential.

The man was very happy. He requested the bottle of beer he rejected earlier before the demonstration. He considered himself blessed and opportune, to be involved in such a highly classified corporate secret. He decided not to go back to work for the day. This was more interesting than work.

This was quick and easy money!

He was astonished with the result. He believed the money Baaba produced was part of the whole contents of the box. However, the three men knew the notes had been 'palmed' – placed on top of the ordinary stained papers.

"My brother will really see me in another light when this business succeeds. I will be the richest man in the family and the best thing about it is that he wouldn't know how I made my money. I will not tell even my wife," he assured Baaba and Henry.

Meanwhile, ChiChi's curiosity got the better of her. She had got into the habit of peeping through the keyhole sometimes when Baaba had these secret meetings with his friends. And this occasion was another development she was closely following. Baaba is the one man she qualifies as a daredevil.

They all relaxed with the beer, and ChiChi served them food.

"How much do I have to put in?" the victim asked.

"We can't discuss that yet. Firstly, you have to spend the money I have just produced," Baaba replied.

"I will give you the money to spend so that you can believe it is genuine. If you have any problem spending the samples, then we know we have a problem.

You have to take it to the bank and deposit it. You also need to take it to your suppliers and the market. When you have confirmed it is genuine money, then we will talk about sponsorship of the business. For now, I am not interested in your money."

Baaba handed the client the washed notes. Henry was not very pleased with this move. He had no money and hoped that at the end of the demonstration, Baaba would give him some of the sample notes.

However, he could not argue with Baaba. He could see he knew what he was doing.

The man left with the samples from the box, the genuine notes. But, of course, he was oblivious to this fact. He returned the next day with a big smile on his face. He had gone into his bank and deposited part of the money. He also paid his supplier and purchased some items from the market, just as Baaba had instructed.

He was now convinced that the money was real!

"How much, how much?" he asked enthusiastically, as he sat down in Baaba's sitting room. "I spent the money and it was genuine. My bank accepted the notes with no problem. If the bank could accept the notes, what more proof do you need?

"Let's talk business, please," he said, pleading with Baaba, who was trying very hard to suppress his excitement.

"The first thing is to pay the man from the bank, who arranged for the box to be released. If we don't pay him quickly, he would want his box back."

"How much does he want?" the *mugu* asked.

"We then need money to buy the chemicals and the drying powder," said Baaba, ignoring the man's question.

"Okay. How much in total?" he repeated.

Baaba told him the amount. Henry could not believe how much Baaba had raised the stakes. Never in his dreams would he think Baaba could ask the *mugu* to pay such a large sum. However, Baaba had noticed the man's enthusiasm and raised the bill amount.

The victim agreed to the bill without any arguments. He informed them that the money would be available the next day.

Henry was still shocked at Baaba's ingenuity. "This man must be from another planet." He was amazed at how Baaba had turned a few-hundred-naira business into a thousands-of-naira deal.

The next day, the man returned with the money as agreed. He handed the briefcase to Baaba. Baaba asked Henry and Emi to count the money, made up in 25 thousand-naira bundles.

Baaba promised to complete the work within two weeks. They agreed a meeting date to share the printed fake notes. They all exchanged handshakes and Baaba reminded the *mugu* of their allegiance to each other.

Baaba followed him to his car and bade him farewell. He came back to the room; the three men jumped and screamed, hugging each other.

"I told you I am the Baaba of Wayo. Do you believe me now?"

Henry laughed. "I believe! I believe!"

They looked at each other and stared at the money on the table.

Emi muttered, perplexed, "But the man looked very intelligent, how could he fall for this trick?"

"Shut up and take another look at the money on the table, my friend! If he thinks he doesn't have enough money and wants to make more this way; that is his problem. We will help him to spend the money he already has."

Baaba gave Henry his share, which was more than he had ever earned in his lifetime. Emi also got his share.

"This calls for celebration. Emi get a bottle of brandy from the shop. No more beer, we are big men so we should drink brandy," Baaba declared.

Henry offered to pay for the brandy, and Emi left to go to the shop.

"Don't get carried away yet, this is only the beginning of his bills. We have to prepare for the next stage," Henry said. "He has only paid for the paper. The next story would be that the ink had gone off and more money was needed to buy new ink."

The 'ink' was only a bottle of iodine and would not cost ten naira. However, Baaba intended to give the man another bill, running into a few thousands of naira to purchase another bottle of ink. He would say that, at some point in storage, air had penetrated into the bottle. This had rendered the ink ineffective.

"After that, he would have to pay for the washing powder. By the time he has paid for the powder and the ink, we will get a few more thousands of naira from him."

Baaba and Emi, who were new to the business, were astonished at how easy the 'game' was.

They gave the man the second bill, which he paid without much resistance. He could not afford to lose the money he had already invested. He still had hopes of making easy money.

Baaba kept on inventing stories; and he kept paying. In the end, he was very despondent and asked that they return his money. His reason was that there seemed to be no end to the mishaps. It seemed that every time he paid, something went wrong. The ink was expired; air had got into the chemical powder; the paper needed to go back to the Central Bank for further processing. The stories were endless; he could not see an end in sight.

He refused to pay any more money; instead, he demanded his money back.

Baaba got nasty and asked him to go to the police. He also banned him from coming to his house, if he could not afford to keep up with the payments.

Baaba created a scene and they had a row. He left and vowed never to return.

He could not go the police. He thought, "What would I tell the police? That I was printing fake notes?"

THE 419 CODE

His business capital had gone to these crooks. He had learnt from the experience. He would concentrate on his genuine trading business. No more 'get rich quick schemes' for him.

Of course, he was too ashamed to tell anybody, including his wife. He realized he had been duped. But the method of the deceit was what hurt him most. He could not tell anybody that he wanted to print counterfeit notes. That was a criminal act and any mention of his experience might get him into trouble.

Meanwhile, the business flourished.

ChiChi also became part of the team. She was responsible for hiding the money and the materials.

She was due to give birth to her fourth child.

Baaba moved them to a bigger house in Surulere. They had off-street parking with spaces for Baaba's four cars. He furnished the house with electronics, air conditioning, a gas cooker, and new furniture. Baaba could also afford the expensive rent. The money-doubling business was doing very well and bringing a large income in.

The family visited the village regularly.

Baaba recruited more boys as catchers from Lagos, and especially from his village. The boys' parents were delighted that Baaba was helping their children. The boys in turn made money very quickly and returned to the village to show off their wealth.

Chapter 29:
ChiChi is Apprehended by the Police

ChiChi's fourth child was a girl. With the birth, she had two boys and two girls. Baaba threw a big party and spent a great deal of money on ChiChi and the baby. He invited all his '419 boys', who arrived with their expensive cars and partied until morning.

After the party was finally over, he held the baby close to his chest and made a promise to all his children, "I will make sure you get the education that I missed," he told them. "You will go to the best schools and will not end up as Wayo People, like your father."

He very much loved his children. He put them in the best nurseries. He spared them no expense; he wanted the best for them. He did what his parents could not do for him.

Two weeks after ChiChi had the baby, there was a loud knock on the front door to the house. Baaba had been celebrating the successful collection of a bill from a client the previous night, during which he'd had too much beer and brandy until the early hours of the morning. Now, he had a debilitating hangover.

ChiChi, who was breastfeeding the baby, heard the noise at the door. She shook Baaba to wake him up.

"This is the police, open the door," came a voice from outside.

"Baaba, it's the police. Wake up," whispered ChiChi.

Despite his aching head, he jumped up from the bed. "Where is everything?" he quickly asked ChiChi.

"Don't worry, they will not find it."

Baaba dragged himself to the door. "Yes, Officer. Can I help you?" he asked as he opened the door.

"We have a complaint that you played *wayo* on this man, and illegally took money from him under false pretences," the officer said, pointing to the man at his side.

"My friend, did I take your money?" he asked, turning to the victim.

"Yes, you did."

"What did I take your money for?"

"I just want my money back."

Baaba smiled and looked at the policeman. "Officer, he does not even know what I took his money for," he said, laughing softly but nervously.

The officer produced a search warrant. He was ready. The victim had told him that Baaba had served in the Police Force. Baaba had also threatened the victim when he demanded his money back. He had also boasted, during their argument, "The police cannot do anything. This is 419 – obtaining under false pretences – it does not warrant a jail sentence."

He also warned him that, if he went to the police, his life would be at risk.

These threats did not deter this victim, who could not afford to lose the money. He was his company's accountant and had taken his employer's money for the business. He had hoped to replace the company money with the fake money. Now he needed the money back no matter what.

His employer had sacked him. The company had reported the matter to the police, resulting in his arrest. They were pressing charges against him for embezzlement of company funds. He was prepared to die. He had family to feed. His problems were too complex to worry about who knew the truth. He had no choice but to tell it all to his employer and the police.

Baaba studied the warrant and then looked at the officer. "Okay, Officer, you can search my house."

Of course, as ChiChi had assured him, the search yielded no evidence. She had hidden everything outside the house in a neighbour's shed.

"You will have to come to the station for a statement," the officer told Baaba.

"Can't we sort this out here, Officer?"

He shook his head. "No, you have to come with us to the station."

With the victim watching, Baaba could not offer the officer a bribe. Worse, this officer had come from a police station where he did not have friends. The officer was very hostile and looked very professional.

Baaba thought, "At the first opportunity I will offer him money; they all fall for bribery because they are not well paid in the force."

Baaba asked for time to change his clothes. Then, when he was ready, he was taken to the police station and locked up in the cells without interrogation. When he asked the officer to take his statement, he was told that a senior police officer, the District Police Officer (DPO), was to carry out his interview.

He would have to wait until the next day when the officer was available.

Baaba relaxed in the cell. This was not his first time in the cells; it was part of the business. If it does not work, you end up in a cell. There was no sense in worrying about it. He had no doubt that the police would release him the next day and he would go back to his family.

He sat on the cell floor, listening to the other inmates wailing and being disruptive. Surprisingly, his thoughts centred on ChiChi and his children. He hoped they were still too young to understand what was happening to their father. His first son was very inquisitive. He had coached ChiChi on how to answer his constant questioning. He had wanted to know why his father did not go to work in the morning, like his friend's father.

At school when asked what his father did, he could not explain. He asked Baaba, "Daddy, why don't you go to work in the mornings like my friend's daddy?"

"I work from home because I am a businessman." Then he told his son to tell them that his father was a trader and a businessman.

Baaba was so confident that he would be out the next day that he fell asleep as if he had no cares in the world. This was despite the mosquitoes that inhabited the cells, as if they owned them. The next morning, a policeman woke him up and asked if he wanted breakfast.

"I don't want breakfast," he yelled at the man. "I want your officer so that I can go home."

"Well, that is not my problem. If I were you, I would have breakfast because we don't know when the DPO will come in today. Sometimes he does not get here until late afternoon."

This infuriated Baaba; he had promised ChiChi that he would be home in the morning. That's how confident he was that his bribery strategy would work.

Even angered, he didn't see the sense in getting riled. He calmed down, sat back on the mattress on the floor, and requested the local porridge and fried bean balls for his breakfast. He thought, "It won't be as good as ChiChi's."

He fell asleep again after his breakfast. He did not care about being in the cells. Why should he worry? Being locked up was part of the game, after all. When released, he would have enough money to care for himself. That was a consolation. They could not send him to jail because this was 419. No one was sent to jail for obtaining under false pretences. There are two sides to every 419 story. And, obviously, the complainant was hesitant in revealing the full details of the business. Moreover, he was ready to tell the police that the man wanted him to break the law by producing fake money. What he did not know was that the accountant had already told them the truth.

He felt it was better to go to prison than face the shame.

A loud rattle of keys and noise on his cell door at about four in the afternoon woke him up. The policeman said, "The DPO wants to see you now."

Baaba got up and put on his shirt. The heat in the cell was unbearable. He could not have his shirt on in that oven. The mosquitoes had fed on his blood all night, and he was itching from their bites.

He walked into the DPO's office and, to his surprise, ChiChi with her young infant was sitting in a corner of the office.

"What is she doing here?" he demanded. "She has nothing to do with this." He looked at the DPO with disgust. "How can you bring her and the child to this place?

"This is wickedness. Do you have no child?"

The DPO was unmoved by Baaba's anger. "She is here because the complainant has given us information that she knows where the materials you use for your *wayo* are kept.

"According to the complainant, she passes them to you from the bedroom during your operation, so apparently, she knows a lot."

"When did you bring her here with my daughter?" Baaba shouted.

"Last night. Now sit down and shut your mouth," the DPO replied in a stern voice.

Baaba shook his head. He slumped into the chair in the DPO's office and held his head in his palms. He could not look at ChiChi. He was so ashamed that he had brought ChiChi and his two-week-old daughter to this stinking hole. He did not mind spending time in the cell himself, if that was what it took to make the big money. However, seeing his young family at the mercy of policemen was too demeaning for him.

All his efforts to keep his family out of his criminal activities had failed. They probably knew that his family was his life; without them, he could not function or be happy. He lived for them.

His thoughts switched immediately to another concern. "I hope no policeman has abused my wife," he snapped. This horrible thought made him look up at ChiChi. If she avoided his eyes, then he would conclude that she had betrayed him. However, if she looked him straight in the eye, he would know that she was sincere.

ChiChi looked up and winked. Baaba winked back at ChiChi and then felt relieved.

"That's my girl," he thought to himself. He could always trust her. He had made a good choice in marrying her. He took the baby from ChiChi and held her very close, trying to protect her from the ugly situation.

ChiChi gave him a big smile. She didn't say a word though, because the DPO was watching all the time.

The DPO got emotional when Baaba took the baby from ChiChi. He asked Baaba, "If you love your family this much, how can you put them through this? Why not look for a decent job and have some respect?" He continued in a very calm voice, "You two are young. You have a little baby. How do you feel introducing your young baby into a police cell and criminal activities?

"And as for you, young lady," he said, turning to ChiChi, "you have been to university and this is the life you have chosen."

The DPO explained that he had taken the responsibility of the case, because the victim was his brother-in-law. He had one goal and one goal alone, to plead that he got his money back from Baaba. He told them that he had promised his family that he would do his best to get the money back from Baaba. If he did not succeed, he would lose respect as a senior member of the family. As a DPO, the extended family expected him to use his position to help them. The family members had piled pressure on him to deal with the matter. This included his mother.

The DPO said that if Baaba paid back the money, he would close the case.

Baaba refused the offer and said to the DPO, "Your brother is guilty as well. What makes him think that I could print money for him. If I could print money, do you think I would do it for someone else?"

Baaba preferred the second option and the DPO said, "Well. It is your choice; I will charge you to appear in court. That way, it will be the judge's decision, not mine. That would exonerate me from my family at least."

He got up from his chair and called out to an officer, "Take him back to the cell, take his statement, and prepare the court papers."

They released ChiChi with her daughter. However, they put Baaba back in the police cell. A few days later, Baaba was taken to court and charged. Baaba was the one to coach his lawyer to refer to Section 419 of the Criminal Code.

Once again, the defence got him off.

During the hearing, the judge asked the victim, "How did you think this man can print money for you?"

The victim could not answer and, in amazement and disgust, the judge dismissed the case for lack of evidence – under Section 419 of the Criminal Code.

On release, Baaba looked up at the victim outside the court and said, "I warned you. You are an accountant and you don't know that only the Central Bank prints naira? You are a stupid man!"

Outside the court, a smiling Baaba announced to ChiChi and his friends, "It worked again." He was all smiles and happiness. "I told you this is the magic word. Any time we get into trouble, we use it to defend ourselves. It is the Criminal Code and they cannot change it. They can only change it if they change the constitution."

He was very confident. "You only need a clever lawyer to use that section of the law."

So it was that the term '419' stuck with the group. They used the term amongst themselves, keeping any outsider ignorant of the meaning. As time went on, Baaba recruited more 'boys' to act as the salesmen.

They left in the morning to hunt for victims, visiting shops and businesses. They approached their relatives and friends. Once these are convinced, they pulled in their rich uncles, fathers, sisters, mothers. They targeted anyone who was greedy. They had no shame about who they targeted, including their parents.

Baaba's boys included all tribes – Ibos, Yoruba, Hausas, and any desperate boy who could communicate effectively with clients. He recruited boys from his village, including ChiChi's brother, who had dropped out of school.

He coached them on the sales technique and sales language. He assured them that if things went bad, he would be there to rescue them. He had a good lawyer who could argue their case based on 'obtaining under false pretences'. He boasted to them about his knowledge of the police and the Criminal Code.

Nothing could stop him. Baaba grew in confidence because he had placed the local police officers on a payroll. These 'police friends' often visited him at home.

ChiChi did her duties: cooking, serving, and keeping Baaba happy. She knew her place and kept away from the room, whenever Baaba was discussing his business. She had decided to stay in the background. She had done this consciously. She never wanted to visit a police cell again and, also, she wanted to have the freedom to plead on Baaba's behalf if he was in trouble.

She had learnt her lesson. She could never forget that her two-week-old daughter spent a night in a police cell. She had to make sure it did not happen again. Baaba agreed with her and said, "Whatever I am doing, I don't want the police touching you or my children."

And so, with each passing month, Baaba polished the 419 business. He recruited more boys who returned with rich clients. There was serious money rolling in now. The 'boy from the village' was now a self-made king.

He had many subjects who respected him.

Baaba compensated the boys more than fairly. Everyone wanted to work for him. But he was very particular about the kind of person he had working for him. He inducted and trained new recruits and bought new clothes for them to look corporate.

He reorganized his house, separating his business area from the family area. In this way, his boys came and went without disturbing his family. He also made sure Henry moved to a better area of Lagos and into a more deserving apartment.

He was an emperor and he was running an empire of rogues.

ChiChi's father was not impressed. He called Baaba's house 'the den of thieves'. He refused to visit the couple. Baaba tried several times to appease him. He sent elderly men to ask for his forgiveness. He offered him money but the old man refused. He said it was dirty money, and that he would not stain his hands with such money.

He preferred his miserly police salary; he had always been comfortable with his genuine earnings.

Baaba made sure he took care of ChiChi's mother financially. He wanted to make her father jealous for being obstinate; but the old man was not interested.

Baaba, meanwhile, treated himself in a lordly fashion. He had expensive cars, expensive household goods, and fine clothes for his family. He developed an insatiable taste for electronic goods. He spent time and money at Alaba electronic market, buying the latest music sets in the market.

He made sure his mother lacked nothing. She was the envy of her friends in the village. He moved her from the thatched hut to a new brick house that he had built very quickly for her. He said to her with deep pride, "Now I have very big friends who may visit me, I can't have you living in a thatched hut. That's a sign of poverty and your son is not poor."

Baaba's mother was happy to support her son's trade. Her attitude was that if he could make money, it was all good. It did not matter how. The family had always been very poor and she had envied her peers who had rich sons that looked after them. She had had enough of poverty.

And she knew that most rich people got their money by cheating others. So she was happy to live in the house her son had built her with cement. She had an electric generator and got water from the taps.

Baaba dug a borehole in his mother's compound. Other villagers had to go to the stream, which was two miles away, to fetch water. However, Baaba's mother had the luxury of just turning on the taps in her kitchen and bathroom for water.

He even had a separate tap for the rest of the family members. His aunties and other relatives came to get water from his mother's compound.

So it was not surprising that his mother defended his *wayo* vehemently. After all, he was helping many poor people in the village, and taking their sons to Lagos. This was something they would not otherwise have the opportunity to do. To go to Lagos, one needed money and relations already living there, who would offer accommodation and help.

The villagers knew people lived on the streets of Lagos because they could not afford accommodation. The villagers who lived in Lagos brought these stories home. But not those who went to Baaba. Baaba, on the other hand, provided money, accommodation, and a trade for their sons. It did not matter what type of trade it was. The main thing was that they brought back riches to the village.

His boys stayed in his servant quarters until they made enough money to find their own feet. He fed and clothed them well. As long as they worked hard at being catchers their success was guaranteed in a short time. They only needed to catch a rich *mugu* and they were made nearly overnight.

Baaba decided to build a family house in the village. He assigned ChiChi's mother to locate some suitable land.

Baaba's empire was growing beyond recognition. On occasions when he found himself alone, he would look around him and reminisce on how he started with Ogo.

Ogo, who had served his term in prison, was now living in the village. Baaba had a special place in his heart for him. He gave him money and never forgot that he was the one who first took him to Lagos.

He had no contact with Amaka, who was living in England with her new husband. News had reached Baaba that she had more children and had trained as a midwife.

He also took special good care of Emi. He was his best friend and he loved him like his own brother. He put Emi above all his boys, almost making him an equal in their business dealings. The other boys were jealous of his relationship with Emi and accused him of favouritism, as Emi was lazy and was more interested in showing off his money to girls.

He had many girlfriends and introduced a few to Baaba. It was Emi who introduced Baaba to Lagos' nightlife and Fela's Shrine, where they became regulars.

ChiChi stayed at home. She did not like Emi because she felt he was a bad influence on Baaba. However, she dared not say anything. She knew that Baaba was very protective of Emi. Baaba had asked her to give Emi the same respect and service that she accorded to him.

Oh, how she detested this; Emi took advantage of this and constantly created a bad atmosphere between the couple.

"Baaba, ChiChi, come here, sit down, I have found a wife!" Emi announced one day. He told them that morning that he had a date with a girl he met a few days earlier. He was to take her out to lunch.

"Did you have lunch with the girl?" Baaba asked.

"No, she disappointed me. Nevertheless, as I was leaving her office, I saw a girl standing by the roadside, waiting for transport. Her beauty dazzled me. She wore a customs officer's uniform. Well, I mustered the courage and spoke to her. I offered her a lift. She accepted my offer and I took her to lunch. I am so in love with the girl; I am going crazy. She is so beautiful, but she is a law agent." He frowned. "I am not sure how she would react to our line of business."

He closed his eyes and his face took on a dreamy expression. "Baaba, ChiChi, she is so beautiful. I can't imagine her falling for me. If she does fall for me, I am in luck. This is the only girl I want to marry."

Baaba was happy for his friend. He had advised him to settle down, get married, and stop running after Lagos girls who were only interested in his money. He encouraged Emi in his infatuation. "You must bring her here on your next date, so that I can talk to her. ChiChi will have to cook very nice food for her. Do not take her to a restaurant; we need to plan this properly. Leave the talking to me, there will be no mention of the business yet. That would come after she has fallen in love with you. I will tell her you are a shipping official."

"No, Baaba, she is a customs officer, so you dare not mention anything about shipping. That is her work and she will know you are lying."

"Ah," Baaba said, remembering what Emi had said. "In that case, I will change the story. You are an electrical goods trader."

They agreed to tempt her with money. They would show off by counting a large sum of money in her presence. This seemed to always work on girls.

"She could not have seen nor handled big money in her life. After all, she is a civil servant on a monthly salary."

Her salary was meagre compared to the money they made.

Emi left to pick her up on the appointed day in his new Renault car. He brought her back to the house and she found herself mesmerised by the affluence around her. As Baaba expected, she fell more for the affluence rather than Emi, but she pretended she had fallen in love with Emi.

They started a relationship and she became a regular visitor to Baaba's house.

For convenience, Emi immediately searched and secured accommodation. He needed his own privacy where he could live with his wife-to-be. He moved out of Baaba's house, and this alone was a reason to celebrate his relationship in ChiChi's mind. His presence had become unbearable as his influence on Baaba was taking him further away from her.

Chapter 30:
The Wedding

ALTHOUGH THE POLICEMAN FOUGHT TO get his daughter back, he relented in the end. He could not continue to fight against reality. ChiChi now had four children. Most importantly, Baaba was doing very well financially. He was kind to everyone in the family. He renovated ChiChi's family house in the village. The whole family was benefiting from Baaba's wealth. The old man also benefited indirectly through his wife and other children who Baaba helped. Baaba brought ChiChi's siblings to Lagos. He paid their school fees and they lived comfortably with him. He also helped them to find jobs in Lagos. ChiChi's big brother decided to become one of Baaba's boys and made quick money in the process.

Her father was relieved that it had not all been doom and gloom with Baaba. Although she had not become a doctor, she was still in the medical field. She was a graudate. It had not been nearly so bad after all.

He was finally on talking terms with the couple. He was a difficult man but he could not stand apart from his own grandchildren. He did plead with Baaba to let ChiChi get a job but Baaba refused.

"I have enough money to look after my family; what is she going out there to do? Is it not to earn money?" Baaba shook his head. "How much would she earn; and what would she use the money for? She can't even earn her weekly housekeeping money as salary in a year," he added.

But her father continued to argue. "What if your business went wrong? She could end up being the breadwinner."

"No. My business will not go wrong; I know what I am doing. Besides, if it did, she would have enough money in the bank to take care of herself and the children."

During the second year of their life in Lagos, Baaba had insisted they marry in the court registry. He wanted to make sure that she did not leave him. He also felt that her father could not separate them if they were legally married in the court. He invited a friend to witness the marriage and he kept the marriage certificate to prove their agreement.

However, as time went on he thought the time had come to officially celebrate their union. He wanted to marry her in their native marriage ceremony. He had promised her a big church wedding but with four children, he did not feel it was necessary. But the native ceremony was important to him. He asked his uncles and parents to approach her father and ask for her hand in marriage, following the customary route.

And this time, the old man said yes.

THE 419 CODE

They fixed a date. They sent out invitations to friends and relatives for the wedding. He paid the dowry of sixty naira, the equivalent of thirty pounds. The colonial masters had set the dowry fee at thirty pounds and the villagers still maintained that custom. Although the colonial masters had left Nigeria since independence in 1960, the villagers were still following the laws they left behind. If the wife wanted a divorce in the future, her family would have to pay back the thirty pounds. That was the rule. Moreover, until she did, she was not free to remarry.

They performed the ceremony with the villagers as witnesses. Baaba spent a lot of money on the ceremony. He bought live cows, goats, and chickens. There was excess food and drink for the villagers. The marriage celebration lasted a full week. Most of Baaba's friends came from Lagos, showing off their expensive cars and fine clothes. They chatted up the village girls, who were fascinated with their big cars.

Some ended up in tears when they found they were pregnant after the men had left.

CHAPTER 31:
BAABA'S TRANSFORMATION

CHICHI'S MOTHER SECURED SOME SUITABLE land for the family house. Baaba purchased the land; he was now set to build the family house. He needed to supervise the work in the village. He could not trust the builders to meet his high standards.

He told ChiChi, "You know I have to spend time in the village until the building is completed. I do not trust the builders. They use poor quality materials, so I have to be there to supervise the work." They agreed that Baaba should visit the village every other month and spend a maximum of one month on each visit.

ChiChi told him that the family would miss him, but the house was equally important. They needed their own home. His father's house was not suitable any more. It was time. Some of his boys had already completed their houses in the village.

Initially, Baaba kept to his word but as time went on, he was spending more and more time in the village. He returned to the village after a very short time in Lagos.

ChiChi remained in Lagos with the children. She spent months on her own and found herself missing Baaba very much. She was not used to being alone without Baaba since they had arrived in Lagos. She found it strange being on her own. He had always been with her since their youth.

She told him how she felt during one of his short visits. He asked her to be patient. "When the house is completed, you will love it. I am only doing it for you and the children."

"Can I go with you to see the house?"

"No. I need you in Lagos to take care of the children. I don't trust the servants and the driver to take the children to school."

As the work progressed, his only visits to Lagos were to pick up more money for the project in the village. Occasionally, his boys would secure a client, inform him in the village, and he would come to Lagos to 'execute' the deal. Then he returned to the village immediately after the deal concluded and the money was paid.

The only other reason he came to Lagos was to secure the release of his boys from police cells. He used his police connections effectively. The police were on his payroll and were supportive of his business deals. It was a win-win situation. The more people Baaba duped, the more money the police made.

During his short visits to Lagos, ChiChi noticed that Baaba was less attentive to her. He used to hold her hands and cuddle her; but he barely touched her on his visits these days. He seemed to have a lot on his mind. His only concern seemed to be the house in the village.

On one of his visits, ChiChi tried to hold him in bed but he would have none of it. "I am tired," he snapped. "Don't you realize the amount of work I have to do on the house?"

"But, you have been here for two days and you are well rested."

He shouted at her angrily, threatened to leave for the village the next morning, and turned his back on her.

"What have I done?" she cried. "You have not been here for several months and you are acting very strangely. What is wrong?"

Without answering, he immediately got up from the bed, put on his shirt, and left the house. It was only later she found out he spent the night at Emi's house.

It was true. Baaba had changed. She was confused. She had been a good wife, attending to his needs and respecting him.

She loved him and produced lovely children for him.

But he was distant and moody. He kept to himself during the day and spent his evenings and nights at Emi's house. He did not eat ChiChi's food though she continued cooking as usual. He simply ignored the meal on the dining table.

He spoke only to the children.

ChiChi could not understand. Why had he changed from her Baaba? He made excuses to avoid spending time with her. He could not wait to get as far away as possible from her. She could not understand.

They had always talked about everything but now Baaba completely shut her out of his life. Each time she tried to talk to him, he stormed out of the house in anger. He used to look lovingly at her and admired her eyes; but now he avoided eye contact with her.

She couldn't bear the pain of this change and so, one morning when he came back from Emi's house, she summoned up enough courage to ask him what was wrong. "Have I offended you? I need to know why you have changed."

"You always seek attention. Your father spoilt you."

"No," she said. "Baaba, I do not seek attention. I seek affection from you."

"You are enjoying my money, why are you complaining about me not being here? Is this not what your father wanted – money? Would a doctor's salary earn you as much money as I give you?"

She shook her head. "Baaba, it is not the money. Money cannot replace our love for each other. I miss you so much." And then she burst into tears.

But he was unmoved. "You see, that is the problem. You said you would not marry an illiterate; so what are you doing here?"

ChiChi was shocked at how he had changed. Something was wrong and he would not tell her. She had been a faithful wife and had maintained her integrity. She only loved Baaba and knew no other man. Now, although she was very comfortable financially, she was not happy. She spent all her time in the house when the children were at school, but started seeking comfort in food. This made her put on weight and she kept buying new clothes because she grew out of her clothes very quickly.

Baaba would not discuss the progress of the village house with her. He kept her out of his life. Intimacy was non-existent. Her beautiful children were her only contentment. Caring for them kept her busy. She had no friends because Baaba had warned her not to have friends.

"I don't want any outsider coming in here to know my business. I am 419 man, and women like to gossip about their husbands."

For his part, Baaba couldn't bear her constant hectoring. On his next visit to Lagos, he decided to sleep in the lounge instead of the bedroom. If he went into the bedroom, she would only start asking the same annoying questions and seeking attention.

For her part, ChiChi wished he had gone to Emi's house; she did not want the servants to know what was going on between them. She continued to pretend to the outside world that all was well.

"Why don't you come to bed?" she asked him in the night.

"I don't want to. And I want to be left alone," he replied angrily.

"Baaba, please talk to me. What have I done to deserve this treatment?"

"Your father said I was not good enough for you. Will you leave me alone?"

"But that was a long time ago, we are all settled now. Please talk to me and come to bed."

"I said, leave me alone!"

"How can I leave you alone, when our house is on fire?"

"Whose house is on fire?"

"You know how we used to be with each other. I want that back."

"If you don't leave me alone, I will get angry with you."

"I can't leave you alone. You need to talk to me like we used to."

"Are you forcing me to talk to you?"

"No, Baaba, but I can't stand this treatment from you any longer."

"Why are you in my house if you cannot stand the treatment I give you? Why don't you go back to your father?"

"Stop bringing my father into our conversation."

"What if I did?"

"It's not fair because I can never disrespect your parents."

"Why did you mention my parents?"

"I was only saying …"

Before she could complete the sentence, he lashed out at her. She cried out loud, more from shock than the pain. "Baaba, you hit me?"

"And if you don't go back to the bedroom, I will hit you again."

She cried on her way to the bedroom. She lay down on the bed, and wondered what was happening to him. She could not believe that Baaba who had treated her like his queen could raise a finger to hit her. She lay on the bed and tried to think of any reason for his behaviour, but could not come up with an answer. She knelt down beside the bed and prayed to God to bring her Baaba back.

The next morning, he woke early and got ready to go back to the village.

"You have only spent three days with me and the children, we miss you a great deal, please stay with us."

"Why don't you go and stay with your father, he can marry you because I am not interested any more."

"Has anything happened between you and my father?"

"You know what has happened; he said you were too good for me. Even with your qualification from the university, are you better than I am? You sit here and spend my money and yet you are not satisfied."

With that, he said goodbye to the children and left with his driver.

Baaba's visits to Lagos became less frequent. ChiChi became used to being on her own. She concentrated on taking care of the children and relied on food for comfort. The more she ate, the fatter she got. Neighbours commented on her weight but she could not care less. She had no reason to maintain her good looks. Baaba was not interested in her looks; he was the only one that mattered in her life.

She came to dread his visits to Lagos because she would surely receive a beating from him. He would deliberately create a scene as an opportunity to beat her up. ChiChi still could not understand the change in his behaviour. She ended up in hospital on several occasions from the injuries he inflicted on her.

Soon, the common gossip within their local community was all about them. "That's the man that beats that beautiful woman all the time. Why is she still with him?"

Neighbours advised her to leave but she still loved him. She ran away from him on numerous occasions, but he begged for her forgiveness. He would promise not to beat her again but did not keep to his word. The police could not help her because they were his friends. Her father could not help because he was still angry that she had disobeyed him and stayed with Baaba. She found herself dealing with all the issues alone.

Baaba banned her mother from visiting her in Lagos. ChiChi wished she could talk to her mother. Her mother was the only one she could really tell how she felt. She was the one person she could open her heart to and tell about her pain. The man she loved had turned into a monster. She blamed it on the money. He worshipped money. He felt that the world belonged to him.

On one occasion he visited Lagos, he beat her the same night he arrived, and for what? For not providing the exact meal he wanted.

"I did not know you would come today. I would have made sure I went to the market."

"You should be ready at all times with my food."

"But you are in the village. How do I know when you would come to Lagos?"

With that, he lashed out at her. The children witnessed the beating and started crying with their mother. She held them close to her and took them into their room.

Baaba waited until they were asleep and he called out to her, "What did you tell my children, did you tell them I am a bad father?"

"No. I did not. I did not have to tell them anything. They saw you slap me."

He lashed out again; the sharp end of his ring cut her lips, and she was bleeding. She tried to run away from him but he caught up with her and gave her more beating. She struggled out of his hold and escaped to the road opposite the house. She stood half-naked, staring at the house.

It was almost midnight.

"Don't you try to come back to this house or I will kill you. Your father can come and pick up your dead body," he screamed at her, shutting the front door.

ChiChi stood beside the road, wondering what to do next. She had no footwear; she was half-naked with only a short nightgown. She walked along the road away from the house, crying. She was scared he would come after her.

"Is this how much he hates me? He should be worried about me outside the house at this hour of the night. Bad people could attack me. He really does want me dead."

After about half an hour sitting by the roadside, a car pulled up beside her. The driver asked her, "What's wrong, madam, are you all right?" The stranger noticed the bloodstain on her lips. "Come into the car, I will take you to the hospital. Who attacked you?"

ChiChi had a quick look down the road to make sure Baaba was nowhere in sight. It was past midnight, he should be worried about her safety, but he did not care about her welfare any more. As far as he was concerned, she was as good as dead. She couldn't fight it any longer. She got into the stranger's car, still crying. He comforted her and offered her a lift to the nearest hospital. She declined and said, "I need to run away from here. Not the hospital … please hurry before he catches up with me."

"Who are you talking about?"

"Please move the car … please," she pleaded with him, looking around nervously.

The stranger started the car and drove on. When he had driven a while, he stopped and asked her, "Where do you want to go? Who did this to you?"

"My husband," she replied, still crying.

He took out a white handkerchief from his trouser pocket and offered it to her to wipe the tears from her face.

He watched her and commented, "You are so beautiful; does he not see your beauty? If I had a wife so beautiful, why would I want to hit her? Did you sleep with another man?"

"No. Please do not say that. I can never sleep with another man."

"So what did you do to deserve this treatment?"

"He said I did not cook his favourite meal."

"That is just so ridiculous, you cooked for him but it was not his favourite meal; are you joking?

"I am taking you to my mother and sister. They will take care of you. You can have a bath in our house. They will give you a change of clothes and anything else you may need as a woman, and then we can sit down and talk about your plight."

"No. I can't go to anybody's house. If he finds out he would kill me."

"I insist. I am not letting you out this late on a Lagos road. It is dangerous. I care about your safety even if he does not." Without any word, he drove to his house. He kept quiet in the car. She was also very quiet, thinking about Baaba and her children. When they arrived, he left her in the car, went into the house, and spoke to his mother briefly.

He came back to the car and asked her to come into the house.

His mother immediately took ChiChi into her bedroom. Unable to hold her feelings in any longer, she told her about Baaba, crying all the time. She was happy to find someone she could talk to about her predicament. She opened up her heart to this stranger who somehow reminded her of her own mother.

When she stopped talking, the woman said, "From all indications, he has got himself involved with another woman. That is the only reason men start mistreating their wives. Believe me, I am an experienced woman. I have been there. My husband is dead but that was his style when he got a new lover."

ChiChi had never given a thought to Baaba cheating on her. Astonished, this was the answer to her questions. And to think that it was coming from a total stranger.

"But my mother will tell me, she is in the village. Now I know why he banned my mother from visiting me in Lagos. He also banned me from visiting the village."

Now it all suddenly made sense. This woman had opened her eyes. Baaba had not slept with her for months. He always had an excuse to keep well away from her.

"Thank you, Ma," she said to the woman.

Her new-found family made her comfortable that night. She had a hot bath and they offered her a snack, which she accepted gratefully. The woman left her and went into her son's room. She overheard them discussing her plight. His sister was asleep in her room and couldn't be bothered.

"Mama, I like that girl. She is so beautiful. I can't understand how a man can beat her up. It's insane. Can you convince her to sleep in my room? Please, Mama." He was a mama's boy all right!

"Okay, I will try," she replied and came back to her bedroom.

ChiChi had finished eating the snack.

"My daughter, are you all right?" she asked ChiChi.

"Yes, Ma."

"I need to go to bed. It is almost 3 a.m. You need to sleep as well."

"Where can I sleep, Ma?"

"You will sleep in Kelly's room, my daughter."

"Can I sleep here in your bedroom or the sitting room, Ma?"

"No. Kelly is your age group, so you can talk to him."

"Okay, Ma."

She thanked her and went into Kelly's room.

ChiChi did not look at Kelly in the car. She was too focused on her own problems. She now had a good look at him. She thought he was very handsome and spoke very good English. He was educated and had good manners, which Baaba lacked.

And he seemed gentle. She felt safe.

They talked until the early hours of the morning. He told ChiChi he worked in a bank. He had no girlfriend. His last girlfriend left him to marry a man from America. She wanted a ticket to America and did not care for the man. He confessed to ChiChi that he had not liked her very much anyway.

ChiChi told him more about Baaba and her children.

Suddenly, they fell into each other's arms. It was like magic. They blended like one. ChiChi wished the night would last forever.

She fell asleep with her head on his chest. They spent the remaining hours wrapped in each other's body.

In the half-sleep of dawn, she mused over how she used to spend her nights with Baaba. "I thought that was where I belonged. Why did Baaba have to ruin everything?"

He had thrown her to the wolves. Now, she has slept with another man. However, to her surprise, she had no regrets. On the contrary, she was happy that she could give her lovely body to another man instead of that monster.

The ill treatment from Baaba had injured her sense of who she was. She was not sure she loved him any more. One should have good thoughts about one's husband, not horrible memories. When she thought of him, all she could see was his hands raised to beat her up.

Moreover, he was a strong, muscular man. She had scars on her body to show for it too.

"I have to get back to my children, they are all I have; I cannot abandon them," she said, getting up from the bed in the morning.

"But I like you so much and would marry you if you want. You made me so happy last night. I have never felt that way with any of my girlfriends. Please stay with me. We can look after your children together. I can also fight him if he wants a fight."

She shook her head. "No, Kelly. It is more complicated than that. I would not want to involve you in my problems. We can remain friends, and see each other occasionally. Baaba spends most of his time in the village. When he is away, we can be with each other.

"I do like you very much. You are very handsome and tall. Most importantly, you are educated and civilised."

Kelly was satisfied that she wanted to see him again. That was sufficient, for now. She might change her mind in the future and their friendship could turn into a serious relationship.

He took the day off from work and they spent hours together in bed until late afternoon. Then he drove her to the end of her street. "If he gets violent, please promise to come back to our house. You are welcome at any time," he told her.

She thanked him and walked towards her house, with fear of the repercussions she would face from Baaba.

When she went into the house, he shouted at her, "Where have you been?!"

"I slept on the road."

"I wish robbers had killed you."

She muttered under her breath, "You will die, not me."

"What did you say?"

"Nothing," she replied.

"You said something and I want to know what it is."

She kept quiet and this infuriated him.

He lashed out at her. She was placid. She focused her thoughts on Kelly, and the encouragement he gave her. Now she could ignore Baaba's madness. She was beyond care.

He left for the village two days later. They did not speak to each other during those two days. Her suspicions got the better of her. She remembered every word Kelly's mother said. Baaba must be having an affair. If it were true, she would definitely leave Baaba. She would leave him and she would marry Kelly.

She found herself thinking about him all the time. She had never slept with another man, apart from Baaba. She had been a virgin when she met him. Now, she knew what it was like to sleep with another man. This was a wonderful revelation and all thanks to Baaba's bad behaviour.

He had pushed her to it.

Life continued with Baaba spending more time in the village and ChiChi finding a way to keep herself busy in Lagos. He had absolved himself of all his matrimonial duties; he did not care about her welfare. He also cared less for the children.

Surprisingly on one of his visits, he did try to sleep with her. But now it was she who made excuses. "I am ill," she told him.

He would not take no for an answer; and literally raped her. "You are my property and I can take you whenever I want, ill or not," he shouted.

The rape led to another pregnancy. Of course, he was gone, well before ChiChi found out that she was pregnant. "Why is it that every time this man touches me, I end up pregnant? He need only walk past me and a baby jumps into my tummy."

She cried herself to sleep and considered an abortion. She was planning to leave him, not to have another baby. She already had four children. Baaba wanted her to be either pregnant, or nursing a baby. Pregnancy was a way of keeping her in the house.

Since her life with Baaba as a couple, she was either pregnant; nursing a baby; or being impregnated by Baaba. It was only now she realized this had been his dubious plan all along. While she suffered with the early morning sickness, Baaba was in the village with a warning that she must not visit the village. She also had to care for the other children.

She thought, "This is what Baaba wanted, to keep me at home as a full-time housewife. I should have listened to my father." But, of course, it was too late. The old man had been right about Baaba.

Seven months into her pregnancy, Baaba visited Lagos. Although she was heavy with the pregnancy, an argument ensued and he beat her. She fell down and hit her back on the sofa.

His reason was that the house girl had prepared his food because ChiChi was ill with the pregnancy.

She had a miscarriage and lost what turned out to be two babies. She had been pregnant with twins – two boys. She spent a week in hospital. She covered up for him and told the doctor that she tripped and fell down.

Surprisingly, Baaba felt bad. He has a conscience after all. He regretted his actions. He begged for her forgiveness; and promised that he would never beat her again. But she had learned. She did not believe him. He had made such promises in the past and still beat her. It was a vicious circle – he beat her … apologised … promised not to do it again … forgot his promise, and beat her up again.

She refused to speak to him until he left for the village.

She vowed never to have another child. Her priority was to protect herself and her children. She needed to get them as far away as possible from Baaba. He had turned into her worst nightmare. She could have lost her life with the termination of a seven-month twin pregnancy.

The doctor said she was lucky to be alive.

On his next visit, she kept well away from him. She made excuses to keep herself busy. She spent most of her time in the kitchen when he was around, or concentrated on fussing around the children.

He left after a week; the atmosphere was too irritating for both of them.

ChiChi was relieved on his departure, and immediately found her way back to her lover. She had kept away from him because of the pregnancy.

His reaction to the news of her pregnancy when she told him was, "I think you are mad to get yourself pregnant again by that man, have you not heard of birth control? He does not care about you and the kids, and you are still having more children."

She explained that she had never used birth control. She dared not use any contraceptives. Baaba would kill her if he found out.

Kelly promised to take her to his doctor discreetly. She also wondered why her lover could not get her pregnant. She had slept with him several times. Maybe she had a natural bond with Baaba. It never occurred to her that she could have slept with Kelly at the wrong time of the month. Baaba had lived with her for years and could figure out her ovulation period.

A few months passed by and ChiChi grew happier. Kelly treated her very nicely. He cared.

On his various visits to Lagos, Baaba spent his time buying expensive cars and electronics. He sent all his cars and electronic gadgets to the village. He even went as far as taking some of the goods in the house to the village. Piece by piece, he moved every good thing they had to the village.

ChiChi advised him to go easy on the money. She wanted him to stop the 419 business. She advised him and set up a medical laboratory for her. A colleague from the university ran a laboratory and hospitals referred patients to her. It was a successful venture.

"Since you spend most of your time in the village, why don't you set up a medical laboratory unit for me? It will keep me busy and I will make money running it."

His attitude towards her had changed since she lost the twins. For her part, she was thinking of her children, not him. He could go to jail for all she cared. She would be better off if he ended up in jail. If he were in jail, it would be an opportunity to reorganize her life.

Baaba shouted at her, "Do you really think your laboratory will give you the kind of money I spend on you and your family?"

"I can't just sit at home while you have your life in the village. All I do is eat and get fat."

"How dare you talk to me like that?"

"I can talk to you the way I want. Are you God? You begged to marry me. I did not force you."

Baaba was furious with how she spoke to him. He lashed out at her; and in a few seconds, she was bleeding from the wounds he had inflicted on her.

"You have the audacity to touch me again after causing me to lose twins from your beating?"

She was not scared of him any more and he could tell, which made him crazy with rage. But for her part, he could beat her as much as he wanted. She had a plan and that was what mattered. He left for the village the next morning, threatening to stay away as long as he could.

"Good riddance!" At last, peace! She felt relieved. His presence irritated her. He had now become everything she did *not* want in a man. Her relationship with Kelly made her realize the difference between educated men and illiterates, like Baaba.

As soon as Baaba was gone, she was right back in her lover's arms. He was her comfort zone, he was very caring, and he was hoping she would change her mind and get rid of Baaba and marry him.

"I don't want another woman to bring my children up," was always her answer to his request. "You should go for a woman who has never been married nor had children, like me," she advised him.

"I don't want another woman. You are all I want in a woman. Just looking at you makes me happy, what more should a man ask for?"

ChiChi still said no to him but they continued to see each other at every opportunity.

Chapter 32:
Baaba Plans Polygamy

ChiChi decided – out of curiosity – to investigate Kelly's mother's certainty that Baaba was having an affair. She was very close to one of Baaba's personal drivers, so she decided to talk to him.

She had always been kind to him. He was also a distant relation of hers. She promised him that whatever he revealed to her was to remain confidential. She persuaded him to talk about his master's affairs.

He was willing and divulged Baaba's secrets to her. It was true. Baaba was living with another woman in the village. Most shockingly, he had married her in the native law and custom. She was also pregnant.

Baaba's servants did not like her, because according to the driver, she was devilish and treated everyone as a slave whereas ChiChi always treated them with respect.

"She is pregnant?" she asked the driver.

"Yes, and she will soon have the baby."

"She has been living with him for over a year. You are a major obstacle to them. My master is confused; he does not know how to tell you about his second wife. I would advise you to stay in Lagos, because you are safe here. She is a JuJu woman. She would hurt you and your kids, so as to have Baaba to herself," he added.

"Does my mother know about this?"

"Yes, but what do you expect the poor woman to do?"

"What about my mother-in-law?"

"Oh, she knows, all right. She is all for it. She reckons Baaba needs to marry another wife; he is rich and will be given a chief's title soon. And you know, chiefs traditionally have more than one wife.

"She supports him based on this reasoning."

"I did hear her say, 'My son has enough money to feed ten wives'," ChiChi thought. She had also said that ChiChi would have to accept that her husband was now a 'big man'.

"Please, Auntie, stay in Lagos. They will kill you if you go to the village," the driver pleaded with ChiChi.

She told him not to worry and repeated her promise of confidentiality. Then she thanked him for volunteering the information. In a curious way, ChiChi was relieved that Baaba had fallen for another woman. This would make it easier to leave him; he would focus on the new wife. Surely, he did not love her any more. She definitely felt nothing for him.

She wanted Kelly.

She left the driver, went into her bedroom, and jumped up with joy. At last, she would be free from Baaba. She could not wait to give her lover the good news. She thought, "I will still not marry him; I have four children and that is not acceptable. He is not their father. He will never love them as their natural father. I am better off without a husband or a man. I will take care of my children the best way I can."

Meanwhile, the very thought of Baaba disgusted her; she vowed she would pay him back by leaving him. This time she would fight him with no help from anyone. She now had a valid reason to break away from him. She was only in her mid-twenties, and still very beautiful.

She would also find a job and become a professional. She felt the sort of relief she never imagined. To celebrate her freedom, she played and danced to her favourite song, Marvin Gaye's 'Let's Get it On'. Her children joined the dancing but had no clue of the reason for the celebration.

Whether intended or not, Baaba's behaviour had an effect on his children. They were scared of him during his visits to Lagos. He was always shouting or beating up their mother.

What was the guarantee he would not beat them as well?

None.

CHAPTER 33:
BAABA TAKES 419 BEYOND NIGERIAN BORDERS

HER NEW-FOUND HAPPINESS LASTED ONLY a short time, a mere two weeks. Baaba returned to Lagos suddenly. He told her that a friend had contacted him, regarding an international business.

ChiChi was indifferent and did not let the secret about his woman out. She kept her distance. She feigned illness to avoid him sleeping with her. Whenever she was near him, she bemoaned the serious malaria she had. She bought malaria tablets from the chemist, but left them on the bedside table.

For his part, Baaba was so busy with his friends that he paid little attention to her. He had a series of meetings with his boys. The only time he spoke to her was to ask for their meal. He did not care about her illness. In the past, he would have known that she wasn't really sick. Now he didn't care enough to see through her act. She spent all day in the kitchen. His friends were at the house from morning until late at night. Two of these men were new; she had never met them until this visit. And she had always known all his boys.

But these two arrived with their luggage and stayed in the house.

She paid no attention to any of the secret discussions going on around her. At least they kept Baaba busy and he had no time to find fault, which usually resulted in violence. He seemed to be under some strain, but she did not care.

His meetings with the men lasted until late at night, and eventually after a week, they lasted through the night until morning. The group grew from four men to six, including Emi.

ChiChi had no doubt that Emi knew about Baaba's new wife. He was his closest friend. Yet he had said nothing to ChiChi. That meant he supported his friend's decision. She paid no attention to him; and only greeted him with good morning or good night.

The second week into the activities, Baaba said to ChiChi, "We need to talk tonight when I finish with my friends."

"About what?" she asked.

"Do I have to tell you in advance when I need to talk to you?" he said with a frown.

She ignored him. He was not worth her time or concern.

When he finished with his friends, he said to her, "Come into the lounge so we can talk." She sat down on the sofa and folded her arms, defending herself from what she suspected was coming.

"You must have noticed the meetings I have been having with my business mates."

"Yes," she replied, without looking at him.

He told her that his friend had made a new business connection from Ghana. It was an international business. He went on to explain that the two men staying in the house lived in Ghana. They were in Nigeria solely for the business.

One of the men had met a girl in a nightclub in Ghana. She introduced him to a government official in Ghana. This official intimated that one of the African countries wanted to overthrow the government of Nigeria. Their reason was that they did not like the ruling military men. They wanted to work with army officers to organize a coup, which they would sponsor.

He told her he could not reveal the name of the country.

The men staying in his house had promised they would source army men in Nigeria, who would carry out the coup.

Baaba decided it was an insult. "Can you just imagine an idiot from another country planning to disrupt our country? We are more intelligent than they are; they think they can come here and tell us what to do. Whatever is happening in our country is our business. They have no right. We have decided to use 419 and take their money. We will 419 them until their government goes bankrupt!" He was furious with the idea that he would be used in such a way. "What a cheek."

Baaba explained that the numerous meetings were to organize his boys to act as army officers. They needed army uniforms and army vehicles. Arrangements were already in place to obtain the materials required. They needed to convince the foreigners that they were army officers. The plan was to introduce Baaba as an army colonel, Emi would act as an army major – and his deputy.

Two other boys were from the lower ranks. They needed to recruit more men to make it look authentic.

The two men were going back to Ghana the next day to ask for bribery money. The story would be that they needed the money to bribe other officers to join them in the coup.

"We will be travelling to Ghana to meet the men from the other country, in the near future."

ChiChi felt a chill run down her spine. "This is madness," she thought. "And Baaba is crazy."

"The next stage would be to ask for money for arms," he said. "That is the main 419 money from the business.

"When we collect the money for the arms, we would have to disappear from Lagos. The men are very dangerous. They would come after us if we fail to produce results. They would not hesitate to kill us.

"You have to be ready to leave Lagos with the children once we collect the money for the arms," he told her.

"What?! Have you gone completely mad?"

He made a face. "Don't ask stupid questions. Just do as you are told! I have no time to listen to your rubbish. Just be ready, that's all I can say to you."

ChiChi was upset. She thought, "There goes my plan of leaving this man." In addition, she was frightened. His plan was insane and unbelievable. How could he pretend to be in the Army? The reigning military government was merciless. They dealt with any opposition ruthlessly. People disappeared overnight, without a trace.

He really had lost his mind.

The two men left the next day, back to Ghana. Baaba was in and out of the house like a man possessed. He spent whole days with Emi and his two other friends. They talked, went out and came back to talk some more.

It was all hush-hush and troubling.

A week later, the two men returned from Ghana. They had a long meeting. After the meeting, Baaba brought a bag into the bedroom. He handed it to ChiChi. He asked her to open the bag and look at the contents. She opened the bag; it contained bundles of American dollars in five-hundred-dollar bills. Thousands of them.

Usually, Baaba was excited when he received money from a client; but this was a different Baaba. He showed no emotions. However, ChiChi knew him well enough to see through his façade, he was very anxious and nervous.

"You have to take this money to the village tomorrow. I am not taking any chances. Armed robbers could attack us in the night and kill us. I don't trust anybody. Any of the men in the group could arrange for armed robbers to attack the house, for the money."

"Why can't you take it? I don't want any part of this. I am scared."

"You don't have to be scared; no one knows that you are going home with the money."

He gave her further instructions on what to do when she got to the village.

She had to go to the village on a day's notice! After Baaba had banned her from it for two years.

His friends left past midnight. They came back in the early hours of the morning, with suitcases and bags.

ChiChi suspected that the suitcases and bags contained the army uniforms.

Baaba issued more instructions. She should spend one day in the village. She was to follow his directions on how to secure the money. She was to return to Lagos immediately, because he had to travel with the men to Ghana to meet the foreigners.

Her heart was palpitating. "What has he got himself into this time?" The present Nigerian government would skin them alive, if they found out they were impersonating army officers. This was a government matter, not 419. Maybe he could get away with duping individuals, but not a whole government. Nevertheless, when it came to such matters, Baaba was fearless.

He became very creative, guiding the men on military processes. He trained them on how to salute effectively. He even trained them on their conduct as army officers.

For the first time in years, his experiences in the Army paid off. Baaba and Emi had served as officers in the Biafran war; they called on their former experience to execute this business. They had been good officers in the Biafran war. They were familiar with military language and the tone of voice.

ChiChi left for the village in the morning. She had no time to contact her lover. She spent her time in the car thinking of him. She thought about where Baaba would end up with this new frightening venture. Then her thoughts centred on the wife Baaba was supposed to have left in the village. How would she react to her presence? Baaba did not mention her nor did ChiChi.

What was his game?

On her arrival, there was no woman in the house. The driver informed her that Baaba had sent her away to her village, before he travelled to Lagos; that was why he was not worried about ChiChi travelling to the village.

She left the village the next day as instructed and came back to Lagos.

A few days later, the six men travelled to Ghana with the bags. They returned a week and half later.

Baaba handed ChiChi another bagful of American dollars and sent her to the village the next morning, telling her, "This is the part of the money for the arms. We had to go to the country concerned and meet with their president.

"We have convinced them. They were impressed and are certain that we could carry out their coup." His eyes were wild as he told her this. His face shiny with excitement. "Idiots. They are all idiots. They have no brains and they want to rule Nigeria. We should be telling them how to run their country. Whatever gave them the idea that we are fools!"

It was ironic. This was the first time Baaba had gotten angry at a paying *mugu*. He was very patriotic. In his opinion, Nigeria was a leading country to other African nations.

"We have asked for more money for arms to be delivered in Ghana next week. The two men will collect the money from Ghana. We now have to come up with another story following the receipt of that money. I would advise my friends that we exit the scene after that." He shook his head. "Bastards, they took our pictures in army uniform," he moaned. Then he looked at ChiChi as if he was seeing her for the first time. "Whatever happens, you will be safe with the children in the village. The foreigners do not know the village. Just make sure you remain alert to any strangers."

ChiChi left again for the village the next morning, with the money. The men all went with their loot as well, probably to hide it as Baaba was doing.

On her return, Baaba was waiting for the two men to return from Ghana.

On their arrival, he asked her to pack whatever she needed. She quickly packed some clothing for her and the children. She left that night in two cars.

Baaba decided to wait for the rest of the money; but he was not putting his family at risk. He arrived a week later, with more bundles of American dollars. Emi also returned to the village with his family. They went underground for fear of the consequences.

This was a highly sophisticated 419.

Months passed and still no one came after them. One of the men from Ghana, who had disappeared earlier, visited Baaba in the village. He informed him that the foreigners were scared; they had found out the men were civilians. They worried that they might expose their plan to the Nigerian military government. That would be serious between the two countries.

Planning a coup against the ruling government could result in Nigeria breaking all relationship with the perpetrators. "They will not be coming after you for their money," he said. They were on the run themselves.

"Good. If they come here, I will kill them! How can they play with Nigerians? We will topple their own government if they are not careful!"

Still, Baaba was not going back to Lagos. He decided to settle in the eastern states. He had made enough money to invest in legitimate business. He had lost interest in 419.

He had run his last 419. Even he, Baaba of Wayo, had been in over his head on that one. He never wanted to feel that way again.

Still, he had established the 419 legacy.

He settled in a town some forty miles from his village. He rented a nice house. He also bought other houses for rent and then set up a thriving business, selling building wares.

He completed his house in the village and settled his children in schools.

Life was back to normal. For him.

Then one day, when he was drunk, he said to ChiChi, "Stupid foreigners, they think Nigerians have no brains. We have shown them we have more brains than they do. Imagine trying to dictate what happens in our country. Whatever happens here is our business. Now they know you don't mess around with Nigerians."

ChiChi begged him to keep his voice and his thoughts quiet. It was still too soon to rule out repercussions from the foreigners.

"Nothing will happen," he said confidently. "They are fools, I am waiting for them. If they dared, I will report them to our government. I will tell the whole story to our government, if they want trouble."

But all was not well for Baaba. He had a friend who knew about the coup and who had an uncle who was a high-ranking officer in the Army. He had fallen out with Baaba and, out of revenge, reported him to his uncle.

He told his uncle about the planned coup. He did not tell his uncle that it was a 419 coup.

The uncle was furious. He reported the matter to his army colleagues who took the matter very seriously and arrested Baaba a year later. The government of Nigeria eventually learnt of the deceit and released Baaba after six months. They wanted to find out the truth about his involvement and activities in the planned coup. They also wanted to know if there was truth in the story.

However, when they found out that it was only a fraud, they released him.

With all the drama of the preceding months, one would have thought that Baaba would have the good sense to settle down and be a good husband. But it did not take long for Baaba to go back to his old ways. He disappeared regularly. He spent nights outside the new home. ChiChi knew he went to the other woman. But now she did not care; she still had plans of leaving him. She was not in love with him any more.

She couldn't have cared less for his 419 money. Her wish was to get as far away as possible from him. She was a very jealous woman and was not prepared to share her man with another woman. She knew that if she did not leave, he would eventually force her into polygamy. She would rather die than live in a polygamous home.

She knew only too well what happened in such homes. Wives were allocated different days to be with the man. If he was married to more than two wives, each wife had to wait for weeks before they had the opportunity to get close to their husband. That was no life for her.

And, of course, the beatings had started again. Her new neighbours sometimes witnessed Baaba's aggressiveness towards her.

Baaba had his own plans about his other woman. He had to find a way to bring her into his home. The hiding and secret meetings were no longer acceptable to him. He wanted to bring her into the family home.

Occasionally, he would beat ChiChi and send her to the village so that the other woman could spend time in their house with him. She already had his baby, and was pregnant with the second child. She was also harassing him because she did not want to be the 'other woman'.

She wanted to be a proper wife.

Chapter 34:
ChiChi Leaves for England

BAABA'S AFFLUENCE ATTRACTED NEW FRIENDS in the new town; new friends who were not in 419 businesses but genuine entrepreneurs. Most of them had no idea how Baaba came to be very rich. They only knew that he had the kind of money that could help them. He became a popular individual amongst them.

One of them, Sam, became a very close acquaintance. Sam had studied economics and marketing abroad. With his advice, Baaba ran his shop effectively and profitably. He visited the house regularly and got friendly with ChiChi. He introduced his family of two children and a wife to Baaba's family. The two families exchanged visits at the weekends and socialised.

Sam was well educated. He had studied in America and England. He treated his wife with respect. Seeing this, Baaba pretended that all was well between him and ChiChi. But at night, he would sneak out of the house and go to his other woman.

ChiChi did not mind his behaviour because she could not stand him. In fact, she was desperate to leave him. She often toyed with the idea of going back to Lagos. However, she knew Baaba would find her in Lagos. She wanted and needed a clean break. She needed to go to a place where he could not reach her.

She thought about going to the northern states, knowing he was not familiar with the states in the north. But she couldn't be certain. Her uncertainty made it difficult for her to sleep at night.

"If I leave, I have to take my four children. I am not leaving them behind for another woman to bring them up." On this point she would not compromise. She prayed every night for an answer to her dilemma.

God answered her prayers in the most amazing way. During one of Sam's weekend visits, he announced that his family was going on holiday for a month to England and Paris.

"They usually go every summer to do their shopping," he said.

Baaba immediately thought, "Wouldn't that be fun?" He was thinking only of taking his other woman to Sam's house, in his wife's absence.

ChiChi, however, saw Sam's holiday as an opportunity to escape.

"Yes," Sam continued. "I have a house in England; I am also buying one in Paris. I don't like them staying in hotels. My wife does not like hotels."

ChiChi listened with interest. She sighed. "I wish I could go on holidays to England, but I don't even have a passport," she said despondently.

"Baaba, why don't you let ChiChi and the children go with my family; at least they would keep each other company."

"Next week is too early; they haven't even got passports or any of the papers that would be required."

"But they don't have to go next week, we can apply for their papers quickly; and they can join my family after one week." Sam was very earnest and honest in his feelings. "My wife would really appreciate company. She is spoilt and loathes being on her own. She wants me to go with them. If she knows that your family would join her, that would make my life easy." He frowned. "I am not ready to go abroad yet, because I have urgent business to attend to."

ChiChi maintained absolute silence, holding her breath in anticipation of Baaba's response.

"Anything that would take her away from here," he said harshly. "I need a break from her. If they go for a month, that would give me enough time to play around," he said disrespectfully.

Sam was angered by Baaba's words. "Baaba, even if that is the case, you don't say that in your wife's presence."

"I can say what I like to my family, if she does not like it she can go to hell," was his cynical response.

"I am sorry, Baaba, but I have a lot of respect for my family; and you must learn to respect your wife. She is the mother of your children."

"Okay," Baaba said, annoyed by Sam's sanctimonious tone. He was ready to give in to the holiday. "You would have to make all the arrangements. I have never been abroad, and don't know how to apply for passports and all that," he added carelessly.

Sam smiled. "I will do all the paperwork next week and they can join my family the week after. My wife likes your wife a lot and really wants to be her friend. She does not keep friends but she has taken to your wife; and I would like them to be close."

ChiChi's heart was beating very fast. Was this really happening? She had to pinch herself to convince herself it wasn't a dream. Would she wake up and find it was all just like smoke on the wind?

She thought the army coup 419 had brought her only misery but she learned anew that God works in mysterious ways. If they had not moved to the new town, Baaba would not have met Sam. Life was full of surprises and patience often pays off in the end.

She could not miss this opportunity. She *would* not.

Baaba was an illiterate village boy who had no idea about holidays abroad. He himself had never been abroad. He always bought goods from people who had been abroad. Because the goods were foreign, he paid exorbitant prices for them. He had money to go abroad for his shopping like his friends but lacked the confidence.

He once joked to his friend, who had come back from America, "I understand the police stop you at the airport and use magic to find out if you are a criminal."

In addition, due to his 419 business, he was scared that he would be arrested if he went abroad.

He agreed to Sam's suggestion only because it created an opportunity to bring in his other woman. He would bring her into the house, the very day ChiChi left for England. And, he told himself, he would keep her in the house when ChiChi got back from abroad. If she were already in the house, it would be easier to convince ChiChi to accept her.

It was a fantastic opportunity! He was amazed at how God worked in such wonderfully mysterious ways!

For her part, ChiChi walked around in a daze in the next few days. Hard as it was to believe, it was real. It was no dream.

God had heard her prayers.

All the papers were completed. Sam warned her that it was very cold in December in England. So she went to a woman who sold used clothing at the town's market. The woman picked out some warm clothing for her and the children. She also bought used woollen hats and gloves.

It was only when she arrived in England that she realized that the woman had sold her dressing gowns instead of winter coats. This made her laugh. Baaba bought suitcases for them; he insisted that one of the house girls travelled with them, to help look after the children.

During this preparation period, Baaba broke the good news to his other woman. "Immediately they are gone you could move into the house," he told her.

"But that is only on a temporary basis, I want more than a temporary arrangement," she argued. "I am also your wife," she reminded him.

"You have to be patient; I will handle it my way. When she comes back from England, you will be living in my house. She cannot ask you to leave. I say what happens in my house. She will have to accept you as an equal."

In the days that followed, ChiChi's prayer was simple, "Please, God, don't let me wake up from this dream."

Her only sadness was when her thoughts shifted from the present circumstances to her lover in Lagos. If she went abroad, they would lose contact for good. She would have no means of contacting him. She had been missing his care and kindness; but for now, she had to come first. She knew he was missing her too. She had sneaked out of the house to tell him about her move to the village. They cried in each other's arms. She promised that if she were ever to come to Lagos, she would visit him.

In the days before she left, Baaba too was very happy. He tried to get close to her.

"He wants to get me pregnant. I am too clever for him this time." Her lover made sure of that. He gave her contraceptive pills he got from a doctor friend which she took religiously. Even so, she pretended to enjoy his attention whenever Baaba touched her. But she knew that actually going abroad would mean that she would have to pretend that nothing was different. After all, he could still stop the trip.

"You cannot come back before the date on the ticket. I don't want you back here in less than a month."

ChiChi thought to herself, "Do not worry about that!"

When the plane finally took off, ChiChi looked out of the window and breathed a sigh of relief. Freedom at last. So sweet. So sweet. She leaned back in her seat and made sure her children were comfortable.

Whatever it took to live in England, she would do it. There was no way she was going to go back to Baaba. Her visa was for one month but she would rather go to jail in England than go back to the hell that Baaba called home. She looked at the scars on her arms from his beatings, and was more determined to remain in England.

After their arrival, the hours in England turned into days. The days turned into weeks. The month went very quickly. She did not go to Paris; she was happy to remain in England while Sam's wife went to Paris to complete her shopping.

"No. I am not going to Paris."

"What do you mean, you are not going to Paris?"

"I am not returning to Nigeria either."

Sam's wife was shocked. "Have you gone mad, who will take care of you and the children? You cannot survive here without a job. How long do you think the shopping money will last with four children?"

But ChiChi was unperturbed. She had tasted freedom and she liked it. "God will take care of me and the children. Just please don't tell Baaba of my decision to stay."

"That is not my business," she said with a shrug. She had never liked the way Baaba had spoken to ChiChi. "I will tell him I waited for you in Paris, but you did not show up so I left."

With her confidentiality reassured, she thanked her. "Please thank your husband for me. He made this trip possible. Tell him I will never forget him as long as I live."

And then she was alone in England. She had her work cut out for her. How would she survive with four children, all under the age of ten years, in London?

When Sam's wife returned after the month, Baaba could not contain his anger. When ChiChi failed to return to Nigeria he blamed Sam for putting ideas in her head. That broke their friendship. He tried in the few years that followed to bring ChiChi back to Nigeria to no avail. When his threatening and aggressive behaviour failed, he resorted to persuasion. He promised that he would not abuse her ever again, but it was far too late for those lies.

She had made a life in England for her four children and herself.

Baaba regularly visited the airport, to give letters to people who were travelling to London. ChiChi read his letters and laughed. She could not understand why he wanted her back. "What about his new wife?"

THE 419 CODE

A friend ChiChi met in London told her that Baaba now claimed that, "She had used black magic to confuse him." She had made a fool of him. If he could get her back to Nigeria, he would make sure she does not walk.

The same friend told ChiChi that Baaba's new wife had left because he beat her up.

He was alone.

"Good riddance," was ChiChi's only thought.

Chapter 3:
ChiChi Divorces Baaba

AFTER A FEW YEARS IN England, ChiChi did go back to Nigeria. Without Baaba's knowledge, she applied for a divorce in the same court where they had once been married in secret.

In England, she had returned to college and improved on her education, got a good job, and settled the children into schools. The world was a good place again. She no longer existed in Baaba's world, or more correctly, Baaba's 419 hell.

She worked hard to provide for herself and the children. She eventually met a man who was educated and caring. Nigeria was a closed chapter in her life.

There were times when she would sit and think about the madness she lived through. She would think of Baaba and his 419, her lover in Lagos, her father, and all the madness Baaba put her through, especially the beating and bullying.

If Baaba were living in England, he would have been sent to jail for physical and mental abuse. There was law and order in England, no man has a right to abuse a woman, married or no.

Chapter 36:
Baaba Degenerates into Drugs

Baaba could not get over ChiChi's absence. Despite his horrible behaviour towards her, he still longed for her and his longing drove him mad. His other woman had left; he even blamed her for contributing to the breakdown of his family.

In his distress, he began to dabble with hard drugs – cocaine and heroin. Whatever money remained from the army 419 business was lost on drugs. He sold most of his assets. He became very wretched. His friends abandoned him. Creditors took what was left in the shop. He pledged his cars for drugs.

The landlord threw him out. He could not pay his rent.

He eventually ended up in the village permanently, exactly where he started. With Ogo.

Ogo had served his sentence. He looked older than his years. Prison had emptied his soul. He had no will to play the card game any more.

He married a widow from the village. The woman could not produce any children, so he ended up childless.

Amaka, a fully qualified midwife, visited the village on holidays. His daughter from Amaka was training as a lawyer in England. He met her only once, on one of their visits.

Baaba, meanwhile, survived on gifts from the 419 boys he had earlier initiated into the business. There is honour amongst thieves and they did not forget that he was the Baaba of 419. He was the originator and had introduced them into the trade.

They visited him when they were in the village to accord him his due respect.

A few of them tried to reinvent the wheel and bring him back into the business. However, Baaba was too deep into hard drugs to handle any sort of business negotiations. In the end they gave up and decided to hand him crumbs whenever they came round.

When ChiChi heard of his plight, she sent him money to get into a drug rehabilitation clinic. "After all," she reasoned, "he is still the father of my children. They may need their father sometime in the future, especially the boys, who look like Baaba."

CHAPTER 37:
A VILLAGE BOY TURNS INTO A NATIONAL AND INTERNATIONAL VILLAIN

4 19 BECAME A HOUSEHOLD NAME in Nigeria. A high percentage of the boys who grew up in the late 1980s and 1990s abandoned school to look for easy money through 419. They had witnessed people like Baaba, Emi, and the others acquire incredible wealth with almost no effort. To their minds then, there was little point in going to school and 'wasting' all those years for a meagre salary.

The next generation of 419 elevated the business to an international level. They modified the system and introduced other kinds of 419 – just as Baaba had modified Ogo's trade. They duped businessmen and rich men from all over the world.

419 changed from when Baaba initiated it to a highly skilled trade. The computer and the use of the Internet created another avenue for communication. It became easier for perpetrators to contact businesses abroad by email. They also identified businesses and business directors from the Internet, and could dispatch thousands of emails to potential *mugus* with the click of a button.

They formulated letters telling potential *mugus* that there was easy money to make. Some of these letters were so ridiculous and filled with errors that it was clear that illiterates wrote them.

Even women participated in the trade, using their bodies to lure men into the 419 fraud.

Everywhere, people fell for the various stories about making easy money. The foreigners were aware that Nigeria was a very rich country with oil resources. With their eyes blinded by greed, all they saw was easy money. That made them believers in these outlandish schemes.

Soon other West African countries joined the trade. The boys moved their bases abroad and sent the letters from various countries. The new 419 boys formulated additional methods of conning people, ways that were far too technical during Baaba's time.

They made big money and life improved for most of their families. They built mansions in the remote villages, employing foreign contractors. They built roads and installed electricity where none existed. They set up goods production factories and created local employment. 419 contributed greatly to the local economies.

Individuals were able to provide the infrastructure where the central or state governments could not.

The 419 boys became prominent members of society and coronation was commonplace; they showed off their wealth by becoming village chiefs, buying their titles with money. The traditional method of inheriting royalty disappeared.

As long as you had money to afford the bribery, you could buy the kingmakers.

Some of them rebuilt schools and hospitals and offered scholarships to poor families. Musicians sang their praise. They were honoured and adored ... but, in the end, every good – or bad – thing must come to an end.

419 became an ill in the society. International governments complained to the Nigerian government. The government made the decision that it had to fight 419. With the government finally fighting them, most of the old 419 men ended up in jails, both in Nigeria and abroad.

Still, new 419s sprang up with no fear of the repercussions.

Fraud squads were set up in countries to tackle the crime. People, all over the world, lost money through this crime, including judges, magistrates, doctors, entrepreneurs, the police, and pilots.

There were no borders on greed, and no amount of understanding seemed to guard against it. People everywhere seemed to want one thing and one thing alone – easy money. That made them easy prey.

Banks issued warnings but still the scams worked. 419 haunted the country and damaged its image internationally. Legitimate businesses avoided doing any sort of business with Nigerians. When it was absolutely necessary to have a transaction with Nigerians, participants carried out extra checks to ensure the business was legal. Even banks and the Central Bank of Nigeria had been involved with the 419 boys. It was difficult – almost impossible – to know which business was genuine.

The greedy officials of these banks provided cover for the boys and authenticated false documentation for the fraud.

As long as greed is real, fraud will find a way.

ChiChi remained in England where she lives to this day with her children. As for Baaba, he is still desolate in the village, practically penniless.

Sometimes, ChiChi would find herself reading about 419 in the newspapers and on the Internet. When she did, she had to shake her head in amazement. It was so difficult to get over the fact that what she'd always thought was one of Baaba's jokes ended up being an international plague.

Sadly, most of those who 'succeeded' with 419 came to sad ends too. After all, they too were motivated by greed. Why should their greed have a happier ending than those who lost money by being defrauded?

Most boys from his village who had gone into 419 became destitute because with the fall of 419, they all went back to the village. Some who had started building empires like Baaba could not afford to complete the projects. Too old to return to school, the village is now full of these men, hopeless and sad, without education or jobs.

It is nearly impossible to find a town or village that has not been afflicted by this fraud. It ruined youth and education in most towns and villages. Young people roam about in the towns and villages, getting into other criminal activities. Some of the more clever ones went into politics. Nigeria, known for its corruption, provided other avenues for them. Money could buy political positions in Nigeria. So they bought their way into the House of Representatives and other political positions.

Sometimes, ChiChi will spot their names on the Nigerian Internet site. It always astonished her. How could a 419 boy she knew in Baaba's days become a member of the House of Representatives? Then she would sigh in amazement, realizing that nothing is impossible in her beloved country – Nigeria.

Although a British citizen, she still returned home on holidays. She always gives Baaba money when she goes home. For good or ill, she finally realized that she could never love any man as much as she loved her Baaba.

Ah, well. Nevertheless, life goes on.